Tea for Two

**Center Point
Large Print**

Also by Trish Perry
and available from Center Point Large Print:

Tea with Millicent Series
The Perfect Blend

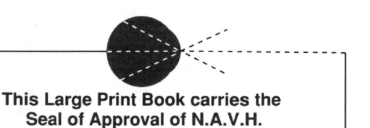

Tea for Two

TRISH PERRY

CENTER POINT PUBLISHING
THORNDIKE, MAINE

This Center Point Large Print edition
is published in the year 2011 by arrangement with
Harvest House Publishers.

Scripture quotations are taken from the Holy Bible, New International Version®, NIV®. Copyright © 1973, 1978, 1984 by Biblica, Inc.™ Used by permission of Zondervan. All rights reserved worldwide.

This is a work of fiction. Names, characters, places, and incidents are products of the author's imagination or are used fictitiously. Any resemblance to actual persons, living or dead, or to events or locales, is entirely coincidental.

The text of this Large Print edition is unabridged.
In other aspects, this book may vary
from the original edition.
Printed in the United States of America
on permanent paper.
Set in 16-point Times New Roman type.

ISBN: 978-1-61173-060-9

Library of Congress Cataloging-in-Publication Data

Perry, Trish, 1954–
Tea for two / Trish Perry.
p. cm.
ISBN 978-1-61173-060-9 (library binding : alk. paper)
1. Tearooms—Fiction. 2. Large type books. I. Title.
PS3616.E7947T43 2011b
813′.6—dc22

2011001603

For my mother, Lilian Hawley,
with love for her amazing strength,
unfailing love, and mischievous smile.

Acknowledgments

It's never easy to write an entire novel, but I'd like to thank the following people for making *Tea for Two* a smooth and entertaining project for me:

Tamela Hancock Murray, for being my fantastic advocate, counselor, and friend.

Kim Moore, for catching what doesn't make sense. A phone call from you is always a joy, and I know how blessed I am to be able to claim that!

The Harvest House family, for treating me as if I'm a valued member. That does *not* go unnoticed. Thank you so much for being such a kind group of people to work with.

My readers, for your encouraging emails, reviews, encouragement, and support.

The people of Middleburg, Virginia, for the kindness and helpfulness extended toward me while I imagined fictional people and places within your lovely town. I hope many readers will get a chance to visit both fictional and real Middleburg and enjoy it as I have.

American Christian Fiction Writers, Romance Writers of America (FHL), The Girliebeans, and Capital Christian Writers. I learn something new every day, thanks to these fellow writers.

Vie Herlocker and Mike Calkin, my dear friends and critique partners. I can't believe you haven't blocked my email address yet.

Betsy Dill, Gwen Hancock, Barb Turnbaugh, and Wendy Driscoll, for your dear friendship and prayers of support. I miss all of you!

The Saturday Night Girls, The Open Book Club, and my Cornerstone Chapel friends, for making me think, laugh, and cry—sometimes all in one sitting.

Chuck, Lilian, John, Donna, and Chris Hawley, my ever-supportive parents and sibs.

Tucker, Stevie, Doug, and Bronx, for filling this past year with new beginnings.

My precious Lord Jesus, for patiently bridging that gap between uncertainty and assurance, and for drawing my focus back to where it belongs—on You.

"I know the plans I have for you," declares the LORD, "plans to prosper you and not to harm you, plans to give you hope and a future."
JEREMIAH 29:11

Tea for Two

ONE

Zack Cooper wasn't your typical male, and he knew it. He couldn't simplify life by innately compartmentalizing its various issues. If something was wrong at home, that something tried to go with him when he left for work. And this rainy June morning, as he made a delivery to Millicent's Tea Shop in downtown Middleburg, that something felt like a passenger sitting beside him in the front seat of his truck. Or maybe like *two* passengers, because his teenagers, Dylan and Sherry, were what was wrong at home.

He stopped in front of the tea shop and hurried to remove two boxes of produce from underneath his truck bed's tarp. A chatty group of women walked toward the front door and blocked his path toward the shop's back door, so he waited for them to file into Milly's. He would have tipped his baseball cap were his hands free, but they didn't seem to notice him anyway.

Most of the ladies shared umbrellas, squeezing together to avoid the rain. The lone woman at the end of the group, while the last to enter, somehow seemed in charge. As she neared Zack, she tilted her umbrella back to look at him.

"I'm sorry. Please excuse us."

Zack experienced a momentary ability to compartmentalize. The kids were nowhere in his mind just for that instant. Neither was work.

This was one great-looking woman. Exotic, with dark hair and warm brown eyes. Even though he hadn't said a word, her lips tugged into a subtle smile, and she looked at him as if he had the driest wit imaginable.

On the contrary, he stood in the rain, holding fruit, and struggled to string words together. "Uh, yeah. Sure. I mean, yes. Or, no. No problem."

Her eyes twinkled at him briefly before she turned and entered the shop.

He shook his head and spoke aloud. "Real smooth there, Zack." He hefted his boxes and continued around to the rear of the building.

Milly didn't answer the back door right away. Zack figured she was up front in the dining area, greeting the same ladies he had just passed. She was expecting his delivery this morning, though, so she had probably unlocked the door for him. He shifted the boxes to one arm and was about to reach for the door knob with the other when he heard a sweet young voice from behind.

"Who's that handsome farmer? Locked out, are you?"

Zack turned to see Jane, Milly's assistant. He grinned at her as she tossed back the hood of her slicker and shook out her red hair. Like Milly,

Jane always managed to sound upbeat. And both of them were British, so Zack loved listening to them talk.

"Morning, Jane! I'm not sure if it's locked. Haven't tried the knob yet, but Milly didn't answer. I knocked with my elbow, though, so she might not have heard me."

Jane pulled a set of keys out of her purse even as she reached for the knob. "Ah, there we go. Not locked."

Zack lifted his chin at her. "After you." The moment the door opened, he could smell the irresistible pastries freshly baked or still baking in one of the shop's ovens. He wondered if Jane could hear his stomach grumble. He'd missed breakfast this morning.

Milly walked into the kitchen just then and broke into a warm smile as Jane and Zack entered.

"Sorry I'm late, Milly." Jane removed her slicker and swiftly exchanged it for an apron. "I'll never get used to how timid drivers get around here when a single drop of water falls from the sky."

Milly set a serving tray on the counter and pointed to a mat near the door. "Mind you dry your shoes off so you don't slip, Jane. You're just in time for Tina's group. Would you mind bringing them a pot of English breakfast? Tina's asked for a tray of the apple-cranberry scones. To start, anyway."

Jane prepared the teapot, cups, and saucers. "Is Carmella with her today? I saw her over the weekend, and she said she didn't care how early in the morning they were meeting or what else they were ordering, she planned to get some of your little berry shortcakes before leaving."

"We'd better go ahead and whip up some cream, then." Milly turned her attention to Zack. "Oh, Zack, I'm sorry. Here, here." She patted the counter near the sink. "Set those right down. Such a wet morning for you! Do you have time for a cup of tea?"

She turned away and poured a cup without waiting for his answer.

"I'd appreciate it." He set the boxes of berries, cucumbers, and watercress on the spacious counter. He was always impressed with how tidy Milly's kitchen was, considering how much she produced in it. He removed his hat and tucked it in his back pocket. "Had another one of those mornings with the kids. Didn't get to enjoy my morning coffee, so I could use the caffeine." He took the delicate cup and saucer from her as if they were priceless museum pieces.

"Milk?" She stepped to the refrigerator, but he waved her off.

"No, this is great." He glanced toward the kitchen door, the one that led into the dining area. "You've got a good-sized group already, I see." He wasn't about to ask outright about that woman

14

he saw earlier, but he wondered if she was Tina. Or Carmella.

"Yes, one of my regular groups. We have a few that come in on a scheduled basis."

He watched her prepare a three-tiered tray with lacy paper things and what he assumed were the scones she mentioned. His stomach growled again, and she looked up at him.

He grimaced. "Sorry."

She smiled and pulled a tall chair over to the counter. "Have a seat, young man. Something tells me you missed more than your coffee this morning."

Zack obeyed her, and she placed one of the scones on a fancy flowered plate and retrieved a bowl of dense cream from the refrigerator.

"Here, now. You start off with that, just as my ladies out front are going to do." She spooned a generous portion of the cream onto his plate. "We call this clotted cream. Use it like butter, only more generously. I think you'll like it. If you want to try the little berry shortcakes Jane was talking about, you'll have to stick around a few minutes. Interested?"

He shook his head as he bit into the amazingly perfect pastry. "Mmm." Apple-cranberry. His new favorite combination. He quickly swallowed and washed it down with tea. "Can't stay, no. But wow, that's something!" He held up what was left of the scone. "I need to make a few more deliveries this morning before heading home. I got off to a late start."

Milly had resumed her work, spooning the thick cream into a serving bowl. "You said the kids gave you a rough morning. Is everything all right?"

He shrugged his shoulders as he swallowed another warm bite. Without his asking, Milly placed another scone on his plate. "Thanks, Milly. No more after this. I really have to go." He sighed. "I don't know. Seems like one day Dylan and Sherry thought I was terrific. Their hero. And then suddenly I'm the enemy. We don't seem to be able to get through a single conversation without getting into an argument."

"Typical teenage issues?" Milly stopped working and turned to face him. "How old are they now?"

"Dylan's seventeen. Sherry's fifteen-going-on-get-lost-Dad."

Milly smiled. "I'm sure they—"

Jane walked back into the kitchen. "You have those scones, Milly? Oh, great. Thanks." She took the tray and bowl of cream from Milly and grinned. "I was right. Carmella's already talked some of them into adding the shortcakes to today's order."

"I'll get on it." Milly turned toward the refrigerator, and Zack stood. He hadn't finished his scones, but he had taken up enough of her time.

"Let me get out of your way, Milly—"

"No, hold on a minute, Zack. Sit and finish. I want to give you a few goodies to take home to the kids. We'll have them calling you a hero again in no time."

He smiled and sat for a while longer. "Thanks." He scratched at the back of his neck. "To tell you the truth, I don't know how much of the problem is growing pains and how much of it is the continued aftermath of their mother's leaving. I've never dealt with teenagers before."

Milly nodded as she placed several pastries in a box. "I wondered about that too. How long since Maya left?"

"Four years ago. Still not a word from her, but I've heard through the grapevine she's moved on from the guy she left with. Different guy now. I can understand her leaving me, but I just don't know why a mother would leave her kids like that."

Milly placed the box on the counter. "I imagine Dylan and Sherry wonder the same thing. Poor dears."

Zack's cell phone rang, and he pulled it from his shirt pocket. "Excuse me." His caller ID made him frown. It was smack in the middle of the school day.

"Dylan? Aren't you supposed to stay off the phone during school hours?"

"Um, I'm not at school. I . . . I need you to come get me."

Zack stood. "Now what? Please tell me you didn't skip class again."

"Dad, I'm at the police station. I've been arrested."

TWO

Tina waited for the women to finish their first bites of scone before starting their discussion. "Meredith, how about we start with you today. Is that all right?" She sipped from her dainty, violet-covered cup and used her eyes to smile at the pale young waif beside her.

Tina loved the atmosphere of these group meetings at the tea shop, and she was glad she had implemented them a few months ago. The sweet-smelling dining area was the very picture of comfort and charm, from the lacy tablecloths to the fine china cups and saucers, from the vintage shelves and cabinets to the delightfully British artwork on the walls. The tea and food made the gathering fun, which seemed to enhance openness between the women. Milly kept the shop's music at the perfect level. It set a calm mood and added privacy to their conversations while still allowing them to hear one another. That privacy mattered, now that a few more customers had just come in.

Meredith looked up from her plate as if surprised Tina had recognized her. "I . . . I guess. Okay." She pushed her limp dark hair away from her eyes.

A stillness followed as the others waited for input from Meredith. It didn't come.

Tina prompted, "How did the week go for you? Did you get a chance to talk with your boss about that raise?"

"Or lack thereof, is more like," said Gerry, Meredith's opposite in many ways. Gerry tapped a thick finger on the table and leaned forward. "You ought to tell him you'll walk if he doesn't pony up at least five percent more."

Meredith's eyes widened. "I could never threaten something like that. I need my job. It's just that I know he pays Aaron more for the same work. And we both started working there at the same time. It doesn't seem fair."

Before Gerry could comment again, Tina spoke gently to Meredith. "But you still haven't spoken with your boss about it?"

Meredith shook her head, apparently so ashamed of her weakness she couldn't even speak.

Tina took another sip of her tea. "What do you think would happen if you said to him what you just said to us? You and Aaron started at the same time, you do the same work, and yet he is paid more. It isn't fair. What do you think your boss would do if you said that to him?"

As Meredith struggled for words, Tina found herself momentarily distracted by movement outside. It was that wonderful-looking guy who had waited earlier while her group entered the shop. The rain had finally stopped, and the sun had broken through like a floodlight, allowing her to see outside clearly. Right now he looked as if he were in a hurry, so she didn't get a very good look at him. But the way he had looked at her earlier and the way he carried himself now intrigued her. She liked that he seemed nonplussed by her. He was either shy or attracted to her. Or both.

At that moment he suddenly looked directly into the shop. Directly at her. Taken aback, she actually gasped in the middle of Meredith's halting speech. The look in his eyes? Intense. As a therapist she tried to master the art of reading people's expressions, but she couldn't tell what emotion might be behind that brief flash of . . . passion. Then he jumped into his truck and tore away.

Had he actually looked at her? Could he even see inside the shop?

Someone in the group cleared her throat, and Tina realized they had all fallen silent and were watching her now, the ditzy teacher who had zoned out in front of the class.

Gerry squinted her eyes and turned to look out the same window Tina had. The rest of the group followed suit.

Tina scrambled to draw their attention back to her. "I'm so sorry, ladies. Meredith, please forgive me. You were saying?"

But Meredith remained silent and leaned toward

the window as the others had done. They were like a hodgepodge of garden flowers seeking sunlight.

Next to Meredith, Carmella—who continued eating her scone even while craning her neck to see outside—looked back, disappointed. "What? What did I miss?"

Gerry gave Tina a playful smile. "We all missed it, Carmella. Were you checking out that hot produce guy by any chance, Tina? The one who was here when we arrived?"

And Tina thought she was the only one who had noticed him.

They all turned back to her, their expressions eager and amused.

She had to laugh. "All right, ladies, we're not here to talk about me. Let's get back to all of you. Meredith, please indulge me and start again. Tell us what you envision happening when you approach your boss about that raise."

By the time they had moved beyond Meredith and on to Carmella—who was eager to bare her soul for a while—Milly stopped by their table.

"Jane tells me we're going to need some individual berry shortcakes here. Is that right? Are you ready for them now?"

Carmella set down her teacup with enthusiasm. "Definitely!" She looked sheepish and shrugged her shoulders to the group. "Okay, I know I said I was going to start my diet, but I meant tomorrow. Please don't think less of me for it."

Tina laughed. "That's not why we're here."

"Carmella, honey," Gerry said. "You're the only one focused on 'less of you.' We love you, girl, just like that." She pointed at Carmella's plump figure.

"And as we established before," Tina added, "you're in control of your diet and when—or *if*—you start it. Not anyone else."

"Besides, I want to join you in a second helping of Milly's handiwork." Gerry leaned over and patted Carmella on the shoulder. Then she turned to Milly. "So, Milly, what's the story with the hunky produce guy?"

Tina immediately flushed, despite her effort at remaining cool. Gerry had caught her off guard. "Gerry, I'm sure Milly doesn't—"

"Do you mean Zack?" Milly smiled as if she were talking about her favorite son, although she couldn't be all that much older than he. "Yes, he's quite handsome, isn't he? A dear man too."

"Single?" Gerry glanced at Tina, who rolled her eyes and shook her head.

Milly followed Gerry's eyes and adjusted her tone. "Oh." She looked away from Tina, but not before Tina gave her a quick, pleading grimace. "Well, yes. As a matter of fact, he is single." Her eyes sparkled as she turned back to Gerry. "But I was always of the impression you were a happily married woman."

The others chuckled, but Gerry wasn't dissuaded.

"I am happy. I was just wondering for Tina."

"All right, Gerry. That's enough out of you." Tina gave Gerry a crooked smile to show she could take the ribbing, but she needed to regain control of this gathering. She turned to Milly. "Why don't we all sample those berry shortcakes? They sound wonderful."

Milly gave her a conspiratorial wink and turned away before anyone was able to ask her for more information about Zack. She spoke over her shoulder. "I'll be back in two shakes."

"Okay," Gerry said. "If I don't get to play matchmaker for you, Tina, then tell me how I can do it better with my sister. That's my thing this week. She absolutely refuses to go on a date with my hubby's coworker, who would be perfect for her. She's barely speaking to me after the last guy I sent her, and I need to know how to talk her into trying this guy out."

Tina nodded, and then said, with a more serious tone in her voice, "First let's talk about your need to orchestrate your sister's love life. That definitely coincides with the discussion we had last week." And in no time they moved far from the hot produce guy and closer to their own personal concerns. They managed to finish out their session focusing on the group.

Still, as they left the tea shop, Tina felt she had left something behind. She often forgot her umbrella on rainy days, but no, it was folded up and dangling from her wrist. She had paid the check and left a tip, so . . . what?

When she stepped onto the sidewalk and remembered glancing at Zack from underneath her umbrella, she experienced an "aha" moment. She wanted more information. She wondered what else Zack was, besides Milly's oh-so-captivating, one-word adjective: *single.*

THREE

Zack was sure his heart couldn't beat much harder without his suffering cardiac arrest. He parked the truck at the curb and ran into the police station, angry about whatever Dylan had done but also frightened that his boy was in trouble, his future possibly ruined.

With a small measure of relief, he saw Dylan—not handcuffed—the moment he walked into the station. Dylan sat on a bench and stared at the floor. Zack was struck by how much his boy looked like him, now that he was grown. Same straight blond hair, same lanky build. Dylan's long bangs fell forward and hid his eyes, but Zack imagined shame in them, regardless. At the sound of his father's steps, Dylan looked up and then quickly down again, exhaling visibly.

"Dylan, what happened?"

A tall officer adjusted his belt as he approached them. "I can answer that for you, sir. Are you the boy's father?" His expression was calm but stern.

Zack nodded and put out his hand. "Yes, officer. Zack Cooper. What happened?"

"Officer Reynolds." He shook Zack's hand and lifted his chin toward Dylan. "Your son was in the wrong place at the wrong time. We brought him in for shoplifting at the convenience store."

Zack jerked his head to face Dylan. "Shoplifting? Dylan, what in the—"

He saw fear and anger in his son's brown eyes. His mother's eyes, but less hard.

"Dad, I didn't . . . it wasn't—"

"Apparently your son didn't steal anything, Mr. Cooper. But the store manager didn't know that. We couldn't be sure of what happened until we got the boys down here. We asked the manager to review the security tape. Dylan here was the only one of the boys who appears to have been innocent of what was going on."

"The boys?"

Officer Reynolds nodded. "He was with two others. Older kids. One of them isn't even in high school anymore. They were the ones we actually arrested." He cocked his head behind him. "They're being held on bail. The store manager has had enough and wants to press charges."

Zack looked from the officer to Dylan and back again. "So Dylan wasn't officially arrested? He won't be charged or have a record?"

Reynolds rested his hands at his waist. "Not this time." He raised an eyebrow at Dylan. "You might want to rethink how you spend your school hours, son. And who you hang around with. This isn't the first time I've seen you with those two, and they're not heading in the right direction, I can tell you."

Dylan returned to staring at the floor. He gave a barely perceptible nod.

Zack shook his head and turned his back to his son in order to address the policeman. "What do I need to do? Is there something to sign?"

"No. Just get him back to school and hand out whatever punishment you see fit."

"I'll be sure to do that. Thanks." He frowned and felt his lips tighten. He faced Dylan. "Let's go. You're going to go talk to the teachers whose classes you missed this morning before you go back to whatever class is going on right now."

Zack waited until they got to the truck before letting his anger escape. He felt his voice get louder with each word. "What is the *matter* with you, Dylan? Do you have a *clue* about how a police record could destroy your future? Do you?"

Dylan's voice met his father's in volume, his attitude fitting someone treated poorly. "I didn't steal anything, Dad! I didn't know Piker and Tim were shoplifting. That cop even told you that."

"What were you doing out of school?"

Dylan had already opened his mouth to argue, but he closed it and sighed emphatically.

Zack kept his eyes ahead. "You realize you've ruined my trust in you, don't you?"

Dylan tsked. "Like you trusted me in the first place."

"Don't try to make this about me. I've trusted you in a lot of ways. I trusted that you'd be in school when you were supposed to be. When you've gone out with your friends, I've trusted that you'd go where you said you'd go. But you keep stepping on that trust."

"Come on, Dad. You haven't trusted me for . . . forever. You ask me all kinds of questions whenever I go anywhere, and then you act like I'm lying to you. You expect the worst of me."

"Prove me wrong, Dylan!" Zack stopped and ran his hands through his hair. He didn't mean to verify what his son said—that he thought the worst of him, but he didn't know what to do. He took a deep breath and released it. "You're grounded for a month."

"But I didn't steal anything!"

"You're grounded for skipping school again and hanging around with thieves."

"I didn't *know* they were thieves!"

Zack started the truck. "Well, you'll have a month to hone your skills in evaluating character. Pick better friends." He pulled away from the station and wondered how he could help his son improve on a social level. He used to be such a good kid. But now he seemed destined to gravitate toward troublemakers, and Zack felt helpless. If his own example wasn't enough, what would be?

He reached the intersection where he had to turn

and used the opportunity to glance at his son, who had ceased arguing.

Dylan stared out the side window. He looked furious, his nostrils flaring with every breath.

Well, Zack was angry too. But as mad as he was, his heart broke over this deepening rift between them. He was struck by a sudden memory of one of their fishing trips, years ago, when Dylan was a smaller, happier version of this angry young man, eager to explore nature and spend as much time as possible with his dad. Dylan had left his fishing rod for a moment to explore the area. He returned and proudly showed Zack something he found—it looked like it might be a musket ball. The two of them concocted an entire Civil War battle story, blending their imaginations together and enjoying each other's ideas.

Now, sitting in the truck, facing reality and the opposite sides of their own personal battle, that innocent memory seemed many ages away.

FOUR

Tina leaned back in her chair and laughed. Then she pushed back from her computer. On tea shop days she tended to work through lunch, and she had begun to edit her notes from her last session. But her best friend, Edie Llewelyn, had called to discuss their dinner plans for the following evening. Tina was seldom able to pass up a conversation with Edie, especially not conversations like this one. They hadn't even gotten around to discussing dinner yet.

"Come on. You're padding this story." Tina wiped tears from the corners of her eyes.

"I swear I'm not. Cows, I'm telling you. Four of 'em. Right out there on 626. Dispatch sent Ned and me. Said this lady was trying to get to a baby shower, but there were these cows in the road and she couldn't get past them. She was freaking out about being late for that shower, the dispatcher told us."

"Wouldn't that be something for Animal Control to handle? Not the baby shower part, but, I mean, what did the lady expect the police to do?"

"She just called nine-one-one. She didn't care who came—fire, police, whoever. She considered this quite an emergency, being late and missing baby bingo or blindfolded diapering."

"I usually pray for reasons to miss those shower games."

"I hear you, girl. But not this lady. It's a good thing she wasn't armed, or those cows would've been dead meat. Literally."

"How did the cows get there in the first place?"

"One of the farmers out there left a gate open, is all. And they liked it just fine on that paved road, I'm telling you. They had absolutely *no* plans to move out of that lady's way. She was laying on her horn and sweating bullets by the time we got there, she was so worked up. She's yelling at us, 'You open up a lane for me! That's what you're here for. That's why there's a "serve" in "serve and protect," isn't it?' And Ned goes, 'Lady, I can't just arrest a cow. This could take a while.'"

Tina walked to the window. She saw her next client getting out of her car. "I have to run, Edie. What about tomorrow night? When and where?"

"Hmm. You know, I thought maybe we could drive out to Upperville. The Blackthorne Inn. You up for that?"

"I'd love that. I haven't been out there in a while. I'll be finished with my last client at six tomorrow. You want me to make reservations?"

"No, I'll do it," Edie said. "I'll come pick you up at your place around six thirty. And be prepared, lady. It's karaoke night in the pub."

Tina's client walked into the waiting room just outside her office and smiled at her. Tina returned the smile, raised her hand in a casual wave, and signaled she'd be off the phone shortly. She couldn't argue about karaoke night in front of her client, so she let it go and said her goodbyes. Who knew? Maybe she'd be in the mood for that kind of evening tomorrow.

She walked to her office door. "Good to see you, Brandy. Come on in."

"Thanks!" The perkiness in Brandy's step and voice contrasted significantly with her mood several weeks ago. Tina closed the door as Brandy settled onto the loveseat, pulling her slim legs up and crossing them. With her retro '60s clothing and long wispy hair, she looked far more childlike than would be expected of a twenty-five-year-old woman. In a matter of seconds Tina was able to smell Brandy's trademark musky perfume. The girl was definitely into the whole hippie-chick thing.

Tina sat in the chair adjacent to the loveseat. "So, I take it this week went as well as last week? You seem upbeat."

"Great week!" Brandy nodded emphatically. "I think the new meds are helping *so* much. I didn't have a single episode since I saw you. Of course, it was a pretty stress-free week, but I think I like what Dr. Kendrick is giving me."

"Wonderful. I heard from him on Tuesday, and

he said the same thing. He thought you were on the right track."

Brandy gave Tina a shy smile. "But we might have to mess with the doses in a little while, you know, like we've had to during my periods."

"Oh?" She could tell Brandy was about to pop with some piece of news. "Why is that?"

Brandy bounced once on the loveseat, her voice in a near squeal of delight. "I tested at home yesterday. Mike and I are going to have a baby!"

Tina laughed with pleasure. "Congratulations, sweetie! What a blessing." She stood and leaned over to give Brandy a hug. "I know you were both eager for that, weren't you?"

Brandy rolled her eyes about herself. "I've been dying to try." She calmed for a moment. "But with my meds and my episodes . . . well, you know how concerned I've been. I didn't want any of that to interfere with the baby."

"What did Dr. Kendrick say about that? Have you talked with him since you found out?" Tina sat back down and wrote a few quick comments in her notebook.

"Just on the phone. I'm meeting with him tomorrow. He wants to watch me closely and adjust if we need to. But he says none of my stuff is terribly risky to the baby. And he said he was going to call you and talk, now that it's for real." She squeezed her eyes shut and drew happy little fists up to her chest for a moment. "I can't believe it."

Tina grinned. "And how is this news affecting your marriage so far? What does Mike have to say?"

Tina seldom worked with Brandy or any of her other bipolar clients without thinking of her own husband, Phil. The passage of years since his death—had it really been fourteen?—enabled her to reflect on him without fresh heartbreak. And God had used the loss and Tina's need for answers to guide her to her chosen profession.

"He's thrilled, of course," Brandy said. "But he's a little worried about finances and baby care, and all that kind of stuff. I guess I am too. I'm looking forward to being a mom, but there seem to be an awful lot of things I need to, you know, organize. I'm trying not to let that stress me out."

"All right, let's work on that today, then. Let's look at what your tasks and jobs are right now and how they'll change. We'll take some of the mystery out of the process."

She knew this client thrived on order. By the end of their time together, Brandy's worries seemed diminished, though not completely eliminated.

"Thanks, Tina." Brandy stood at the door before she left, her hand resting on her stomach as if she could already feel the baby there. "You know, when I started coming to see you last year, it was all I could do to get here and keep myself together.

It's never been that easy for me to juggle an entire day's worth of responsibility without *some* kind of meltdown. I sure wouldn't have thought I could handle marriage and a baby."

Tina smiled. "You've worked hard to get to this point, Brandy."

"Well, I just wanted to say thanks. Now I feel like almost anything's possible."

After she left, Tina sat at her desk to work on her session notes before it grew too late in the day. Not that she had anything of consequence to rush home for. She enjoyed her home and her privacy and her freedom, but she wouldn't mind a little more complication in her life, frankly. Maybe even male-generated complication.

She had dated a few men during the years since she lost Phil. None of the relationships had panned out particularly well. Why was she even thinking this way this afternoon?

A brief vision of the produce guy flitted through her mind. So that was it. She came across a set of crystal blue eyes and a rugged, square jaw—and, yes, she seemed to remember nice lips—and immediately she began to pine away for the man of her dreams, whoever he might be.

She was being silly and romantic. For all she knew, the man of her dreams was nothing but that: a dream. But Brandy's last comment kept her distracted from working on her notes: *Now I feel like almost anything's possible.*

FIVE

D ylan?" Zack called up the stairs, but he heard
pounding music in Dylan's room and
realized there was no way his voice had broken
through that sound barrier. He still held a serving
spoon in his hand as he mounted the stairs, and he
took care to keep gravy from dripping onto the
carpet.

He gave a quick tap on the door before reaching
for the knob—but the door was locked. Zack
didn't mind Dylan's locking his door except when
they were at odds. And they were still at odds a
day after the shoplifting incident. He knocked
again—louder. "Dylan? Open up."

His son came to the door. He looked less surly
than he had on their drive back to school from
the police station yesterday, but an overall
disdain for everything about his circumstances
still lingered. His spoke in a dull voice. "What's
up, Dad?"

"Come on down and set the table for dinner. It's
just about ready. And would you please turn that
music down?"

Dylan looked at the floor. "You're dripping stuff
on the carpet."

"Oh, blast!" Zack cupped his hand under the

spoon and rushed to the bathroom sink. He should have taken the time to put the spoon down before coming up. For that matter he shouldn't have had to come up here. He raised his voice as he rinsed the spoon. "I want you to keep that music down enough that you can hear me when I call you. This is ridiculous."

Dylan, directly behind him, had walked into the bathroom to grab a towel and clean up the drips. Now he stopped and looked at his father, exasperation written all over his face.

Zack cringed inwardly. The boy was trying to help, and he just threw a criticism at him. But for some reason, he couldn't bring himself to apologize. "Look. Thanks." He gestured at the towel. "I appreciate your help."

"Whatever." Dylan turned away.

One of Zack's least favorite expressions was "whatever." But before either of them could say anything else that might spark further conflict, he thought he'd try to defuse the discord between them. And what better way than to keep the two of them from speaking to one another?

"Hey, since it's just the two of us, let's eat in front of the TV tonight."

Dylan looked up from the carpet, his expression more open. Zack didn't normally allow meals in front of the television. "Where's Sherry?"

"She's staying over at Amanda's."

Dylan nodded and finished cleaning the carpet. "Okay. I'll set the coffee table instead of the kitchen table."

A few minutes later they settled onto the couch, switched on the TV, and dug into beef stroganoff. Zack hated to admit it, but their not speaking to each other was the perfect solution. They both focused on the movie unfolding before them as they ate. The film was hilarious. Eventually they not only laughed together, but when they did say anything to each other, it was to repeat and savor some of the funnier lines they heard.

However, once the film ended, Zack sensed a return to tension in Dylan's silence. When he headed for the stairs, Zack said, "Come on and help me with the dishes, son."

He ignored the harrumph of annoyance from his boy and started washing the saucepans. "I'll get these, but please bring everything in from the den and put away those leftovers."

Dylan obeyed silently, but his irritation filled the kitchen.

Zack decided to give conversation a shot. "So. Anything interesting happen at school today?"

A moment's hesitation. Then, "I went to every class, Dad. You don't have to worry."

Zack stopped drying a saucepan and turned. "That's not why I asked. I just wondered how your day went."

Suddenly Dylan set down the plastic wrap he

was struggling with and faced Zack. "I know you want to teach me a lesson about skipping school. I know this is all about consequences and stuff. But we're only two weeks away from the end of the school year."

"Uh-huh. What's your point?"

"It's just, you know, summer's short." Dylan shrugged. "I was wondering if you could shorten my restriction so it ends with the school year. That would still be pretty bad for me. I mean, I'm missing a party tonight, and I'll miss a lot of stuff over the next two weeks. But there will be some celebrations right after the last day of school. It just doesn't seem fair that I have to miss everything just for skipping school one day."

"Are these school-sanctioned celebrations?"

"I don't know." Dylan looked away and picked up the plastic wrap again.

Zack tilted his head and gave his son a world-weary eyeballing. "Dylan, you're a smart kid. Are you talking about school activities or are you talking about parties given by people like Piker and what's-his-face. Sticky Fingers Tim?"

Dylan ripped a piece of plastic wrap away and scowled at Zack. "Piker and Tim aren't having any parties. That's not—"

Zack snorted. "Guess not. They're probably going to be busy planning a prison break."

"You can't decide to hate all of my friends just because of what Piker and Tim did." Dylan's volume rose. "I've got to have *some* kind of life besides school!"

"How can I figure out whether I like your friends or not, Dylan?" Zack wasn't able to control his frustration either. This wasn't how he'd planned the conversation to go. He heard himself yelling as if he heard someone else's voice. "You never bring anyone around here. Either you know your friends are unacceptable or you consider me too clean-cut for your friends to meet. Either situation is a problem in my book."

"You're not so clean-cut. You're just . . . you hate everyone who . . . you don't have any idea how to . . . oh, forget it." He shoved a bowl into the refrigerator and stormed out of the room. "I hate my life!"

Zack clenched his teeth and steeled himself against going after the boy. Neither one of them was doing any good in this argument. He shut his eyes.

Lord, I know I don't come before You often, but I absolutely do not know what to do. I didn't sign up for this single-parenting thing. Please help me.

The ringing phone interrupted him. Caller ID told him the call came from Amanda's home. Maybe his daughter was checking in with him for the night. Odd that she wasn't using her cell phone, though.

"Hello?"

"Hi, Zack, it's Rebecca Sheffield. Amanda's mom?"

"Yes. Hi, Rebecca."

"I'm sorry to bother you, but Amanda's not answering her cell phone, and there's been a change in when she needs to be home tomorrow. May I speak with her?"

Zack frowned. "I . . . I don't understand. I thought the girls were staying at your place tonight."

Silence prefaced her response. "Is that what Sherry told you?"

Now Zack was silent. He paced the kitchen floor. "Did Amanda tell you they were staying here tonight?"

"Yes." Rebecca muttered something under her breath. "I'm going to start making phone calls. Do you know of any parties tonight?"

Zack grabbed his car keys and headed for the door. He forgot he was on the house phone and almost disconnected the call as he walked out. "Hang on, Rebecca. Let's exchange cell phone numbers. I'm going out to look for the girls."

"Yeah, I'll send my husband to do the same—"

"Dad?"

Zack looked at the top of the stairs and saw Dylan, which triggered his memory.

"Hold on, Rebecca. Dylan, didn't you say there was a party tonight?"

Dylan nodded.

"Okay, come on. You're going to take me there."

Rebecca's voice broke through their conversation. "Zack, do you know where they might be?"

"I'm not sure, no. But my son knows of at least one party, and we're going to check it out." He heard Dylan groan but he ignored him. "They might not be there, but at least it's a possibility."

The adults hung up and Zack thought about his prayer. Well, *that* certainly didn't seem to help. His fifteen-year-old daughter was somewhere with plans to stay away all night. Plans to stay somewhere she didn't want to tell him about.

A chill ran up his arms. He hoped he wasn't too late. Anything was possible.

SIX

That evening Tina and Edie couldn't have been more relaxed. Their waiter had just placed their beautiful dinners before them, neither of them had to be back at work for at least twenty-four hours, and they were far enough from town that interruptions were highly unlikely. They were fully free and independent.

"One of my favorite reasons for coming to the Blackthorne Inn is I know nobody's going to expect me to play cop on my off hours," Edie said.

While she looked far more feminine in her pale yellow blouse and brown slacks than she did when in uniform, there was always a little of the tomboy about Edie. She took a bite of her seafood cassoulet and closed her eyes with the pleasure of it.

"No chasing down cows tonight, then?" Tina cut into her grilled lamb chops and smiled. Exactly medium rare. Perfect.

Edie shook her blond bangs out of her eyes. "No cows, no teens, no domestics—nobody at all to mess with my chillaxing."

Tina laughed. "Okay, homegirl. Don't get too cool on me there. What's Rob up to tonight?"

"Not sure." She shrugged. "He stopped by the

station earlier today and chatted with Bucky for a while. I think they might have made plans."

Tina nodded. Officer Bucky Reynolds. She didn't want to comment on Bucky and slide into another conversation about him. In the two months since she'd stopped dating him, she and Edie had talked his strengths and faults to death.

Tina's smile slid sideways. "You think you're any closer to accepting Rob's marriage proposal?" One sure way of moving the conversation away from Bucky was to get Edie to focus on Rob.

"You know better than to ask me that." Edie stabbed at a scallop. "The man's going to drive me nuts with his asking."

"How long do you plan to wait before you finally say yes?"

She shook her head. "He's forty years old, just like me. I love that he's Christian, just like me. I love that he's smart, that he's an associate professor. But he has two more years of exorbitant child support to pay, and I don't want to get married to a man who's barely making ends meet, which he is." She held up her palm as if she were taking an oath. She reminded Tina of someone from Manhattan, rather than a homegrown country gal. "That might sound cold, but I've seen too many domestic issues that arise from financial worries. It's not going to happen to me."

"No, I understand." Tina swallowed a delicious bite of wild mushroom couscous.

"Plus," Edie said, "even though he didn't want his divorce, he *is* divorced. That's not nothing."

"Sure, you're right. I just thought I remembered your saying you might at least say yes to a long engagement, for when he's more financially stable."

"I changed my mind. Who's to say what will happen over the next two years? I want to see how he handles himself once he's really free. I'm not in a hurry. I've been single all my life. I'm doing just fine." She shook her head. "I just didn't expect to fall for a divorced man going to the singles group at church."

"Well, the divorce wasn't his idea, Edie, like you said." Tina smiled. "And I believe there are a few other sinners in the congregation, including me."

Edie jerked her head up from focusing on her meal. "Oh, Tina, I'm sorry. I didn't mean to insinuate anything against you. I know you would have done anything to prevent Phil's actions. The divorce, the suicide—"

Tina waved off the issue. "I'm teasing you. I know how you feel about all of that."

But suddenly Edie wasn't paying attention. She was staring over Tina's shoulder.

"Well, speak of the devil."

That sent a shiver up Tina's spine, since she felt they were speaking about her deceased husband. She turned around and saw Rob walking toward them. And Tina's old boyfriend Bucky Reynolds was with him. Her stomach dropped.

"Oh, please no."

Edie laughed. "You do know you just said that out loud, don't you?"

Tina shut her eyes for a moment, praying a quick plea for graciousness. When she opened her eyes she took it all in: Edie's narrow glare at Rob, Rob's shrugging as if his choice of location that evening had been beyond his control, and—worst of all—Bucky's sorry attempt to act surprised to see Tina there.

Edie nearly hissed. "Rob. What in the world— this huge world, full of billions of restaurants other than this one—are you two doing here?"

Before he could respond, Bucky put his hand on Tina's shoulder. "Well. You're looking super hot as usual."

"No, Bucky." Tina felt she couldn't stop him soon enough. She knew other diners could hear him. Comments like this were exactly why she had cut their relationship short. As a policeman the guy could operate with all the authority and decorum of Lord Horatio Nelson. But on a personal level? Maybe a seventeen-year-old. He was forever resorting to behavior and comments that made Tina's teeth hurt, she clenched them so hard. "No comments from you, please. Edie and I are trying to enjoy a lovely dinner, just we two women. We aren't attempting . . . hotness. Okay?"

Unfazed, Bucky grinned. "I know that. It just comes naturally for you. Can I help if it—"

"No!" Tina turned in her seat to face him more squarely. "No," she said sternly. She knew she sounded as if she were scolding a dog with a penchant for messing in the house, but nothing else seemed to penetrate Bucky's density.

Edie said, "Rob, you're too smart for this. If you want me to start keeping secrets from you about where I spend my time away from you, you're doing great."

"Hey, it wasn't my—" Rob stopped defending himself and tapped Bucky. "Come on, man. This was a bad idea. Let's head back to town for dinner."

Bucky looked at Tina, his brown eyes suddenly forlorn. Inquisitive. As if he actually needed her to signal further whether he should stay or go.

Tina blinked slowly and nodded. "Bye, Bucky."

"Oh. Okay. See you around." He nearly hung his head as he turned away.

If Tina hadn't experienced this kind of thing before, she would feel inclined to call him back and make the dismissal less harsh. But he was a hard one to repel.

"I do *not* know what happens to that man around you," Edie said to the back of Tina's head.

Tina turned back to the table. "Welcome to my world."

"I swear, Tina, it's like a part of his brain works

backward when he sees you. Was he like that around you before you two dated?"

Tina took another bite of lamb and sighed that it had cooled. "Not like that. This is the weird kind of behavior I told you about. He didn't seem like this in the beginning. You know, he's all tall, dark, and . . . swarthy. He seemed so manly when we first dated."

"Yeah." Edie nodded. "That's the way he acts around the station. He always looks like he needs a shave. A tough guy, you know?"

"But the more he liked me the harder he tried to be . . . I don't know. Cool? He was forever embarrassing me. He didn't sound cool or young. He sounded—"

"Stupid?" Edie spoke at her plate while scooping up a forkful of crabmeat. "Ignorant?"

"Yes. I guess that fits. A very odd guy."

"Well, he's not like that on the job. He's a good cop." Edie shrugged. "You just don't know how a guy will handle love until he's knee-deep in it."

"Oh, that's not love." Tina jerked her thumb over her shoulder. "That's something else altogether."

"To you, maybe." Edie dipped her bread in the cream sauce on her plate. "But that boy thinks he loves you. I'd bet my favorite diamond earrings on that."

Tina frowned. "You don't own any diamond earrings."

"If I did, I'd bet 'em." She pointed in the direction of Rob and Bucky's departure. "He's hoping to heat things back up with you, I'm absolutely certain."

Tina sighed and motioned for the server. "The only thing I'm interested in heating up at the moment is these lamb chops."

Edie smiled. "And then the pub's karaoke stage?"

"Oh, Edie." Tina groaned and then laughed at her friend's pleading face.

"Please? I don't know when I laugh so much as when we do karaoke. And you just never know who you might meet."

Tina rolled her eyes. "Something tells me if God has someone in mind for me, he's not spending the evening waiting for me in a pub."

Edie gave her a sly smile. "Maybe not. But maybe he is. Who knows how Mr. Right is spending his time tonight?"

SEVEN

Tired and stressed, but also relieved that his daughter was safe, Zack never wanted to spend another night as he had this last one. And he didn't have the luxury of sleeping in on Saturday morning, so he decided his kids wouldn't either.

At eight o'clock he readied his truck, preparing to pull away from the Middleburg Community Center, where the Farmers' Market did business every Saturday during the warmer seasons. Both Dylan and Sherry waited in the front of the truck, sulking. They had been recruited to load produce on the truck early in the morning and to help Zack and his right-hand man, Lorenzo, set up for the market's opening.

Now they were to accompany Zack while he made a special trip to deliver produce to Milly's tea shop for an event she was helping to cater with one of the local restaurant owners.

"You sure you'll be all right on your own, Lorenzo?" Zack rested his hand on his friend's shoulder.

"What, all right? I do this all the time. You know that." Lorenzo, while born and raised in the States, was the very picture of the Italian male. His

Roman nose and the dark curls of his receding hairline caused many to expect an accent before he spoke. He had worked for Zack for years, and the men had grown close.

"Yeah, I know." Zack smiled, glad he could lean on Lorenzo after such a rough night. "But this is a gorgeous morning. You know it's going to get crazy busy."

Lorenzo waved the comment away. "You're not going to be gone that long. I'll be fine on my own." He glanced at the truck. "You going to tell me what's going on with the mopey twins over there?"

"Yeah, but it's a long story. Later." He turned to the truck, saw the tops of two blond, lowered heads, and looked back. "And the mopey twins will be working here all morning just as soon as we get back."

"Ah." Lorenzo smiled. "It will be good for them."

Zack drove to the other side of Middleburg and pulled up in front of Milly's. Neither he nor the kids had spoken much this morning. While Dylan and Zack hadn't argued any more beyond their words after dinner last night, Zack and Sherry had had quite an exchange. Now her pretty blue eyes were puffy from crying, and her lips were pushed out in a spoiled pout.

"All right. Let's go, both of you." Zack yanked the emergency brake up and got out of the truck.

The kids joined him at the truck bed, where several boxes of produce were stored. "Dylan, you take those two in, and Sherry, you take those two smaller ones. I'll be right behind you."

Milly met them at the back door. "I thought I saw the kids! What a nice surprise. Come on in, all of you." Her voice remained pleasant and chipper, even after Zack was sure she gave the Cooper family enough of a once over to have understood all was not well. "Goodness, those peaches look lovely. Here, right over here on the counter, Dylan. Sherry, you're looking so grown-up these days."

Sherry attempted a smile, but she looked as if she could break into tears with very little effort.

Milly's expression was kind, and she acted as if nothing were wrong. "I have several trays of shortbread I've just pulled from the oven. Why don't you all try them and tell me what you think?"

Dylan eyed the trays, clearly already hungry despite a big bacon-and-egg breakfast back home. "Is that what smells so good in here?" His manner was still subdued, but Zack knew Milly would bring the kids out of their slumps in no time. That's how she was.

She laughed. "I'm not sure if that's what you smell, but I'm glad it smells good. Thank you. Here, try." She encouraged both teens toward the rack of cooling trays.

Zack couldn't help but smile. Just for a moment, his kids looked young again. He'd give anything to erase the last several days of conflict and have his contented kids back again. Never would he have expected his children to become so rebellious. So disobedient. But he knew their straying hadn't happened overnight. They had been pulling away from him and his authority for . . . well, for a few years now.

"Zack, why don't you and the kids sit up front and enjoy a bit of tea and pastry?" Milly's eyes studied Zack as she spoke to him. "It won't take me but a minute to get a pot of Formosa oolong together, yes? It's wonderful with sweets."

"Thanks, Milly, but we can't. We need to get back to the Farmers' Market and help Lorenzo with the customers."

Her smile widened. She sighed and crossed her arms. "Ah, Lorenzo! I haven't seen enough of him lately. How is he doing? And Ilsa and the boys?"

Zack waved his hand in the air, as if including all of the people she mentioned. "Doing great. Fantastic little family." He didn't mean to, but he looked at his own kids when he said that last bit. Then he looked back at Milly and dropped his gaze. When he met her eyes again, she had the warmest, most accepting expression on her face.

"Uh, look, kids," he said. "There are a few more

boxes in the back of the truck. I need you to bring those in for me, please."

Neither of them balked. Milly had already affected them in a positive way. The moment they walked out, she spoke.

"What happened at the police station the other day? Is Dylan in great trouble?"

He shook his head. "Not this time. They didn't actually arrest him, but his so-called friends were in the holding cell when I picked him up. Shoplifting."

Milly put her hand to her chest. "Oh no. But Dylan wasn't involved?"

"So he says. He claims he didn't realize the other two were shoplifting. But I grounded him for skipping school, so I'm the bad guy right now."

"I know that's one of the hardest roles for a parent to play. I've never been happy about missing motherhood, but I do consider it a blessing I haven't endured the trials many of my friends have with their children."

"Yeah. It's especially hard to do it on your own." He pressed the heel of his hand against his forehead. "I have to admit I haven't been much of a praying man these last few years, but those kids are definitely bringing me to my knees."

Milly's blue eyes were full of sympathy. "Sherry too? I assumed she was upset about what happened with Dylan. That's not why she's been crying?"

Zack felt a headache coming on. "No. She's a trial all on her own." He looked back at Milly. "She lied to me about where she was spending the night last night. She and a girlfriend planned to stay out all night. She went to a party she knew I wouldn't approve of, and she figured she could just sleep there. The boy having the party was fine with that."

"Where were the boy's parents?"

Zack huffed. "Obviously they thought they could trust their son on his own when they had to spend the evening in Washington at some political function. It was only by God's grace I found out that Sherry lied to me. I realize that now. Who knows what might have happened—"

Dylan and Sherry walked back in, each carrying a box full of fruit and vegetables. Both teens glanced from Zack to Milly and away. Zack knew they were sharp enough to gather their father had shared with Milly what they had done.

"Thanks, kids!" Milly's manner was completely devoid of judgment. "Those can go with the others." She turned away from all of them and put several items from the cooling trays in a small box. She handed it to Dylan. "For the two of you to share."

They both smiled. "Thanks," Dylan said.

She rested her hand on Sherry's shoulder. "I

wonder if you two could give me another moment with your father."

"Sure they can." Zack opened the door they had come in. "Wait for me in the truck. And don't go *anywhere.*"

Their smiles faltered as they walked out. Sherry spoke over her shoulder. "Thanks for the goodies, Milly."

"My pleasure, dear. Come by anytime." Once the door was closed, she poured a cup of tea and handed it to Zack. This time he didn't turn it down. Milly tucked her graying blond curls behind her ears and said, "You know they're good kids at heart, Zack. That's your doing."

"Yeah, they are good at heart. But I could still lose them. I'm afraid one of them will make a life-changing mistake that can't just be attributed to adolescent ignorance. When they start lying like this, it's impossible to warn them against everything they might be doing. Or considering doing." He sighed and looked at the ground. "I'm so out of my league here."

"Well, I'll keep you in my prayers, of course. I hope you know that."

He looked up and nodded.

"But I also wonder if you'd be willing to get some professional guidance. Some guidance for the kids, maybe."

He frowned. "You mean, like a shrink?"

"No, just a counselor. It's not unheard of, Zack.

She might give all three of you some tools to cope with this tough stage in the kids' lives."

"She? You have someone in mind?"

"I have a customer who's a counselor. She seems quite popular. She's a dear woman too."

Zack stuck his hands in his back pockets and shook his head. "I don't know, Milly. Not only would it be near impossible to get those two to cooperate with something like that, I can't afford the cost. I know I may look like a wealthy man of leisure—"

Milly laughed.

"—but farming isn't the most lucrative of careers. Not for me, anyway. I get by, but I haven't given Lorenzo a raise in three years. I can't believe he stays with me."

She patted his arm. "Lorenzo's a good man. He recognizes one of his own kind."

"Thanks."

The truck's horn honked, and both of them looked in that direction, even though they couldn't see out the front of the shop from where they stood. Zack looked back at Milly, shock on his face.

"Can you *believe* those two? It's like the condemned man yelling at the governor."

Milly chuckled. "The pastries must have run out. I'll let you go. But consider the counselor idea. Maybe something could be worked out."

He nodded and left.

Zack didn't have anything against counselors, really. He'd even come across one or two in his time. But if he had ever crossed paths with one his kids would meet, he certainly wasn't aware of it.

EIGHT

The sermon Sunday morning at Tina's church seemed designed specifically for her. Of course, she knew the best sermons made everyone feel that way. As the closing music played and she and Edie filed out with everyone else, she ran some of the pastor's encouragement through her mind again.

Edie seemed to read her thoughts. "You really can't go wrong with that verse from Jeremiah, can you?"

"I was just thinking the same thing." Tina grinned. "'I know the plans I have for you.' You hear that one so often that it's easy to forget how encouraging it can be. Plans to give us hope. I love that."

They walked toward the youth room. Tina was scheduled to help out there this week.

"Yeah," Edie said. "I usually only think of it when things are messed up, but it made sense to me today too. Made me even more certain about not saying yes to Rob yet."

"Really? How did that happen?"

Edie shrugged. "It just verified that I don't need to rush. I don't feel really pressed to be married. Maybe it's not in God's plan."

Tina didn't respond. Until that moment she hadn't realized she had come to expect that she would remarry someday. She didn't feel pressed either, but it was something she took for granted. Here she was, thirty-four years old, though, and not a prospect in sight. How much of that was God's plan, and how much of it was due to her own choices?

"Hey, Tina!" A teenage girl's lively voice interrupted her thoughts. "Are you in youth today?" She was passing so quickly, headed toward the youth room, that Tina had to call out her answer.

"Yeah, I'll be right there, Casey."

"Okay, I'm out of here," Edie said. She raised her hand in a wave as she stepped back.

"Come with me, Edie. It'll be fun."

"Nothing doing. I want to go home, enjoy a leisurely lunch, and take a little nap before Rob comes over. I've got the late shift tonight at the station." She fluttered her eyelashes. "You don't get this beautiful missing too much sleep."

Tina laughed. "You might be beautiful, but as you heard the other night, *I* am super hot."

The mother of one of the teens walked past Tina as she spoke. She glanced back to see who had claimed super hotness.

Tina felt a flush run up her cheeks. The woman moved on before Tina could explain herself—as if she *could* explain herself. In embarrassed dismay she looked at Edie, who raised her palm in mock disdain.

"And *this* is who we have leading our youth group. Shocking."

Tina smacked at Edie's hand. "Oh, go on home and get your beauty rest, you little diva."

"Talk with you later, girl." Edie turned and left.

By the time Tina got to the youth room, the small group of musicians had already started playing. The teens, on their feet, clapped and sang along. She made her way to the back of the room, where she relaxed against the wall.

The youth pastor, Vince, gave an animated talk about Joseph and his many jealous brothers, and Tina enjoyed it as much as the teens did. Suddenly she became aware that Antony, one of the other adult helpers, had come to stand next to her. They smiled politely at each other. She didn't know him terribly well. The two of them had had a few chats in groups, but none of their conversations were of great substance. Antony was a big hit with the boys in the teen group. He was athletic and upbeat, as far as Tina had seen.

When Pastor Vince made the kids laugh with one of his real-life examples, Tina's and Antony's eyes met, and they laughed together. That was when she realized—by the directness of his gaze—that he was interested in her as more than a fellow youth group helper.

Oh. Now she would have to adjust her view of

him, like focusing a camera lens to focus on details rather than the broad panorama. He was suddenly Antony, the possible suitor, rather than Antony, the fellow Christian.

She hadn't even looked at him all that closely before. She honestly couldn't say whether or not she found him attractive. Obviously, he hadn't stunned her with his looks, but that didn't really mean anything definitive. Men had grown on her before. That was how it was with Phil when she first met him.

She forced herself to return her attention to the pastor's message, which sounded as if it were nearing its end. When he finished in a prayer, Tina added her own—that God would guide her in all matters, including this fellow standing beside her.

She needn't have worried. As soon as the group stood and became a big mingling mass of blue jeans and chatter, Antony was surrounded and caught up in a boisterous, friendly argument about paintballing with a group of the more athletic boys.

Tina worked the crowd, seeking girls who appeared shy or alone and in need of someone's attention. One of the more outgoing girls practically skipped up to her, pulling with her a chunky girl Tina didn't recognize.

"Tina!" The energetic girl grabbed her in a gangly, intense hug, her long brown hair in Tina's face. She made Tina laugh.

"Faye!" Tina mimicked Faye's animated greeting. "I saw you *way* into the music when I walked in, as usual. Who's your friend?" She and the other girl exchanged smiles.

"This is Heather. She's new. Well, not new everywhere, just here. She's my BFF at school, right, Heather?" She said this last as if she were mocking young Hollywood socialites.

Heather laughed softly. "Right."

"Welcome, Heather. You know, I think I heard a group of the teens were planning to meet at Teddy's for pizza. Are you girls interested in going?"

Faye shook her head. "Not today. My mom's taking Heather and me into Washington. Kennedy Center. Opera seats for *Mary Poppins*. Isn't that awesome?"

"Wow! That should be—"

"My mom loves her," Faye told Heather, pointing at Tina. Apparently they were finished talking about *Mary Poppins*. "Tina takes my mom's group to Milly's tea shop—you know that place? She takes them there once a week. Isn't that awesome?"

Tina gave Faye a crooked smile. She was so like her mother, Carmella. Or, like a younger, far thinner version of Carmella.

Before Heather or Tina could answer either of Faye's questions about awesomeness, Faye brought the conversation to an abrupt end.

"Well, gotta go. Mom will stress if we make her wait. See ya, Tina."

"Oh. All right. See you later. And, Heather, I hope—"

But Heather was whisked away, barely able to throw a cursory wave and smile in Tina's direction.

"That one's quite a ball of energy, isn't she?"

Tina turned at the deep voice behind her.

Antony.

Time to go back on alert and sharpen that camera lens, both inside and out.

She knew her laugh sounded polite rather than genuine. "Yes, Faye's quite a character. I'm glad to see she's bringing friends from school."

"She's probably hard to say no to."

He was far more attractive when he smiled. Definitely plenty of women would find him attractive. Manly. But he had just the slightest touch of Neanderthal about him. She wasn't sure she could think of him romantically unless he had one doozy of a sense of humor. And, now that she looked closely, she thought he might be quite a bit younger than she.

She watched his game face suddenly take shape. The smile shrank, the dark eyebrows lifted, and a retrieved thought widened his eyes. Here it came.

"Say, Tina, I was wondering if you'd be interested in getting together for coffee sometime. Maybe even this afternoon?"

This afternoon? Goodness. He just dived right in there.

"You mean right now?"

He shrugged. "Sure." He smiled. "It's just coffee. I'd suggest lunch, but I actually have to work this afternoon."

"No, no. Coffee is fine." She could certainly handle investing the time it took to drink a latte, couldn't she?

A noisy group of boys and girls descended upon them then, several of them talking to Tina and Antony at once. Tina was barely able to decipher that they were asking the two adults to join them for pizza at Teddy's.

"I can't today, guys." Antony jingled his car keys in his hand and shot a quick glance at Tina. "Have to work this afternoon."

Protests from the kids nearly drowned him out.

"Come on, man, that's what you said last week."

"Yeah, and last week you said you'd come this week. You work too much."

"It *is* the Lord's day, Antony."

He smiled at that. Outnumbered, he looked at Tina as if asking her permission.

Okay, he was flexible. That was good. Of course, there was always the chance he was cheap. He was too busy to take her to lunch, just the two of them, but he seemed willing to put the work off to go to Teddy's. Doing a group lunch meant every man for himself (or every woman for herself) when the check came.

She shook off that thought. How cynical she was becoming!

She smiled and shrugged. "Sounds good to me."

So Teddy's Pizza it was. Tina actually liked that idea better. It would give her a chance to consider Antony without feeling the same pressure she would had they gone out one-on-one.

Nevertheless, as she drove to Teddy's, she called Edie.

"Am I interrupting your leisurely lunch?"

Edie's relaxed voice reflected the effectiveness of her leisurely lunch. "Not a problem, girl. I'm finishing up some amazing leftover chicken Marsala and an article about Clive Owen's new movie. Very important stuff, but I'll make time for you. What's up? You missing me already?"

"Of course, but that's not why I called. Do you know that guy Antony from church, by any chance?"

"Antony. Antony. What does he look like?"

"Tall, short dark hair, chronic stubble, possibly Italian-American, kind of big lips—"

"Is this the guy who helps with youth sometimes? Nice-ish but looks a little like a brute?"

"That's the one."

"You interested in him?"

"I don't think so. But he asked me out after the youth meeting today."

"Out where?"

"Coffee. But now we're joining some of the teens for pizza instead."

"So how may I be of service, ma'am?"

"I think he's going to ask me on a date, and I wanted some input from you."

"Hmm. My input is see how he behaves at lunch. If he eats with his mouth open, forget it. If he's cool with the kids, polite with you, and manages to string words together coherently, give him a shot."

Tina pulled the car up near Teddy's. "You certainly aren't setting the bar very high."

"Hey, what can I say?" Tina could practically hear Edie shrugging. "It's not as if your dance card is overflowing, right?"

"Why do I call you, Edie?" Tina sighed. "I suppose I should get to know him better before completely writing him off."

"There's the spirit. Sounds like love to me."

Tina laughed. Then she actually blushed, all by herself in the car, before speaking again. "Um, you know the guy I mentioned last week? The farmer-type guy?"

"The handsome one in front of Milly's shop?"

"Yeah."

Tina lifted a shoulder. "It's just, I don't know, the spark of attraction I felt there. That's what I'd like to feel—at least that—before going on a date. You know?"

"Well, sure. Who wouldn't? But you can't always get what you want, lady. You can't measure each guy that comes along by a shared glance with someone you'll never see again."

"You don't know that. I might see him again. Middleburg is a small town."

"And what do you know about him?"

"He . . . looks really good in a baseball cap."

"Exactly. I believe my work here is done. Now you must go forth and eat pizza."

Tina sighed. "Yes, I must. All right. I'll try to be open minded. Talk with you later."

By the time the group settled in at Teddy's, their number had diminished to eight. Definitely manageable. The teens grabbed their seats so quickly that Tina and Antony ended up sitting at opposite ends of the table. Again, Tina didn't mind, because she was better able to observe, and she could still hear a fair amount of what he had to say.

She loved these teens. They were respectful, godly, and fun. The fact that they were so drawn to Antony was a huge point in his favor. And she could tell he genuinely enjoyed them. Another point on the "yes" side.

Then, on top of the ease she felt during lunch, he surprised everyone by picking up the tab for all of them. So much for his being cheap. Ashamed for her earlier suspicion, she gave him three points for his generosity.

Regardless of the fact that there was still a point—maybe two—on the "not terribly attracted to him" side, he truly was more attractive when he smiled. Her mind was made up by the time they all went their separate ways outside the restaurant.

Once they were the last two standing, Antony tried a second time. "So, now that we've survived a group lunch, maybe we could give dinner a shot. Are you available Tuesday evening?"

She thought of Edie's recommendation. Plus, if one of her own clients asked her how to handle this moment, she knew what she would advise them. She figured she should take her own advice.

"Tuesday evening would be fine."

NINE

While Zack showered late Sunday morning, he couldn't help but hope. He, Dylan, and Sherry had spent several hours in the field that morning, picking strawberries, raspberries, and blackberries. Despite the kids' natural inclination to gripe about working on a Sunday, they both ended up enjoying themselves. Much of the tension seemed to fade away under the early morning sun as they worked side by side. Happier days—before Maya left—came to mind.

His offer to take them to the movies only added to their enjoyment. They might both be on restriction, but that didn't mean they couldn't entertain themselves as a family.

For a moment the old twinge of guilt about skipping church flashed through Zack's mind. He used to love going to church, and the kids did too. But Maya hadn't held his beliefs and had balked weekly in front of Dylan and Sherry. Zack and Maya's quarreling about church eventually painted black the entire experience.

He could certainly start back again now—could have four years ago, after Maya left. But by then he was out of the habit, and the kids no longer wanted to go. He currently had enough battles with them to avoid adding that to the mix right now. Maybe in time.

Now a knock on the bathroom door brought him out of his reverie.

"Come on, Dad." It was Dylan. "I want to get there early enough to see the previews."

Zack turned off the water. "I'll be right out."

Within minutes he was dry and in a T-shirt and a fresh pair of jeans. He ran a comb through his damp blond hair, and a few strands fell back onto his face. He needed a haircut. And a shave. With a shrug, he muttered to himself, "Good enough for the movies."

The closest theater was forty minutes away from home. Zack didn't notice how hungry he was until they began their drive.

"How about we stop for lunch on the way? Say, Teddy's Pizza?"

Dylan nearly whined his response. "Aw, Dad, if we do that we'll be late. Why didn't we quit working earlier?"

"The point of this trip to the movies is to give ourselves a reward for working, Dylan. No work, no reward." Zack gripped the steering wheel just a little tighter. He really didn't want to get into an argument.

Sherry piped up. "Why don't we just get lunch at the multiplex? They have hot dogs and nachos. I think they have pizza too."

Zack hesitated. No doubt the food was

ridiculously expensive there, but how often did he and his kids go out together anymore? "Good idea. We'll do that."

By the time they reached the theater, paid for their tickets, and picked up lunch at the counter, Zack had spent more than $50. When the employee at the snack counter told Zack what their lunch cost, Zack felt both of his kids watching him. He figured they feared he would get upset. Any sane man would rave about spending so much on so little, but he didn't want to spoil this outing. He told himself it was an investment in his relationship with his kids and let it go.

When they chose their seats, Dylan deliberately waited for Sherry and Zack to enter the row first. This put Zack in the middle of his son and daughter, a seating arrangement both kids knew Zack preferred. When Dylan gestured for Zack to enter before he did, their eyes met.

"Thanks, son."

Dylan half smiled and shrugged. "No big deal."

Zack couldn't have orchestrated a better time for the three of them. They managed to see all of the preshow features and trailers, as Dylan had hoped. Two of the film previews prompted Dylan to whisper to Zack, "Let's go see that one."

The feature film itself—a big budget fantasy in 3D—had them riveted throughout. They teased each other about their goofy 3D glasses, but the movie's adventure quickly intensified, and they were drawn into the story. One of the scenes surprised viewers with a shocking visual jolt, and Sherry grabbed Zack's arm in fright. She released him just as fast, but she and Zack both laughed once she let go.

Even their expensive movie lunch was a pleasure, as far as Zack was concerned, because it evoked memories of trips to the movies when the kids were younger and more eager to spend time with their father.

As they were walking toward the theater's exit after the show, they passed a group of teens. One of the girls called out. "Sherry!"

Sherry's expression became animated and surprised. She gave the group a lively wave and immediately headed in their direction.

"Uh, Sherry?" Zack's frown said more than his words.

"Just five minutes, Dad? Please?"

Zack looked at the teens again. Mostly girls and two bored-looking guys. "Five minutes."

"Come on, Sherry, I don't want to wait all day for you." But Dylan was too late to stop her.

"Don't worry. She won't be long." Zack gave Dylan's shoulder a quick pat. He knew better than to display any affection more obvious than that in such a teen-centric environment. "Let's walk through the lobby and check out the movie posters. See what else is coming up."

They walked along one wall, talking about whether or not each film interested them.

"This one looks just a shade too stupid." Zack faced a poster of a buddy film he couldn't imagine sitting through. It featured a chimp in a three-piece suit standing with the two male stars. When he looked at Dylan, he realized his son wasn't paying attention to him. He was looking over at Sherry and her friends.

Zack turned around to see what Dylan saw. One of the formerly bored-looking guys had his hand on Sherry's back and was making a subtle, crafty descent lower. If Sherry noticed, she wasn't reacting.

Zack immediately thundered toward them, but just then the group sauntered away from Sherry to enter their movie, and Zack wasn't sure he wanted to follow them into the theater.

Sherry turned toward Zack and didn't seem terribly concerned about his approach. She did frown, however, once he got closer. "Dad? Are you okay?"

Her nonchalance threw him. He stopped abruptly in front of her. She didn't act the slightest bit guilty.

"Sherry, who was that guy?" He cocked his head toward the theater where the group had gone.

She looked in that direction. "Which one?"

He tried to keep his voice down, talking between clenched teeth. "The one giving you a rubdown."

She frowned, clearly puzzled. "Rubdown?" Then realization dawned in her features, and she giggled. "Oh, Dad. You must mean Matt. He's just a friend."

Well. Now he was stumped. She looked absolutely innocent. He took a deep breath to calm himself. "Sherry, it's not a good idea for you to let boys get that physically familiar with you. His hand was roving, whether you realize it or not."

She rolled her eyes and gave him the smile teenage girls tend to give their silly, overprotective fathers. "Okay, Dad. I'll pay better attention."

"Good, then." He nodded. "Come on, let's head home. I want you two to have time for your homework before dinner."

They rejoined Dylan and headed out of the theater, crisis averted.

But one thing still puzzled Zack. Even though Sherry had been perfectly calm while they spoke about "just-friend Matt," the tiniest beads of perspiration had broken out along the top of her lips.

TEN

The next morning Tina's ten o'clock client had to reschedule for later in the week, so she decided to splurge and spend the hour shopping at Gigi's, one of her favorite boutiques in town. Maybe she'd pick up something to wear tomorrow night on her date with Antony. The weather had been warm enough for her to feel comfortable in a dress and heeled sandals at church yesterday, so that's what she planned for their night out. She had seen a number of lovely outfits in Gigi's display window on her way to work last week.

Mikaela, the shop's owner, approached her after she had milled about the shop for a few minutes. She eyed the sleeveless floral silk dress Tina held. "Business or pleasure?" she asked with a smile.

Tina smiled back at the shapely and elegant older woman. She had never seen Mikaela with a single one of her dark, beautifully coifed hairs out of place. Tina sometimes felt as if she had to get dressed up just to shop here, but that was her own hang-up, not Mikaela's. Like all of the shop owners in Middleburg, Mikaela displayed a welcoming spirit with everyone who entered her boutique.

"Definitely pleasure. I can't see wearing

something this pretty in the office and expecting my clients to take me seriously."

"Understood. Very feminine. Although I can't imagine anyone not taking you seriously. You're such a serious woman."

At first Tina chuckled, but then she frowned. "Am I?"

"Very." Mikaela nodded.

Tina hung the floral dress back on the rack. What, exactly, did that mean? "Do I . . . do I seem severe?"

Mikaela's face registered surprise. "Oh, what have I said? No, not severe at all. You are simply very mature for such a young woman."

"Well, I'm not so young. I'm thirty-four." Why was she getting so defensive?

"I just meant that you are not at all flighty. You come across as very responsible, Tina. You know people's darkest secrets and have to keep all that information to yourself—" Mikaela stopped abruptly and threw her hands up. "What do I know? Don't listen to me. I'm—"

Tina laughed and put her hand on Mikaela's shoulder. "It's all right. I'm being overly sensitive. I *am* sometimes very serious." She pulled the floral dress from the rack again. "But not tomorrow night."

"A date?" Mikaela's eyes sparkled.

"Yes." Tina grimaced. "A first date with someone from church. I don't know him well."

"An adventure, then!" Mikaela pulled another dress from the rack. "You must try this lavender as well. And this one." She withdrew a black-and-red halter dress and held it up.

"Oh, I don't know." Tina took the lavender dress but studied the other one. "I don't know if that's—"

"Serious enough?" Mikaela wiggled her eyebrows, a crooked smile teasing Tina.

Tina grabbed the dress. "Give me that. You're a crafty one, lady. I'm on to your game. I can be as flighty as the next chick."

Mikaela laughed as they walked to the dressing room. "I'm glad you have aspirations."

Tina tried the black-and-red halter outfit first. Her first impression had been right. This was one flirty dress. Way too sultry for a first date, especially with someone she might have no real interest in. But the lavender and floral dresses were both perfect. Still, she couldn't bring herself to buy two dresses so similar, so she tried them both on several times.

"Do you need help in there?" Mikaela asked from outside the dressing room.

"I can't decide between the lavender and the floral."

"Come show me."

Tina walked out in the lavender, and not only did Mikaela emit a gasp of approval, but another voice also exclaimed from within the shop.

"Oh, my! You're stunning, Tina."

Tina would know that British accent anywhere. She spun around. "Milly!" She laughed. "I thought you *never* left the tea shop! What are you doing here?"

Milly smiled. "Why, shopping, of course. I wear more than my apron from time to time, you know."

"I know that, but it's the middle of Monday morning and here you are wandering away from the shop—it's unheard of!" Tina feigned shock.

"You're right, of course. I'm a slave to my work. I'm too happy there, I suppose. But I have an unexpected event to attend this evening straight from the shop's closing. So Jane is taking care of our deliveries and customers while Mikaela works her miracles on me." She linked arms with the shop owner, and the two of them studied Tina as if she were a sculpture.

"Okay. Then you can help me decide which of these two dresses to buy."

Mikaela lifted her palm. "But why not buy both?"

Tina laughed. "You haven't even seen the other one yet. And I can't justify buying both. So?" She posed like a fashion model, limp wristed and bored looking.

"I love it," Milly said.

"Hang on." Tina dashed back into the changing room, switched into the floral dress, and stepped back outside. The other two women had begun looking at items for Milly, but they both turned around when Tina emerged.

Their faces said it all. This was the dress.

Mikaela put her hand to her cheek. "Fabulous. Just fabulous. The colors suit your olive complexion."

"*So* pretty, Tina," Milly said. "You're spring all over, dear. I'd go with that one."

Tina sighed, relieved. "Thanks, friends."

"Now you can come help me decide." Milly handed a few dresses to Mikaela, who walked them over to a dressing room. Then she lowered her voice. "I wanted to ask you something rather personal anyway."

"Oh?" Tina raised her eyebrows.

Mikaela walked past them as another shopper called for her help. "You ladies let me know if I can be of assistance, okay? I'm just up front."

"Let me change, and then we can chat." Tina turned toward her dressing room. "I'd offer to go somewhere more private, but I have an eleven o'clock—"

"No, no." Milly waved her hand. "It won't take long. We can just talk here quickly."

Tina was changed and back out in minutes. She and Milly walked to the back of the shop, and Tina silently waited for whatever her friend had in mind.

"I wanted to ask you, dear, if you do what the

attorneys call pro bono work. Do you ever counsel people for free?"

Well, this was surprising. Not only did Milly not seem in need of counseling, but she certainly didn't seem financially stressed. Especially if she was shopping at Gigi's.

"I try to allow for a little of that in my schedule from time to time, yes. I consider it kind of my way of giving back. To God, you know. For His blessing me with such success in my work."

Milly nodded and obviously wanted to form her next question with care. "Good, good. And do you ever work on a . . . a very casual basis? What I mean is, would you be able to chat with someone and offer your professional wisdom without your . . . client actually knowing you were counseling them?"

Tina frowned and smiled simultaneously. "Milly, what exactly are we talking about here? *Whom* are we talking about?"

Milly looked around them before answering. "I have a friend who—really a lovely man—who is raising his two teenage children on his own. His wife ran off with some scoundrel four years ago, just when the kids needed her the most. Well, I suppose there's never a good time for a mother to desert her children, let alone her husband."

Tina nodded but said nothing.

"Well, he's been having some problems with the

teens lately. They're good kids, really. But they've been—"

"Rebellious?" Tina had a pretty good idea where this was going. This development wasn't unusual, even with teens in two-parent families.

"Yes." Milly put her hand on Tina's arm. "The police have been involved recently."

"Oh. Not good." She wondered if Edie knew them from their trouble with the police. Or her old beau Bucky, even. "And there's a problem with finances?"

"I gather that, yes. But there's also a problem with a lack of willingness on the children's part. At least, that's what the father expects. I don't think he's suggested counseling to them. *I* actually suggested it to him, but he says he probably can't afford it and they probably won't be cooperative."

Tina lifted her eyebrows. "I'm not sure if it would be fair, my observing them without their knowing I was doing it."

"That is a good point. I suppose I just assumed you generally observed people through your professional eye whether you were treating them or not."

Tina realized there was some truth to what she said. "Hmm . . . still, it would be difficult getting them into the office without their understanding why they are there."

"Well, that's where my idea comes in. I thought perhaps you and the father could act as if you were friends, or at least acquaintances, in front of the children. Perhaps you could run into each other at the tea shop while he just happens to be treating them to some tea and pastries? And you could join the group and get the lay of the land, as they say."

"Rebellious teens are willing to hunker down for teatime?"

Milly smiled. "*Pastries* was the operative word, my dear. I've formed many a friendship with my sweet concoctions."

Tina patted her thighs. "Don't I know it." She glanced at her watch. "Oh, I've got to run." A mere moment's thought. "Okay. Sold. I'd be happy to try just kind of being around to observe and maybe offer some counseling here and there, all loosey-goosey." She wiggled slightly, like a standing noodle, as she spoke. "How about that?"

Milly chuckled. "You're wonderful. I haven't mentioned this idea to Zack yet, not in detail. I didn't want to without checking with you first."

"All right." Tina pulled a business card from her purse, handed it to Milly, and stepped toward the front of the shop. "Tell him to give me a call, and then we can plan a pretend serendipitous crossing of our paths at the tea shop."

"I will. Thank you, Tina."

"Sure. I'm sorry I can't stay and help you decide which outfit to buy."

"Not a problem. Mikaela will do that."

Tina bought her dress and headed back to the office, a spring to her step. She knew her happiness had something to do with finding such a nice dress for tomorrow. But there was something else. After studying her thoughts she realized she looked forward to helping—or trying to help—this friend of Milly's. Without giving the matter great thought, she simply felt certain this was something God wanted her to do.

ELEVEN

Zack and Lorenzo loaded the last of the hay onto the truck. Zack removed his gloves and then pulled a handkerchief from his jeans pocket and wiped it across his forehead.

"Right, Lorenzo. The entire truckload goes to Henson's stables. His man is expecting you."

"Why so much? They graze their stock, don't they?"

"They said the lack of rain has hurt them. Not enough growth. They want to supplement. Don't want to overgraze."

His phone vibrated in his shirt pocket. He didn't recognize the number.

"Zack? Is that you?"

British accent. Could that actually be—"Milly?"

"Yes! Hello! I'm so glad I reached you. Is this a bad time? I called the house and Sherry gave me your cell number. I hope you don't mind."

"Not a problem. I didn't realize Sherry was already home from school, but I guess it really is that late." It was odd for Milly to call him in the middle of the work day, especially because he had already made a delivery to the shop that morning. Maybe he had left something out of the order without realizing it. "How can I help you?

Something wrong with this morning's delivery?"

"No, no. The delivery was perfect, as usual. Actually, I had an idea I thought might help *you*. Do you remember that when we last spoke, I suggested you might want to get a bit of advice from my patron who's a counselor?"

"Uh, yes, I remember. But I don't think I can afford—"

"Wait, Zack. Let me tell you what I found out. I talked with her, and she does a little counseling for free every once in a while. It's her way of giving back. I told her what you were facing, but I didn't give her details. I just told her generally that you were having a bit of a time with the kids."

He was about to remind her that he doubted the kids would agree to go to counseling, but she caught him on that before he got out one word.

"And I told her it was probably best if it was done very casually, without the kids feeling they were being studied and analyzed. So we thought maybe you could bring the kids by the shop for a tea-and-crumpet break, and she could casually drop in. You could act as if you knew each other socially, and she could join you. It might be a one-time thing or maybe more, but I think she can help you."

Zack noticed Lorenzo glancing in his direction, obviously curious. "I don't know, Milly. Yesterday was a pretty terrific day for me and the kids. I might not need any help. I think this restriction is making them shape up."

A moment's silence preceded Milly's response. "Well, that's marvelous, Zack. I'm glad to hear it. Just in case, though, why don't you take her number? That way, if you change your mind, you can get in touch directly with her and won't need to call me first. Even if you decide against the counseling, she might be a good person for you to make friends with."

Now, what did *that* mean? He loved Milly, but he honestly doubted this was necessary. Still, it was better to play along than to argue. "Sure. What's the number?"

As she recited it, he repeated it back, but he wasn't writing it down. He wasn't going to call that counselor woman.

"Great. Thanks, Milly. I'll see you Thursday morning."

"Until then. God bless you."

As he expected, the moment he closed his phone Lorenzo grilled him. "What was that about?"

Zack shrugged. "Milly—you know, from the tea shop?"

Lorenzo nodded.

"There's a tea shop customer—a counselor—who's willing to pretend she's my friend so she can hang around us and observe the kids. You know, so she can give me advice about how to deal with their . . . shenanigans."

"This is good." Lorenzo pointed at Zack. "You should definitely do this."

"What?" Zack frowned. "Why?"

"You need some help with Dylan and Sherry, man. You're losing control of them a little, I think."

"I don't think so. We had a blast yesterday. We got along great. And they've both settled into the restriction without any more complaining. They were just testing me, I think. Now that they know I'll ground them, I think we're going to be fine."

"They're just testing you."

"Right."

"So Dylan skipped school and got arrested—"

"Not arrested—"

"Okay, just *brought to the police station,*" Lorenzo said, an eyebrow raised. "And Sherry lied to you and attempted to spend the night somewhere you wouldn't have approved of."

"Yes, but—"

"And they both assumed you'd catch them, which was fine, because they just wanted to test you and see what you would allow. Is that right?"

Zack frowned. Lorenzo was really hard on the kids sometimes. He was Zack's best friend, but Zack didn't like it when he got like this. Especially about the kids.

"No, they didn't think they'd get caught, but—"

"Maybe you're afraid for that counselor to observe you."

"Not me. The kids."

Lorenzo just looked Zack in the eye.

"What? You think I'm afraid she's going to tell me I'm doing it wrong?"

Lorenzo lifted his hands, palms up. "Hey, you said it, man." He walked toward the driver's side of the truck. "I should get this hay delivered."

"Right. I'll see you later. And you're wrong, Lorenzo. I'm not afraid. I don't think I'm doing it wrong."

His friend laughed. Right before he started up the truck he said, "Man, we *all* think we're doing it wrong. Parenting ain't for sissies."

That made Zack smile a little. He waved as Lorenzo pulled away.

All right. Maybe he did worry he was parenting poorly. But everything was fine now. He didn't see any reason to rock the boat. He was certain he'd seen the worst.

TWELVE

Every time Tina tried dating again, she always wished she dated more often. Not because it was so much fun, but simply because it always felt so foreign to her, going on that first date. And the second. She knew herself well—she took awhile to feel comfortable in new settings or with new people. Well, not all people. Just men. And not all men. Just the men she was dating.

But this was what single women did. If she didn't bite the bullet and brave this beginning stage, she'd always be a single woman. On the other hand, if she didn't choose to remain alone, she'd have to keep doing this. Over and over.

So she had her second shower of the day, did her hair and makeup one more time, and studied herself in the mirror, all dolled up in strappy black sandals and her silk dress from Gigi's.

When Antony knocked at her door, she was glad she had prayed a little about the evening. Maybe it was the Lord's will that she and Antony hit it off. Maybe the Lord would help her see him differently when she opened the door.

Nope. Still slightly attractive. Still slightly Neanderthal. A fairly good-looking caveman, nicely dressed and really wonderfully pleasant.

Tina was ashamed of herself for not shrugging off her lack of attraction to him. She worked hard at peering beyond the surface and paying attention to what kind of person Antony was.

He took her to the French Bistro, one of her favorite restaurants in town. A lighthearted accordion tune played softly in the background, which always made Tina think of strolls down tree-lined roads in the French countryside. She breathed in amazing aromas wafting out from the kitchen: garlic, onion, and any number of different meats being grilled and sautéed.

"I love this place," she said, smiling at Antony as they waited to be seated.

He nodded. "Yeah, me too. I'm no food expert. I just know I love their whaddya-call-it. The beef-and-noodle dish."

"Beef bourguignon?"

He pointed at her. "Yeah, that's the one."

"Follow me, please." The maître d' led them to the main dining area. Decorative copper pans and elegantly framed French posters added charm to the room. The golden-yellow walls had been antiqued perfectly.

Antony spoke from behind her as they neared their table. "You look really pretty, by the way. You always do."

The maître d' held Tina's seat out for her, so when she said thank you, she nodded at both men, as if responding to her entourage of two.

The moment the maître d' left them, a server brought warm French rolls to the table and took their drink order. Antony grabbed a roll as if he feared the server might take them away.

"Thanks." Tina smiled at the waiter.

A more senior-looking member of the waitstaff approached them a moment later. He held menus but didn't hand them out right away. While Antony concentrated on his roll, the server spoke to Tina. He occasionally glanced at Antony, who was in no hurry to look away from his food.

"Tonight we have a couple of specials. We have mussels in a garlic-and-white wine reduction, which can be prepared as an appetizer or as an entrée. And we have a lobster thermidor entrée, served with a pine nut rice pilaf and sautéed vegetables."

"Mmm," Tina said. She had a slight urge to give Antony a little kick under the table. Was he aware he was being rude? She decided to give him the benefit of the doubt. He seemed starved. Maybe he had missed lunch and his focus was just a bit off at the moment.

She took her menu, and then Antony put down his second roll to take his. But then he stopped short of opening it and handed it back to the server.

"I already know what I want, to tell you the truth. I want the beef-and-noodle dish."

The server smiled and bowed toward him. "Sir?"

Tina spoke up. "The beef bourguignon."

"Ah." The server straightened up and mild regret settled into his expression. "I'm sorry. The bourguignon isn't on the menu tonight."

Antony stopped eating so abruptly that Tina was reminded of the sudden stillness of prey when a hunter's steps have been heard. Then he folded inward slightly and gave the server a pleading look. "What? I thought that was one of your regular dishes."

"The chef does change the menu from time to time, but we do have several other beef dishes available this evening." He leaned forward again, opened Antony's menu for him, and pointed out his options.

Antony's frown remained. "Yeah, okay. I'll look it over."

Without the slightest bit of disdain, the server smiled at both of them. "I'll give you some time to decide." He moved away, not a ruffled feather showing.

"Man, I was really looking forward to that beef tonight."

Tina gave him a smile while thinking, *Well, mister, life's not always fair, is it?* She had assumed he was really looking forward to spending time with her, regardless of whether he had beef bourguignon or not.

She stopped her negative thinking. She wasn't going to write him off over this. Men did enjoy their food and could become downright childish if—

Oh, she couldn't help it. His reaction bothered her. *Grow up and eat a steak, for crying out loud.*

He suddenly shook himself out of it. "Sorry. I'm being rude. So what, right? I'll eat something else. What do you think I should try? Do you have a favorite?"

Tina smiled. "Let's see what—"

"Of course, that's assuming your favorite is even *on* the menu." Antony glowered around the restaurant as if the wound was fresh again.

Was she going to say something? Was she going to blow her cool and get snippy with him? She breathed in and out. No. Give him a minute to collect himself again.

And he did. "Man, I'm sorry. What a jerk I'm being." He studied his menu. "How about this one?" He pointed to one of the listings. "Have you had that here?"

"The coq au vin? Yes, it's wonderful. I think you'll enjoy it, assuming you like chicken."

He closed his menu with finality and set it down on the table. "That's it, then."

He was even pleasant with the server once he was past the disappointment.

"Can I get some noodles with that chicken, you think?"

"Certainly, sir."

They received salads shortly after placing their

order, and then Antony went back to town on the basket of rolls.

"So, you're like a shrink, right?" He sat back and swallowed a bite.

"Not a shrink, no. That's a psychiatrist. I'm a psychological counselor. A therapist."

He nodded. "I figured that's why you're so good with the teens." He tapped his temple. "You understand how they think. They really like you a lot."

"Well, thank you. I like them too. I felt led to work with them soon after I started going to the church. They're a great group of kids." She dared to reach for a roll for herself. "How about you?"

"Why do I work with the teens?"

"Yes, that, and what do you do professionally? I don't even know."

This was more like it. Maybe this evening would go all right after all, now that they had survived the bumpy part.

"I'm a construction manager. Commercial. Mostly the clearing and excavation part of projects. We've been doing most of our work in the Leesburg area for the past few years. They just keep on growing. Doesn't matter what the economy does, they keep growing."

"That's good for you, isn't it? You always have work."

"Right. I've been blessed."

Dinner arrived, and they talked about the youth

group and then about current films. Tina broached the subject of books, but apparently Antony wasn't fond of reading.

An avid reader, Tina cringed ever so slightly. Not the end of the world, though. They still had a mutual interest in film. Just not the same kind of film, she realized.

As they settled into describing their families, Tina avoided becoming a therapist and worked at just being a date. This was never easy for her, but she had learned to hold off the counseling facet of her personality until she knew a person more fully. Even then, she didn't share her counseling thoughts unless they were solicited. That wasn't why she and Antony were out together tonight, so she talked as much about her family as Antony did about his.

And then it happened. She knew it might seem shallow, but it truly was a deal breaker, considering how lukewarm her feelings were already.

Antony ate with his mouth open.

Tina tried not to stare, but she was mesmerized. She was certain he hadn't done this before. Maybe he only forgot his manners when he was truly comfortable around a woman. Perhaps she should be flattered?

Ew. No. That was pasta he was eating, with lots of sauce. Not flattering.

If he had a cold and couldn't breathe while

eating, he probably would have said something, right? And she would have noticed that. But no. He looked perfectly comfortable, smacking his big lips together and even emitting a few wet noises so revolting Tina couldn't bring herself to eat anymore. She attempted subtlety when she set her knife and fork down on her plate.

Antony stopped chomping at once. Had he noticed his lack of manners?

He pointed at her grilled swordfish. "You going to eat that?"

She nearly sighed out loud. "No, you help yourself."

Now she was glad they had chosen a weeknight for their date. She would have a good excuse to cut the evening short because they both needed to be alert for work the next morning.

Antony was terribly sweet. And his gift of working well with the teens was exactly that—a gift from God. She knew that. But as a date? He was, as her young charges would say, gross.

She was reminded of something she had told one of her clients not all that long ago. The woman was determined to hang on to a man with whom she felt total boredom simply because he was a good, God-fearing man. Tina told her then what she acknowledged to herself now. A single Christian guy could be as bad a fit as a single secular guy. He might be a child of God, but he wasn't necessarily "the one."

THIRTEEN

At four o'clock the next afternoon, Zack called a halt to the work in his field. The rain had become so strong there was the danger that his workers, picking berries, would trample the area into a sea of mud.

Lorenzo hollered to the laborers. "That's it for today. John and Connor, you get the trucks back to the farm. Everyone help unload. Check tomorrow's schedule before you leave, and call me if we have storms in the morning."

Once the last worker departed the field, Zack drove Lorenzo toward Zack's home. He stopped the truck in front of Lorenzo's SUV.

Lorenzo hesitated before getting out. "You and the kids want to come over for dinner? Ilsa's making spaghetti, and she always makes enough for twenty people, let alone the four of us. She and the boys would love to see you all."

Zack shook his head. "I think both of the kids probably have homework. And a trip to your house would be too much fun for them. I already took them to a movie this weekend. They're supposed to be on restriction."

"Oh, yeah. I forgot about that. You're doing the right thing, my friend. They need to learn now, while it's safe to make mistakes."

Zack pushed his damp hair off his forehead. "I just hope their mistakes *stay* safe. Sometimes I feel like I'm barely hanging on to them." He smiled. "But this past weekend was pretty good, considering how tense everything's been. I'm hoping they've learned their lesson."

Lorenzo stepped out of the truck and was immediately pelted with rain. "Just don't get too discouraged if they slip up again. Hang in there."

Zack nodded and drove the short distance to the house. He left his muddy boots on the rack outside the mudroom door and hung his wet jacket on a peg just inside. He called out to the kids. "I'm home. Everyone here?"

A disgruntled mumble of assent answered from the kitchen, and Zack sought out the source.

Dylan sat at the kitchen table, school papers spread out, looking glum. Zack wondered for a moment if he should change his mind and take Lorenzo up on that dinner offer. It wouldn't hurt for the kids to enjoy a visit with Lorenzo's family. Ilsa was probably the nearest thing to a mother they had these days, and both Dylan and Sherry got a kick out of Lorenzo's two boys.

"That's what I like to see. My hardworking son. Where's Sherry?"

Dylan shrugged. "I hate my history class." He held a couple of pieces of paper out to Zack. "I need your signature on these."

Two tests. Each with a vivid red *D* at its top.

"Good night, Dylan! What happened?"

"I don't know. I was distracted, I guess." He didn't look up.

"Distracted? What distracted you *this* bad?" Zack held up the tests. "Did you study for these at all?"

Dylan turned his frown on Zack for only a moment before looking away again. "I thought I did."

"You thought you did? Why didn't you ask for help if you were—"

"I thought I knew it, okay?"

Zack could see that Dylan was distraught. He tried to back off until they could both calm down. He found a pen on the kitchen counter and scratched his name across both tests. He glanced around the room. "Where did you say Sherry was?"

"I didn't say. I don't know where she is."

"Didn't she ride home from school with you?"

"Yeah, but I went upstairs. Maybe she's in her room."

Zack walked to the bottom of the stairs and called. "Sherry?"

Just as that familiar, acidic feeling seeped back into Zack's stomach, there was a knock at the mudroom door. His hopes rose. They all tended to come in through that door when they arrived home because it opened into the garage. But he didn't think he'd locked it when he came in. And she'd have some explaining to do about where she'd been when she was supposed to be grounded.

Before Zack reached the door, though, Lorenzo popped his head in. "Zack? You here?"

"Come on in. I thought you left already."

Lorenzo looked uncomfortable. "Uh, are the kids here?"

"The kids? Yeah. Well, no. Dylan's here. I don't know where Sherry is. She came home with Dylan, but—"

"I don't know how to tell you this, Zack, but—" Lorenzo leaned to the side, seeking Dylan, before lowering his voice. "I think one of the kids took my car out for a drive this afternoon."

"What?" Zack glanced over his shoulder in Dylan's direction and then spoke softly. "Dylan has my old Jeep. I don't know why he would take anyone else's car. And he was in his room after he got home from school, he says."

"What about Sherry?"

Zack's frown returned. "She's not even here, Lorenzo. I'm going to have to start making phone calls."

Lorenzo nodded. "You might want to ask her when you do track her down. I'm pretty sure she took the car out."

"She doesn't even have her license yet, man. I know she's caused a little trouble lately, but I don't think—"

Lorenzo shrugged. "The floor of the car was wet when I got in. Fresh mud."

"But it's storming."

"It was dry when I got here this morning, Zack. Someone took it out during the storm. And we were all out in the field. I'm just saying you might want to check it out."

Zack sighed. It bothered him that Lorenzo immediately thought of Sherry as the culprit, but he didn't want to argue about it, especially now that his daughter's disobedient choice to go out after school reflected poorly on her. "Yeah, okay. I'll see what I can find out. I've got to make some calls, buddy. I'll see you tomorrow, huh?"

"Yes. Tomorrow." Lorenzo headed back toward his car.

Dylan looked up when Zack returned to the kitchen. "What did Sherry do now?" The relief to have the focus taken off of him was so obvious Zack imagined him throwing confetti and blowing a paper noisemaker.

"Don't you worry about it. Just get your homework done." But as Dylan turned gloomily away, Zack filled him in anyway. "She's supposed to be home. And Lorenzo thinks . . ."

He picked up his phone and accessed his contact information, looking for Amanda's home number. He could call Sherry's cell, but something told him the tip-off to Sherry wasn't a good idea just yet.

"What?" Dylan asked. "What does Lorenzo think?"

As he put the call through, Zack said, "Did you happen to take his car out for a drive since you got home from school?"

Dylan's eyes widened for a second before his face registered amused shock. "Oh, Sherry!" He wiped the amusement from his face under Zack's glare. "No, Dad. It wasn't me."

"Hello?" It was Amanda. Considering Amanda's having lied to her parents last weekend, as Sherry had, Zack wasn't about to have any of this conversation with her.

"Amanda? Hi, this is Sherry's dad. May I speak with your mother, please?"

"Sure, Mr. Cooper. Hang on."

Well, obviously Sherry wasn't with Amanda. She hadn't hesitated for an instant when she heard who was calling.

"Zack?"

"Yes, hi, Rebecca. I assume Sherry isn't over there with Amanda, then?"

"No. I'm sorry. Amanda came straight home from school today. Rightly so—she's grounded for the rest of the week."

Only one week's restriction for lying about her sleepover plans. Had he been too tough, giving Sherry two? Clearly the punishment hadn't scared her into obedience if she wasn't home now as required.

"Zack, would you like me to ask Amanda if she knows where Sherry might be?"

"Uh, yes, but first let me ask you something. Dylan says Sherry rode home from school with him, but before going wherever she is now, she might have gone for a little joyride in Lorenzo's car while we were working the fields. Would you know anything about that?"

Not for the first time while he and Rebecca talked about the dynamic duo, his question was greeted initially by contemplative silence. Then, "Uh-oh." She spoke quietly, apparently wanting to keep Amanda from hearing.

"What?" His stomach gripped.

"Was it a blue SUV?"

Zack closed his eyes. "Yes. A 4Runner."

"That little liar." Rebecca nearly hissed and then let out an angry breath. "Amanda was about half an hour late getting home. I saw the car pull up, but it was raining so hard I couldn't see who was driving. She told me it was Denise, some girl I don't know. Probably some girl who doesn't even exist. I have to go. I have a restriction to extend."

"Right." Zack nodded. "But—"

"I'll call you if I can find out where Sherry is right now. I haven't forgotten. I'm glad you called. Neither one of these girls is licensed. *Or* honest."

He hated hearing that, but it was true. He couldn't imagine ever trusting Sherry again.

Now he'd have to apologize to Lorenzo too. He hadn't been unfair to Sherry. He had judged her correctly.

And while she obviously survived driving unlicensed and untrained in the middle of a thunderstorm, now Zack had to wonder how often this kind of thing had happened in the past. And where was she right now? And with whom?

The mudroom door opened, and Sherry fluttered in as if the world were awash in rose petals. She spoke as swiftly as a racetrack announcer. "Hi, Dad! Wow, don't get mad 'cause I went out. I forgot my binder at school." She held up said binder. "And I got Matt—you met Matt at the movies, remember? I called him to come get me and drive me to school really fast before the janitors finished up and locked me out. Phew! 'Cause I have homework, you know?" She giggled falsely. "And I don't want to get in trouble for not getting it done, right?"

Zack heard Dylan snicker behind him.

"I'm curious, Sherry." Zack crossed his arms and leaned against the counter. "Why didn't you just drop by the school to pick up the binder while you and Amanda had Lorenzo's car? Was the school too far out of your way?"

Sherry's smile, frozen in place, flattened ever so slightly. "Uh . . . what?"

"I'd tell you how disappointed I am with you, but I don't really think you care about that."

She said nothing. All pretense of being a happy-go-lucky girl evaporated.

Zack hooked his thumb over his shoulder. "Have a seat at the table with Dylan. Get started on your homework. Tomorrow you'll apologize to Lorenzo, as I have to, for sticking up for you when you were, in fact, guilty as sin. You'll wash his car every weekend for the next month. And your restriction has just been extended by another week."

She gasped and immediately went into whining mode. "What! Are you kidding me? Come on, Dad! That's not fair! It's almost summer!"

"No discussion. No backtalk. No nothing for you. Not for—let me see—two and a half more weeks. You'd just better hope Lorenzo doesn't press charges on you for stealing his car."

Sherry stomped into the kitchen. As she passed Zack, he noted with dismay how short her shorts were. And she had just been out with that hormone-crazed teenage predator.

He had to leave the room to keep from grounding her until her wedding day. He retreated up to his room, his hands in his hair as if he were trying to pull it out by the roots.

Without any further thought, he dropped to his knees and leaned against the bed.

Lord, I don't know where You are in this. I don't see You in it at all, and that scares me. I can't do this alone. I'm sorry I've ignored You, but I need

You. I need Your guidance. Please. I need help.

As he said that last sentence, he felt immediate assurance. Not assurance that all would be well. Assurance that he had prayed something to which he needed to heed. He stopped and thought it again. *I need help.*

He all but heard a reply: *Yes.*

That was it. He *couldn't* do this alone.

He got up and sat on the bed. He waited for his thoughts to settle, and his course suddenly became clear. He knew what he needed to do, first thing in the morning. God was telling him.

He needed help.

FOURTEEN

As usual, Milly was already hard at work when Zack made his delivery the next day. Jane let him in, and then both women fussed over him. Milly's tea shop was his favorite place to deliver.

"You brought the sunshine with you, didn't you?" Jane looked up to the clear sky as she held the back door open for him. "I'm so glad that storm finally passed!"

Zack nodded. "Yeah, but we really needed the rain." He barely had a chance to set down the two boxes of produce he held before Milly began plying him with samples.

"Here, now. Tell me what you think of this."

Whatever she put in his mouth was surprisingly *not* sweet.

"Mmm, that's great, Milly. What is it?" He removed his hat and tucked it into his back pocket.

"That's a ham salad tea sandwich." Her pleasure at his approval spread across her face. "I wanted to try making it with less olive. An improvement?"

He shrugged. "I don't think I ever tried the original version, but that was delicious. And I'm not a big fan of ham. I didn't know you made lunch-type food."

Milly rested a hand on her waist. "But of course I do! You must miss out because you're only here early in the morning. Here, finish these others, will you? I'll make them again later so they're fresh at lunchtime."

He laughed. "I'll eat another, but only one more. I had a full breakfast. You're going to spoil me."

Jane walked back into the kitchen from having carried little flower vases out to the dining area. "You're not here often enough to get spoiled."

"That's right." Milly suddenly seemed to be reading his face for whatever his real frame of mind might be. "You need to come visit us more often, Zack. I don't think you get spoiled enough anywhere. Certainly not out there working hard on your farm and raising two teens on your own."

As he ate the other sandwich, he glanced briefly at Jane. She didn't appear to be paying all that much attention. She picked up crisp, white, lacy tablecloths and then carried them out to the dining room.

"As a matter of fact, Milly, I wanted to talk with you about that. About Dylan and Sherry."

He hadn't noticed her pouring a cup of tea, but she held one out to him. "I'm all ears, dear."

"Dylan brought home a couple of *D*'s yesterday."

"A couple of *D*'s? What are—" Milly gasped. "D *grades?* But he's such a smart boy! Was he upset?"

"I suppose. I was so upset myself that all I

noticed was his looking sheepish and guilty. And Sherry . . . Milly, I think she's worse than Dylan. She took Lorenzo's car without his knowing yesterday."

"I didn't realize she already had her license."

"She doesn't!"

Milly looked nearly as distressed as Zack felt. "Oh my."

"Right. The next call from the police station could be hers. Or worse, it could be *about* her. She drove around in that storm yesterday, Milly. She doesn't have a clue about driving. She could have had an accident. She could have hurt someone else."

Milly poured hot tea in a cup for herself. "Tell me what I can do, Zack. There's nothing more frustrating than not being able to help."

He grimaced. "I know I didn't sound all that interested in your counselor friend before, but I think it's time I got some advice."

"Excellent." Milly nodded. "You're very smart to do that. And I know you'll like her very much."

He waited, thinking she'd get him the name and number. But she looked at him as if she were waiting on *him*. Finally, she moved away from the counter, but she simply got one of her little pastry boxes, wrapped the two remaining ham sandwiches in paper, and boxed them up. She handed them to Zack as if she were sending him on his way.

"Oh. Thanks, Milly."

"If you don't eat them soon, you should refrigerate them. But they'll keep for days in the refrigerator."

"Right. Okay." He scratched at the back of his neck. "Um, Milly, could I bother you for that counselor lady's contact info?"

"Ah!" She laughed. "I was wondering what you were staring at me for." She went to her desk in a small room off the kitchen. He saw her shuffle through items before pulling out her address book. She said when she came out, "I thought I gave you her contact information when we spoke on the phone."

Oops. "Yeah. I guess I . . ."

Milly smiled. "You guess you didn't write it down because you thought it wasn't that great of an idea. Right?"

Now Zack was the one to look sheepish and guilty. "Sometimes I forget you know best, Milly."

She laughed outright. "That's it, young man. Butter me up." She wrote the name and number down and handed it to him. "Her office is right here in town. She knows to expect a call from you, but I'll see her later this morning. I'll remind her."

Despite the troubles with Dylan and Sherry, Zack felt better doing something more than struggling blindly. He couldn't wait to make that call. God wanted him to do this, he was sure of it.

FIFTEEN

That afternoon Tina handed a tissue to Brandy and had to suppress a fond smile. She knew her young client wanted to be taken seriously, despite the obvious melodrama of her concern.

"Mike doesn't understand how important it's going to be." Brandy dabbed at her tears. "Once the baby gets here, we're going to need to be shipshape with everything. He's so laid back about it that I just want to kick him."

Tina was used to Brandy's occasionally histrionic reactions to rather minor glitches in her status quo. It was not only a characteristic of her cyclothymia, but also a characteristic of many a young mother-to-be.

"Let's take a good overall look at this problem, okay, Brandy?"

She brushed her long wispy hair away from her face and attempted to collect herself. "Mm-hmm."

"All right. How far along are you in the pregnancy?"

"Six weeks." Brandy clearly had her answer at the ready. "And probably two days."

Tina struggled not to smile at the "two days." She leaned forward to get Brandy's attention. "All right, so that leaves how much time before the baby is due?" She held up her hand to count fingers. "Let me see . . ."

"Thirty-three weeks," Brandy said. "And about five days."

Tina lifted her eyebrows and then smiled. "You haven't figured out how many hours you'll have to wait on delivery day?"

Brandy frowned. "What do you mean?"

With a pat of Brandy's hand, Tina smiled. "I'm teasing you. Okay, so if you go the full forty weeks, you still have almost eight months left, right?"

"Yeah. Kind of." Brandy looked ready to argue about whatever calming words Tina planned to offer.

"And you're worried because Mike hasn't rearranged his daily schedule yet? One week after you found out you're expecting?"

"But I don't think he ever *will* rearrange his schedule. That's the thing."

"Brandy, remember what we talked about with regard to projecting? About not projecting negative outcomes into the future like that?"

Brandy looked at her lap and nodded. She placed her hand on her flat stomach and spoke softly. "Yeah. I'm creating worries for myself, aren't I?"

"You're not alone in that tendency, believe me. But it helps to step back when we're worrying to gct a grasp of what's happening *today*. What we're doing today. There's nothing wrong with planning for the future. That's definitely one of your strengths. But I'd like to encourage you to give Mike time to grow into your schedule over the next eight months. His speed is different from yours. Not inferior to it—just different. Okay?"

"Okay. But his speed is *really* different from mine."

Tina smiled. "That's why you two are good together. You balance each other out."

Brandy laughed and wiped her hands across her face. "Yeah, we do."

By the time she left, Brandy's view of her problems had calmed considerably. Tina started entering her session notes into her computer when her phone rang. The voice on the other end was hesitant but warm and masculine.

"May I speak with . . ." The sound of rustling paper filled his silence. "Sorry. Tina Milano. May I speak with Tina Milano, please?"

"This is she."

"This is Zack Cooper. I think we have a mutual friend in Milly Jewell."

Ah. The father of the teens. "Yes! I saw Milly this morning. She told me to expect your call, Mr. Cooper—"

"Why don't you call me Zack?"

He had a lovely, comfortable tone to his voice. And there was something take-charge about his manner. Confident. She pictured an older, large man. "I'll do that. And please call me Tina. Can you fill me in some on whatever Milly had in mind? How might I help you?"

"I'm not sure, really. I guess I could use some advice." He laughed, sounding chagrinned. "Actually, that's an understatement. You might say I'm desperate for advice. I'm struggling with my kids, and—"

"What are their names?"

"Dylan. He's seventeen. And Sherry. She's fifteen. They're really good kids, and I love 'em to death, but you'd think they'd been raised by a crazy man. And if things stay how they are, that's exactly who *will* be raising them."

Tina laughed softly and took notes. "And you're raising them on your own, is that right?"

"Yes. My wife—well, my ex-wife—she left four years ago and hasn't seen the kids since."

Tina shook her head as she wrote. She never failed to wonder at such things. It was one thing for a wife to leave a husband—sometimes women needed to escape from brutality, and she knew better than to rule that out in this circumstance before she knew more. But to leave one's children? Even as a woman without children of her own, Tina had a hard time fathoming that one.

Her office door opened, and her next client walked in.

"Mr. Cooper—"

"Zack."

She smiled. "I'm sorry. Yes, Zack. My next appointment just walked in—"

"Let me leave you to that, then."

"No, wait." She brought her calendar up on the computer. "Could you possibly come by my office, say, Monday morning?"

"Sure. I make a few deliveries in town Monday mornings. You name the time and I'll be there."

"Eleven? Just for a few minutes. To meet each other and chat a bit more about this."

"Eleven it is. Thanks, Tina. I'm looking forward to it."

She hung up the phone. He sounded like such a nice man. And she respected his taking this step to improve his relationship with his kids. To improve the way they would be raised. Plenty of men wouldn't bother. As far as she was concerned, he had already shown much about his character.

She waved her next client in even while thinking about Zack Cooper.

Yeah, she had a good feeling about this one.

SIXTEEN

Monday morning Zack stood outside Tina's office for a moment before knocking. Their appointment wasn't for another five minutes, but he thought she might appreciate promptness.

He'd had a little mishap earlier when delivering to one of his clients, and an entire carton of raspberries had smashed up against the front of his shirt. Of course, he *would* choose to wear a plain yellow shirt today rather than one of his plaid or checkered ones. He looked as if he'd been knifed in some back alley.

He combed his hands through his hair in an effort to tame it. He still needed that haircut.

Ah, well. This was who he was. This lady sounded nice enough on the phone. Maybe she'd be understanding.

He almost knocked, but then it occurred to him that this door probably led into a waiting room rather than her office. So he gently tapped a knuckle on the door, pushed it open, and peeked inside.

It was indeed a waiting room, cozy and inviting looking, with its overstuffed couch and chairs. Once he entered he could see directly into Tina's office because she had the door open. She was standing, reading something on her desk, and her eyes widened the moment she looked up at him. He had obviously surprised her, because she had a lot of something stuffed into her mouth. Zack was reminded of younger days when he and his friends would cram entire donuts into their mouths at once, simply because they could.

She made a little squeak and waved her hands in panic. Then she held one hand to her mouth, apparently so she could chew without his seeing. With the other, she held up her index finger, indicating he should wait a moment.

He didn't know much about this woman, but she definitely seemed more human to him now than she had one minute ago. He allowed his smile to show. Her antics were cute.

And there was something familiar about her. Once she swallowed and stopped moving about and covering her face, he remembered. She was the woman he saw in front of Milly's shop a couple of weeks ago. The pretty one who gave him that saucy smile.

She grabbed a glass of water from her desk and took a swallow. She dabbed at her lips with a paper napkin and laughed. He could tell she was embarrassed, just by the nervous tone of her laugh.

"I am *so* sorry about that." She flicked her dark hair away from her eyes and straightened her skirt before approaching him and extending her hand.

"I didn't get breakfast and was trying to fit it in between appointments." She rolled her eyes. "Obviously I was trying to fit it *all* in. You surprised me."

He took her hand and shook it. He liked how delicate her fingers felt. And warm. "I gathered that." He couldn't help smiling. "I'm early. I should have knocked more loudly."

She stared at him as he talked. Maybe she recognized him from that other time. But then she shook her head. "No, no, my clients always just walk in. You're Zack, I assume?"

He followed her into her small, comfortable-looking office. She had a loveseat and chairs clustered in a little nook away from her desk. She sat in a chair and motioned for him to sit on the adjacent loveseat.

"That's me," he said. "Zack. And you're Tina." He didn't know why he said that. The woman knew who she was. He lowered onto the loveseat. A coffee table was in front of it, so he had to turn toward her to find room for his long legs. When he finally got comfortable and looked at her, she was staring at him again. Big brown eyes that darted away for a moment.

Then he remembered the raspberry stain on his chest. "I apologize for my appearance." He looked down at the dark red splotch that appeared to have spread even farther across his shirt. "Had a bit of a fruit accident on my last delivery."

120

But when he looked back up, she wasn't looking at the stain. She was watching him. All of him. She seemed to be taking his measure.

She started and smiled politely. "Don't worry about it."

Again, she seemed as if he had caught her at something. He decided to address it.

"Um, I think you and I might have crossed paths before. Do you remember?"

He watched her make some kind of decision before she spoke.

She nodded. "In front of Milly's shop." It sounded like a confession. But then she smiled. This time it was a real, terrific smile. "It was raining."

He smiled back. "That's right. You peeked at me from under your umbrella."

"My entire group cut you off, as I recall." That slightly nervous laugh returned. "And we made you wait in the rain while we took our sweet time entering the shop."

Zack opened his arms, as if presenting himself. "I didn't melt."

They chuckled together.

"No, you sure didn't." She said nothing for a moment and neither did he. It dawned on Zack that, despite the nature of this meeting, they might actually be on the verge of flirting. Or were they? It had been so long—

At once she sat up straighter and became more

businesslike. "Now, what brings you here, Zack? Tell me about your son and daughter. What's troubling you about them?"

So much for flirting.

He took a deep breath and released it. "I couldn't tell you when things started getting rough between me and them, but I seem to have lost them a little."

"Lost *them* or lost control of them?"

He lifted his eyebrows. "I guess both. They've been pretty good kids up until recently, but now they're getting in trouble, and the only role I seem to play is punisher. What I say, the things I tried to teach them as they grew up, about right and wrong? None of that seems to be in their heads anymore."

"What kind of trouble have they been in?"

"Well, Dylan has been skipping school, so his grades are dropping, and on one of his little adventures his friends were arrested for shoplifting."

"Not Dylan?"

"He was taken down to the station, but they didn't press charges because he wasn't involved with the theft."

She picked up a tablet of paper from the coffee table and jotted a few things down. Zack noticed how pretty her legs were but looked up quickly. It wasn't going to do any good, both of them sitting here, taking turns catching each other staring.

"What else?"

"Sherry . . . well, I feel like she's lying to me about everything. She pulled one of those things with a friend, you know, when each kid tells the parents she's staying at the other's house overnight, and then they both stay somewhere else?"

Tina grimaced. "Yes. And where did she actually sleep?"

"At home. I found out in time and went out looking for her."

She spoke to him while she wrote on her tablet. "Someday she'll appreciate that you did that for her."

Zack didn't know why, but just that comment was enough to make him want to cry. He hadn't realized until now how underappreciated he felt.

She looked up and caught him feeling sorry for himself, he could tell. She looked into his eyes and spoke softly. "Do you want to tell me why my comment touched you, Zack? What emotion are you feeling right now?"

Oh, boy. If she caught me over this, she probably caught me checking out her legs too.

He waved off the question. "Nothing. It's just hard being a parent."

"Mm-hmm. I know it might not seem to matter, but it's a good idea to identify your emotions whenever you can. You'd be surprised at how much better you can communicate with others, including your kids, if you learn to identify your emotions and teach them how to do the same."

Did he really want to get into all of that? It sounded like a lot of work. A lot of navel-gazing. He doubted all that self-reflection was really the way to go.

She spoke again before he could respond. "Anything else?"

"Pardon?" He repositioned himself to stretch his legs in the other direction. Without a word she reached down and pushed the table away to give him more room. And *she* looked at *his* legs. He was in jeans, so it wasn't like a man checking out a woman. She was just being practical. And considerate. She spoke at the same time he thanked her for moving the table.

"Were there any other behaviors that alarmed you about Dylan and Sherry?"

"Yeah. Sherry took my friend's car for a joyride while we were out working the field. She's only fifteen. Not licensed."

A frown furrowed Tina's brow as she made a note. "And any concerns about entanglements with the opposite sex for either of the kids?"

"Absolutely. There's this kid Matt, who seems pretty comfortable putting his hands on Sherry. She says he's just a friend, but I'm not an idiot. I've been a boy before."

The instant he said that he decided he'd choose not to elaborate if she asked. But she didn't.

She sat back and sighed before giving him a smile. "Savvy dad."

He liked this woman. "You don't think I'm overreacting?"

"I know quite a few teenage boys. I work with the youth group at my church—"

"Oh? What religion are you?"

She shook her head. "Nondenominational. I'm a Christian. I attend Middleburg Bible. Are you familiar with it?"

Zack nodded. "I went a few times when my wife . . . when the kids were much younger."

"Well, let me know if you're interested in coming back. I'll keep my eye out for you."

"Thanks."

"Anyway, I work with the teens at church and several of my clients have been young men. I know plenty of the boys in the youth group who develop friendships with girls without expecting anything further." She shrugged. "I can't say for certain, but I think most of the good ones know to keep their hands to themselves. So you're wise to watch that. Touch can be very powerful at that age."

"At any age, for that matter." The moment he said that, he felt his face go red. Why did he say that? It felt as if he were a young boy himself. Tina even looked somewhat surprised.

He saw her swallow. "Yes. Certainly. At any age."

Zack's phone vibrated. A text from Lorenzo about a late delivery. He abruptly stood. "I should get back to work."

"Yes. Of course." She stood too. He was surprised by how close they suddenly were to each other. They just stood there, each seeming to be waiting for the other to do something.

He cleared his throat and looked into her deep brown eyes. "So what do you think?"

"About what?" She nearly whispered. Then she stepped back, alert again. "About what *time,* I mean. What time would you like to meet again? What, uh, what day? That is, assuming you'd like to meet again." She maneuvered herself around the table and walked over to her computer. She spoke directly at the screen. "Because I'm not officially taking you on as a client, we can be very informal." She looked at him. "You understand that, right? Just a bit of advice to help you through the bumpy parts of raising your teens?"

"Sure, sure." Why was she mentioning that now? She sounded as if she were establishing their relationship for an attorney's benefit. "Milly said something about maybe having you meet Dylan and Sherry, but making it as casual as possible. I think that's the only way they're going to go along with something like this, really. Talking with you, I mean."

She smiled. "You mean they'll only agree to it as long as they're unaware of what we're doing?"

He rubbed at the back of his neck. "I guess that's what I'm saying, yes."

"I'm not sure if that's the best approach for us to take, but we can discuss that more when we meet next. When is your next pocket of available time?"

"Friday afternoon?"

She looked at the screen and nodded. "Yes. No. The painters are going to be here Friday."

"Next week, then?"

"I tell you what." She stepped away from her computer. "I'd just as soon not be here when the painters are. Why don't we meet this Friday afternoon at Milly's? At four o'clock? If we're going to make this relationship look less official, we might as well start by changing our venue. Does that work for you?"

Zack put out his hand. "Milly's. Friday at four."

Tina smiled and took his hand.

They took a moment before actually moving, so the clasping of their hands felt suddenly romantic. Zack overreacted by shaking her hand as if she were a water pump.

He thought about his awkward behavior as he walked toward his truck. He was acting like a nervous kid around this woman. Holding her hand had actually affected his body temperature.

Yes, sir. Touch could be mighty powerful at any age.

SEVENTEEN

"Okay, what's going on?" That evening Edie sat across the restaurant table and peered at Tina as if she withheld a juicy secret.

They had opted for the Jasmine Wok Café in Chantilly, twenty minutes out of town. Tina typically loved the spicy, garlicky smell of this place, but she didn't notice her surroundings so much tonight. She squirmed in her seat. "I'm embarrassed to tell you."

"Oh, goody!" Edie rubbed her hands together. "This sounds interesting!"

Their server poured fragrant jasmine tea in their cups and left the pot on the table for them. Tina waited until he left before addressing Edie again. Then she sighed, looked around them, and leaned forward. She spoke in a low voice. "I think I have a teensy crush on my new client."

Edie's eyes widened. "Wow, a crush. Have you caught yourself writing his name all over your geography notebook?"

Tina lifted a single eyebrow and sat back. "I can't *imagine* why I thought this would be embarrassing to discuss with you."

"Okay." Edie laughed. "I'm sorry. This is actually pretty cool. I can't remember the last time you sounded at all interested in *anyone,* client or otherwise. But isn't there some doctor's oath you'd be stepping all over if you, you know, acted on this?"

"Well, obviously I'm not going to act on this. But he's not officially my client, just to split hairs. And I don't know the guy, anyway. I could be whipping up a fantasy personality that isn't even there."

Edie's smile held a healthy dose of tease in it. "But you don't think so, do you? You think you like his personality, don't you?" She grinned. "I can tell."

"He seems really sweet." Tina shrugged. "He cares about his kids, and I like that."

"Kids? He has kids?"

"Look, I'm not going to be able to tell you anything about our discussions."

"So who asked you to?" Edie lifted a shoulder. "I don't care about your discussions." She leaned in. "Just tell me what he looks like."

Tina chuckled as she drank her tea, nearly choking on it. "Just the important stuff, huh?"

"Oh, like you have a crush on his grasp of global economics, right?" Edie took a sip from her cup.

"All right. He's about six inches taller than I am. He has blond, kind of longish hair. Not icky long. Attractive long. Amazing blue eyes. Nice tan from working outdoors. Full lips. Square jaw with stubble darker than his hair. The tiniest cleft in his chin." She touched her own chin while talking.

"Oh my goodness, I think *I* have a crush on this guy."

Their server returned and both women picked up their menus.

Tina smiled at him. "Sorry. We were gabbing too much."

"No, let's just order what we had here last time." Edie scanned her menu. "I'm starving, and I don't want to wait long. How about the pupu platter for two, honey-walnut shrimp, and the Mongolian combo? Work for you?"

Tina shut her menu and handed it to the server. "Perfect. Thanks." She poured more tea for herself and topped off Edie's.

"Anyway, as I said, he's not going to be an official client. He's a friend of Milly's. She's the one who sent him to me. I'm seeing him for free as a favor to her."

Edie tilted her head and batted her eyelashes. "That's just you all over. Give, give, give."

"Hey, when I agreed to talk to him I didn't know he was going to be gorgeous." Tina laughed. "Milly didn't warn me."

"I love Milly. She never actually sticks her nose into anyone's business, you know? But I don't know anyone in town who affects people's lives the way she does. And always in good ways."

"Do you think she knew I'd be attracted to this

single dad farmer? How would she know? I didn't say anything to her about him."

"He's a farmer? You didn't tell me that." Edie frowned. "Wait a minute. What do you mean you didn't say anything to her about him?"

"Hmm?"

"If you hadn't met him before Milly sent him to you, why would you have already said something to her about him?"

"Oh." Tina played with a cuticle on her thumb. "I . . . saw him once before. At Milly's shop."

Their server delivered the pupu platter to their table. They offered a simple prayer the moment he left, and then Edie picked up a rib and shook her head at Tina. "I'm crestfallen. I can't believe you withheld this info from me. Your best friend."

"There was no info to withhold." Tina scooped duck sauce onto her plate and took a spring roll from the tray. "One day he was just there, in front of Milly's shop. I guess to deliver food to her. He was holding boxes of fruit and veggies. We crossed paths and smiled at each other. That was it. I pretty much forgot about him until he showed up in my office."

"But you were attracted to him."

Tina shrugged. "Yeah. He's really handsome."

"And you're even more attracted to him now that you've met him."

After taking a big breath and releasing a degree of disappointment with it, Tina nodded. "Yep."

Neither of them spoke for a moment, finally concentrating on their appetizers. Then Tina lowered her head and pressed her hand against her forehead. "Edie, to be honest, I was almost flirting with him. I had to step away and get all businessy with him at the computer. But then I . . ."

Edie smiled, but Tina could tell she sympathized with Tina's embarrassment. "What? What did you do?"

"I caught myself making it very clear to him that our relationship wasn't official." She looked around them again. "As if I wanted to keep him from thinking of me as a therapist and think of me more as a . . ."

"Woman?"

Tina looked into Edie's eyes. "It's as though I were suddenly a high schooler or something. As though my, I don't know, my hormones took over. What kind of a professional am I?"

"You sound pretty human to me," Edie said. "Frankly, I think it was a good thing, you're establishing what you did. That he's not really your client."

Tina swallowed. "No. None of that really matters, because I agreed to give him advice—"

"Unofficially."

"Right. So I'll just have to deal with the fact that he's kind and handsome and off-limits."

Edie spun the platter and took a spring roll for herself. "Why don't you just tell him you can't give him advice? Then you could flirt with him and maybe things could develop."

"And what excuse would I give for not advising him?" Tina asked. "Sorry, I can't help you professionally because you're just too cute to pass up personally?"

Edie stopped just before taking a bite of her spring roll. "Works for me."

"That is so not me." Tina sighed. "Nope. This will have to be one of those unfortunate circumstances. Maybe I'll find out he's not my type. Maybe he'll turn out to be a slob or something. He did show up with a stain the size of an eggplant on his shirt."

"Eww. That's not good."

"Well, to be fair, he explained that he had had some kind of fruit accident right before showing up."

"A fruit accident." Edie stopped chewing. "That's kind of disarming, don't you think?"

Tina knew there was a trace of a whine in her response. "Yes. It was *really* disarming."

Edie reached across the table to give Tina's hand a little squeeze. "I'm sorry, Tina. But you know what?"

"What?"

"Remember in church a couple of weeks ago, the verse about 'I have plans for you and for your future'? Remember that?"

"Sure. Jeremiah."

"Right, and you and I both said it was a cool verse and we don't think about it often enough?"

"Mm-hmm."

"And I said it helped me feel that I didn't need to stress about what was going to happen—or not happen—with Rob?" Edie dipped the last of her spring roll in duck sauce. "You should think that way about this farmer guy. If God wants him in your future, it's already planned. Don't sweat it."

Tina picked up a rib. Edie was right, of course. But the thing that bothered her, when she really thought about it, was that this was the first time in years—since Phil, really—that she'd felt such a spark about a man.

To use Edie's vernacular, she didn't "sweat" the possibility that God had already planned Zack's being in her future. She didn't sweat that she had to faithfully wait for that to play out.

What she sweated, just a little, was the possibility that God's plans for her didn't involve Zack at all.

EIGHTEEN

The following afternoon, Zack stood in his field and reviewed his roster of scheduled deliveries. It had been a scorcher of a day, and beads of sweat dripped down his forehead, despite his ball cap.

"Hey, Lorenzo, did you tell me you already made the delivery to Jarvis today?"

Lorenzo tied off a truckload of hay bales. "Yep. Delivered Jarvis and Bascombe on the same trip."

"Uh-huh." Zack set down his clipboard on the truck's tailgate and stared across the field. He pulled his handkerchief out, removed his hat, and wiped across his forehead. "How about Bascombe? You deliver Bascombe yet?"

Lorenzo stopped readying the truck and faced Zack. A smile tugged at his mouth. "What's the matter with you, man?"

Until Lorenzo smiled at him, Zack hadn't really paid much attention to him while they talked. "What do you mean?"

Lorenzo chuckled. "I just *told* you I delivered to Bascombe. I delivered to Jarvis too, in case you were wondering. And to Bascombe."

"All right, all right. No need to get smart." Zack shook his head, but Lorenzo made him smile about his own foggy mindedness. "I just have a lot of stuff on my mind, is all."

"About work? Or something to do with the kids?"

"Uh, yeah. Kind of about the kids."

"Sherry did a great job washing my car Saturday. Ilsa had to forbid the boys not to help her."

Zack nodded. "Yeah, you told me."

"*That* you remember, huh?"

"Yep. That I remember."

"And Dylan?" Lorenzo turned back to the hay. "How's he—" He turned back around. "Oh, hey, how about the counselor? Weren't you supposed to meet the counselor yesterday?"

Zack put his hat back on and pulled the brim down. He spoke softly. "Uh, yeah. Met with her."

"Say what?"

"I said I met with her, yeah." Zack picked up the clipboard and studied it intently.

When he didn't hear a response from Lorenzo, Zack looked to see if he had moved on.

He hadn't.

He just stood there. Then he suddenly cocked one eyebrow. "What don't you want to talk about?"

Zack couldn't get anything past his friend. "You're worse than a woman. I think Ilsa's had an influence on you."

"Doggoned right." Lorenzo crossed his arms. "So what is it? Did you do something you can only tell your good friend Lorenzo about? You embarrass yourself somehow?"

"No, I didn't do anything. It's just . . ." Zack furrowed his brows.

"Come on, man, don't make me guess. It's just what?"

Zack kicked at the ground. "The counselor. It's the counselor."

"A problem? You got a problem with her?"

He finally looked Lorenzo in the eye. "Kind of, yeah. She's, um, younger than I was expecting."

He watched Lorenzo break into a huge grin. "Well, what do you know? My man has finally noticed women again."

Zack rolled his eyes and looked away, shaking his head.

"That's it, right?" Lorenzo gave him a punch on the arm. "She's pretty?"

He released a long breath. "Very."

"Well, all right. That is *all right*."

"You sound awfully happy there, sport."

"I am, man. Four years is a long time. Ilsa will be thrilled."

"No, come on, don't tell Ilsa about this. And anyway, there's nothing to tell."

"Not yet, maybe, but just knowing old Zack is back with the living? That's news."

"Hey, just because I haven't been seeing anyone doesn't mean I've been dead. And I won't be seeing this woman, either."

"Why not? You writing her off already?"

"No. But I didn't meet with her so I could find a woman. I met with her because I need some help with Dylan and Sherry."

"Yeah? So? You can't do both? You're one of the most efficient multitaskers I know."

Zack laughed. "It's more complicated than scheduling, Lorenzo. My relationship with her is professional. I don't think she's allowed to go out with someone she's counseling."

Lorenzo raised his hands and shrugged his shoulders. "So she won't go out with Dylan or Sherry. They're the ones she's counseling."

"Hey, let's keep that under wraps too, okay? For now I'd just as soon the kids don't know I've asked for professional help. I think they would clam up so fast we would move backward, not forward."

"Got it, chief. You're probably right."

The two of them climbed inside the cab of the truck. Lorenzo started it up and kept his eyes straight ahead as they headed back to the barn. "She's pretty, though, huh?"

Zack wiped the back of his hand across his damp temples. "Dark hair, dark eyes, slim but curvy, and she's both . . . womanish and girlish at the same time." He looked at Lorenzo. "You know what I mean?"

"Think so."

"And just plain nice. She seems really nice. And smart. Maybe funny too. I like that."

"What did she think of you?"

They both smiled. Then Zack said, "I doubt she thought much beyond when to schedule our next meeting. I'm just a block on her computer screen."

"Not necessarily, friend. Ilsa tells me you're a catch."

Zack laughed out loud at that. Then he straightened his T-shirt as if he were the exact opposite of dusty and filthy from the field. "Ilsa always was more discerning than your average female."

"I'm serious, man." Lorenzo pulled up at the barn. "Don't write yourself off so quickly. Maya didn't leave because of you. She left because of Maya."

Just hearing her name made the moment more somber. Zack nodded and got out of the truck. "I'm stopping at the house for a while to see if the kids are home from school yet. Let me know when you get back from dropping off that load, will you?"

"Will do." Lorenzo lifted his chin to signal goodbye and pulled away.

Maya's image filled Zack's thoughts as he walked in the direction of his home. She had been dark, like this counselor lady, Tina. But Maya would never have done the kind of thing Tina did for a living, helping others. Lorenzo was right about one thing—Maya's only concern was Maya.

He saw the house come into view. Sometimes it was hard to believe she had ever lived there with him. She had become so cold toward him in those last couple of years. Bored, she said. Judging from the guy she took off with, her idea of excitement had changed while she was Zack's wife. *She* certainly hadn't considered Zack a catch.

Well, that was fine. He needed to focus on what was best for his kids right now, anyway. Get them through their teen years and ready to go to college so they could make their way in the world. The last thing he should be moping about was whether or not some pretty counselor considered him more than just another client. As far as he knew, she was all wrapped up in someone far more exciting than he was. Good thing he had a few days before seeing her again. He'd have plenty of time to get over this foolish little bit of distraction.

NINETEEN

Two days later Tina parked in front of Milly's shop and spotted most of her women's group as they spotted her. In their varied shapes, sizes, and summer-toned outfits, the ladies looked as much like an adornment to Milly's shop as did the freesia-filled window boxes.

Carmella appeared a little winded. "Tina, I can't believe that space opened up for you after I walked all the way from my car down there." She pointed down the street.

"For corn's sake, Carmella, you're only a block away," said Gerry. She gave a throaty laugh and hooked her arm through Carmella's. "Come on, honey, lean on me the rest of the way."

Tina smiled at them. They were quite a twosome, and they always kept the group meetings lively. Certainly they were more vocal than shy little Meredith, who had yet to say anything to anyone.

"Meredith," Tina said, "I'm glad to see you were able to get off work again for our meeting."

Meredith perked up. She nearly shimmered with momentary pride. "I actually walked into my boss's office and told him I needed the personal time. I mean, I had the time coming to me, but he gave me such grief about last week's meeting. If I'm going to be paid less than Aaron, at least I want to be able to take time off that I've earned."

Tina put her hand on Meredith's shoulder. "I'm so proud of you! We'll chat more about that inside." Tina glanced around behind them. "I was expecting Sally to come today as well because she's back from her business trip. Maybe she's—"

Tina stopped speaking, walking, and thinking.

Zack had just come around the corner, apparently from the back of Milly's shop. He moved with purpose and grace Tina hadn't noticed before. The man was utterly fluid in his movements, and she felt her pulse quicken. He hadn't seen her yet.

When Tina stopped what she was doing, so did Meredith. And, despite the fact that Carmella and Gerry were about to open the tea shop door, Gerry had turned to make a remark to either Tina or Meredith.

So by the time Zack finally realized that Tina stood at the front of Milly's shop, watching him, there were actually four women watching him. Tina's little posse of gawkers, of which she was the Gawker in Chief.

"Oh!" He stopped on the sidewalk and then suddenly started walking again, as if his feet had hiccupped. He headed toward his truck, doing a double take over the fact that all of those women were staring at him. Finally, he broke out in a half smile. He reached up and tugged at the brim of his ball cap. "Ladies." Then he looked directly at Tina.

This time neither she nor Zack grinned. Not with their lips, anyway. But Tina saw a subtle twinkle about Zack's eyes, and she found it contagious.

He dipped his head ever so slightly at her. "Tina."

"Good morning, Zack." She smiled and turned away. She spoke over her shoulder, nonchalant as a supermodel. "Have a terrific day."

She ran directly into Meredith, who tripped out of her way. Not a single one of the women had moved to enter Milly's shop. They all just stood there, watching her. Gerry had her arms folded, wearing a smart grin and an I-*knew*-it squint in her eyes.

Her cheeks burning, Tina heard Zack's truck drive away as she shooed the women toward the door as if they were errant goslings. "All right, show's over. Let's get on in there."

Milly was already serving a couple at another table when Tina's group walked in. She looked over at them and gave them a smile and a wave. "Make yourselves comfortable, ladies. I'll be right there."

Tina knew she would have to be very deliberate if she hoped to make herself comfortable with her suddenly alert, curious, and distracted group of clients. Even Meredith was looking at her with an unusual expression, as if she had just realized Tina had three ears or something.

Before anyone had a chance to say anything, Milly approached their table. "I have something new for you to try this morning, girls. For starters, anyway. How would you like to try lemon cream tea cakes today?" She used her hands to aid in her description. "Tea cakes filled with a delightful lemon-curd cream filling. They're absolutely perfect with the Earl Grey. Sound good?"

Tina was amazed that Carmella didn't jump at the offer. She was always the first member of the group ready to indulge in the richest pastries Milly had to offer. But no one's attention had yet been fully drawn away from Tina.

"I think that sounds fantastic, Milly." Tina smiled at her on behalf of the group. Then she spoke to the other women as if they were hard of hearing. "Don't you all think that sounds wonderful?" Finally the others engaged with Milly.

"Absolutely. I'm all about the tea cakes." Gerry gave Milly a big grin. "We love being taste testers for your new recipes."

Carmella raised a manicured finger. "Of course, as long as I can still get—"

In unison, everyone said, "Berry shortcakes."

144

"Well, that's fine," Milly said, "but you might want to see how you do with these rich little cakes first, Carmella. They're especially filling."

"So, Milly." Gerry sat back and looked serious. "What's the status on the hot produce guy these days?"

Tina gasped before she looked at Gerry, who wiggled her eyebrows. Tina couldn't help but chuckle. "Never mind, you." She looked at Milly. "They're teasing me, Milly, because Zack and I said hello to each other out front."

"Ah, so he called you." Milly smiled at her. "I'm so glad. You'll do him a lot of good, I'm sure of it."

Tina widened her eyes at Milly, who mirrored them at once with wide eyes of her own. "Oh, dear. What I mean to say is . . ."

Tina wasn't sure if she had ever seen Milly blush before. She wished she wouldn't at this particular moment, but obviously Milly couldn't help it.

"I'll just get those tea cakes for you ladies." Milly backed away. After a glance at Tina's group, she mouthed one silent word to Tina: "Sorry!"

Tina simply smiled and shrugged a shoulder. She'd handled more dicey situations than this one. Middleburg was a small town. She often ran into clients when they were with family or friends. They often preferred that she keep their professional relationship confidential.

"So." Gerry leaned forward, her arms on the table. "What good are you going to do for . . . Zack, wasn't it?"

"Now, Gerry." Tina talked to the woman as if she were the lovable class wise guy. "You know you wouldn't want me sharing anything about *your* business with anyone behind your back. You wouldn't be meeting with me right now if you thought I'd do such a thing."

A flash of disappointment marred Gerry's smile, and she sat back. "Oh no. Are you telling me he's a *client?* That's no fun at all!"

Carmella joined in. "No, it sure isn't! You two would be so perfect together!"

Meredith made doe eyes and nodded with vigor.

Tina laughed. "Ladies, I know him far better than any of you do, and *I* barely know him. I certainly don't know him well enough to make a comment like that. And I didn't say he was a client. I didn't say anything to indicate what my relationship with Mr. Cooper—"

"You called him Zack," Gerry piped in.

"Yes, Zack. I didn't say what my relationship with Zack is, because that's *his* business, not yours. Can I be any more blunt than that?"

The three of them looked at each other and a round of frowns made its way across the table.

"Why don't we get back to what *is* our business, and that's this group. Right here." Tina included them all with a quick sweep of her hand before

146

she looked directly at Gerry. "And since you're especially talkative this morning, Gerry—"

Carmella's lilting laugh interrupted. "What's new, right?"

"—why don't you tell us how this week has gone for you? How about your effort to back away from trying to arrange your sister's love life? Are you still staying out of her business, as I suggested?"

Carmella spoke before Gerry could answer. "Hmm. Gerry, that's what you were doing to Tina, trying to arrange her love life. I didn't realize that until just now."

Meredith leaned in. "Well, to be fair, we all were kind of doing that to Tina."

Gerry ignored them and pointed at Tina. "Now there's something I definitely wanted to tell you. About my sister, I mean. I did back off. Didn't say a word about a guy I thought she should meet. Didn't suggest anyone else, either, for the past two weeks. I just left her to her own terrible judgment."

Tina said, "I'm proud of you. How did you feel about that?"

"You know what she did the other day? She complained! She accused me of not caring enough to keep my eyes open to romantic possibilities for her. *What* is up with that? Does that mean you were wrong about me being a control freak?"

Carmella laughed. "There's no way she was

wrong about that, Gerry. I'm not a therapist, and even *I* can tell you're a control freak."

"How did *you* feel, Gerry, when you backed off?" Tina persisted.

Gerry shrugged. "At first I felt like I would jump out of my skin, knowing how bad she is at reading men, but I did what you said. I kept telling myself that she was a grown-up and her decisions were her decisions, not mine. Her consequences, not mine. I need to stop thinking her happiness is my responsibility."

"Excellent. I think you'll find yourself less frustrated the more you keep that in mind."

"Not if she's going to give me a hard time, I won't." Gerry shook her head, as if her sister were right there, giving her a hard time.

Tina rested her arms on the table and looked at all three of the women as she spoke. "You're often going to find that your loved ones will balk the most at your making healthy changes to your behavior. Families tend to fall into patterns—even unhealthy ones. Some people use the analogy of a dance to describe it."

She mimicked two people dancing by having her fingers dance on the table. "Take you and your sister, Gerry. You're used to leading and she's used to following, and you've both been dancing the same steps for years. If you change the steps or stop leading, your sister has to change as well." She stopped moving her fingers, allowing them to represent two people standing immobile, facing each other. "Now that no one is pushing her, she's on her own. That's good for both of you to acknowledge."

She looked at all three of them. "Change is often uncomfortable, even when it's good for you."

Milly and Jane arrived at the table with the tea and pastries. "Here we go, ladies," Milly said. "You'll have to tell me what you think."

"Oh, those look yummy, Milly!" Carmella's smile was childlike in its enthusiasm.

Jane placed the tiered tray close to Carmella. "They are. Milly's outdone herself with these. I dare any one of you to eat only one."

Once Milly and Jane left, a bit of the mischief had returned to Gerry's eyes. "All right, so I think I'm getting the hang of that. My sis can complain about the dance steps, but it's time for her to take charge of her own choreography."

"Yes." Tina smiled.

Gerry sighed. "But you're going to have to indulge me a little when I tell you that I think you and Zack the produce guy should be thinking about a little choreography of your own."

"Mmm." Carmella had a mouthful of lemon tea cake, but it was clear her nonverbal comment referred to Gerry's suggestion as much as it did to Milly's latest culinary treat.

Meredith sighed and gave Tina an apologetic look. "Afraid I have to agree."

Tina rolled her eyes at the three of them and took a sip of tea. Despite her refusal to engage in further talk about Zack, she could at least admit to herself that the image of dancing with him was something that just looked right.

TWENTY

There didn't seem to be anything that could dampen Zack's spirits that day. After he crossed paths with Tina and her gaping ladies at Milly's shop, he kept catching himself smiling. Even after one of his clients gave him a hard time about the price of peaches. Even after someone in a Jaguar cut him off as he drove to Gourmet Farms, the fresh-food market. Even when a woman's irritable little dog growled at him for no good reason as he passed it on the sidewalk.

He knew there was no logical reason for him to be in such high spirits simply because he and Tina exchanged hellos this morning. But there it was.

And he wasn't the only one who noticed.

"Man, you're sure in a good mood this afternoon." Dylan looked up as Zack walked into the house through the mudroom door.

Zack didn't know quite what tune he was whistling. He simply felt like whistling, so he improvised.

"I'm glad to see you hard at work there, son." He approached Dylan and gave him a hearty rub on his shoulders. "I hope your sister is following your example?"

"I guess so." Dylan shrugged. "She doesn't like

151

working here in the kitchen. She's upstairs in her room, I think." He grinned. "Assuming Lorenzo didn't leave his car outside."

Zack arched an eyebrow at Dylan as he headed for the refrigerator. "Want a soda or something?"

"No, thanks." Dylan had already returned to whatever he was reading.

Zack popped open a can of soda and walked to the bottom of the stairs. He was about to call up to Sherry, but then he decided a personal visit would be better. Tina had encouraged him to focus on his communication with the kids, so this would be a start.

Yeah, that's right. She said it would be good to consider exactly what emotion he was feeling at any particular time. So what was he feeling today? How would he peg this feeling?

Expectation. Was that an emotion? Whatever it was, that was definitely what he felt. Maybe expectation was unrealistic, but he couldn't help expecting things to be better, now that he was talking with Tina about the kids. And about other things, maybe.

He tapped on his daughter's door. When she didn't answer, he tapped a bit harder and then heard her bed creak from her getting up. When she opened the door he saw she had her little earphones plugged in. She pulled them free, and fuzzy, tinny music played out, a young rapper's voice punctuating like an angry ant on steroids.

"Hi, Dad. You home for the day now?"

He leaned in and gave her a peck on the cheek. "Not just yet. I need to finish up in the field and make sure Lorenzo doesn't need me for anything."

"Okay." She brought her earphones back up to her ears.

"Which reminds me," Zack said. "We're opening the field for pick-your-own-berries customers this weekend. I'm going to need you and Dylan to work for a while."

He saw disappointment cloud her face for a moment, but she apparently fought the need to complain. "Yeah. Okay."

"What's the problem?" He took care to ask with a gentle tone rather than a bothered one.

She shook her head. "Doesn't matter. I'm on restriction anyway. It's just . . . Friday is the last day of school, you know?"

He nodded. "Yeah. I know."

"I'm going to miss a few parties. That's all."

"Sherry, don't you think—"

"It's okay, Dad. It's my own fault. I messed up. There will be other parties this summer."

Zack barely nodded. Frankly, he would prefer she not attend any of those parties. He suspected none of them were terribly wholesome. But he didn't want to ruin the day, and it was pleasant to be talking kindly with each other again. They could discuss stuff like parties when Tina came on board.

"All right, honey. I'll be back home in a little while." He turned toward the stairs.

"Dad, wait." Sherry ran back into her room and pulled a piece of paper from beneath the books and binders spread out on her bed. She brought it back to him. "They want each of us to bring in a baked something, you know, like cookies or brownies, or contribute a few dollars for a staff appreciation thing. Because I didn't want to bake anything, I was supposed to bring money in today, but I think I can still bring it in tomorrow."

Zack read the notice and pulled his wallet from his back pocket. "Five dollars okay?"

"I'm sure that's plenty. Thanks."

"Do you think Dylan was supposed to bring in money too?"

"Unless he's baking brownies down there, yeah."

The image of Dylan baking anything was so funny they both laughed.

Zack couldn't remember the last time he and Sherry had openly laughed together. That movie a couple of weeks ago, maybe. Fueled by the upbeat tone of the day, he spoke on impulse. "Say, since you're both grounded this weekend, I could at least take the two of you to that Matt Damon movie you wanted to see. Saturday evening. Kind of a repeat performance of the other week. Interested?"

"Sure, Dad."

"Great. I'll mention it to your brother." With that he headed back downstairs. He pulled another five-dollar bill from his wallet.

Dylan glanced up again when Zack entered the kitchen but looked right back down at his homework.

"Hey, Sherry and I were just talking about Saturday."

"What about it?"

Zack wished the boy would look him in the eye while they talked. But he *was* looking at homework. He appreciated his focus, at least. "I need the two of you to work this weekend. We're doing pick-your-own."

Dylan finally looked back up, annoyance in his expression.

"And then Saturday night I'll take the two of you to the new Matt Damon movie." Zack moved toward Dylan as he spoke, and without giving it much thought he lifted Dylan's backpack from the floor to put in the five-dollar bill.

Dylan started to nod his acceptance of the Saturday plan, but he jerked his head toward his backpack when it became clear that Zack meant to open it. "What are you doing?"

Zack held up the five. "You need to turn this in tomorrow. It's for the staff apprecia—"

Dylan grabbed at the backpack as if he feared Zack were trying to steal it.

Zack was surprised by his son's reaction. He

didn't even have a chance to release the bag before something fell from the small front pocket. "Dylan, what in the world is your problem?"

They both looked to the floor, and Dylan stood abruptly to retrieve what had fallen.

Zack froze. He was a thirty-nine-year-old man. He lived a clean life. But even he knew a pot pipe when he saw one.

Dylan had already replaced the pipe in his backpack, as if he could pretend it hadn't been painfully evident staring up at them from the floor.

Zack silently extended his hand. Dylan paused for a moment before he sighed and pulled the pipe back out.

He placed it in Zack's hand. "It's not mine, Dad."

Zack shook his head and lifted his hand to silence him. "Don't even *think* of feeding me that one." He sank into a chair at the table, and Dylan slowly sat back down. "Dylan, do you want to be grounded for your entire life? Is that the plan?"

Dylan simply stared at the tabletop.

"How do you and Sherry expect me to trust you? Lying. Smoking pot. Stealing cars. Shoplifting. No wonder your grades have dropped."

"I only did half of those things. And that's not why my grades have dropped."

"No? What's the excuse today, Dylan? Whose fault is it today?"

Dylan glared at him. "You didn't even . . ." He bit off his last words.

"What? I didn't even *what?*" Zack's voice rose.

"Why did you let her go so easily? You didn't even fight for her! You didn't try to make her stay."

Tears filled Dylan's angry eyes, and Zack felt as if he had been slapped. He sat up, anger and defensiveness in his veins, but a blanket of guilt weighed him back down. He knew Maya's leaving had to do with more than her feeling stifled by the institution of marriage, but Dylan would never know what pain his mother had inflicted on Zack. At least Zack hoped he would never know such pain.

He didn't want to start yelling or inflicting punishment he'd regret having to bring to fruition. He tightened his lips and stood.

"Just get your homework done. I'm going to go back out and finish with Lorenzo, once I get this pot stink off my hands." He held the pipe out as if it were cow dung. "We'll discuss your punishment later."

He wanted so much to talk with Tina. Right now. But he felt in his gut it would be wrong to call her about this. They were scheduled to meet at Milly's tomorrow afternoon. As far as he was concerned, four o'clock couldn't come soon enough.

TWENTY-ONE

Tina caught herself checking the time more than once during her final appointment that afternoon. Stacy Sumner set Tina's teeth on edge, but if she had any hope of effectively counseling the woman, she needed to get over it, pronto.

The heavily accessorized blonde crossed her tanned, toned legs as she talked. And boy, could she talk. It struck Tina that Stacy always came off as self-sufficient. She never came to Tina terribly distraught or in apparent need of counsel. Rather, she merely seemed to want a sounding board for her complaints. Complaints about customers—she and her husband owned a small bed-and-breakfast in town. Complaints about her fellow townspeople—she didn't appear to have any close friends in Middleburg. And most predominantly, complaints about her husband.

"I'm not saying George held me back in life, mind you. But everyone always thought I'd go far. With my acting. And my looks." She pointed to her long, luxurious hair. "This is my actual color, you know. All of this—" She indicated the entire length of her body with both hands. "All of this is *natural*. Not a bit of surgery. Nada." She punctuated her last word by jabbing her sharp, French-manicured index finger in Tina's direction.

"Yes, I remember your telling me that before." *Like a million times.* "So, Stacy, if you're not saying George held you back, what is it you're trying to say? Are you disappointed in the life choices you made? Are you taking responsibility for your own decisions? Is that what you're saying?"

As if there were a delay in her hearing, Stacy opened her mouth, apparently ready to launch into another round of complaints. But then Tina's question seemed to settle into her mind.

"Well, sure, I'm willing to take responsibility for my own choices. But that doesn't mean my choices . . . I mean, I don't think I should necessarily have to live with the consequences of my choices forever. You know?"

Tina lifted her brows. "Sometimes we do. Which choice are we talking about right now?"

Stacy shrugged. "George, of course."

"You're thinking about leaving George?"

"Oh, *I* don't know." She dropped her shoulders and sighed without any great emotion. You'd have thought she was trying to decide between two different flavors of ice cream. "We've just, you know, grown apart. I realize that sounds cliché, but it's so true in our case. I was swept away by the charm of moving to this little town and running the bed-and-breakfast. But it's *not* charming. It's a lot of hard work. If I'm going to work hard, I want it to be in a profession I enjoy."

"What do you have in mind?"

"Well, *acting* for starters."

"If George were able to hire someone to take your place at the inn, would you be willing to try to hang in there with the marriage and maybe do some local acting?"

Stacy frowned. "Local acting? This is Podunk, USA. Where am I going to act here?"

"There are a number of local theatrical companies in Northern Virginia you could audition for. There are acting troupes in towns and cities beyond Middleburg, all the way into DC. Essentially, all within driving distance."

Stacy shook her head at Tina as if she were the most naive citizen of Podunk, USA. "That's not *acting*. That's pretending to act."

Tina tried to keep her sigh from showing the full extent of her exasperation. "Stacy, what acting experience do you have so far?"

"Well, that's just *it!* I need to be in Los Angeles or New York or someplace like that. I'm not going to get experience hiding away at the Blue Mountain Inn."

Tina clasped her hands together in her lap. "Okay, our time is up, but I have some homework I'd like you to do before we meet next."

"Homework?" The frown that followed was far from surprising.

160

"I want you to find out what you can about local acting companies." Tina raised her hand to stop Stacy the moment she started to object. "And I want you to have an audition or a simple informational interview scheduled before you come back in here. From what you tell me, you've never acted. You've never even auditioned. Is that correct?"

"Yes, but—"

"All right. So by your next visit I want you to have that set up. Before you blame George for your lack of opportunity, you have to make sure you actually *enjoy* acting. This will be your first step."

Tina stood and walked to her desk. "I'll see you once you get that set up, okay?"

Her phone rang, and Stacy stood up. Tina was thrilled to have a reason to cut short any arguing Stacy had in mind. She picked up the phone without even glancing at the caller identification.

"Tina Milano. Hold just a moment, please." She smiled at Stacy. "Thank you, Stacy."

With a quick, indignant sniff, Stacy nodded and left.

"I'm sorry," Tina said into the phone. "Thanks for holding."

"Hey, Tina." A man's voice. "Sorry to call you at work. It's me."

Me. Why did people do that? "Pardon?"

"Antony. From church. From dinner last week?"

Ugh! She had stopped worrying he would call her again once an entire week had passed. "Oh, yes, Antony. How are you?"

"Listen, I'm sorry I didn't call sooner. I've just been swamped on a new job site. Even had to go out of town a few days for some licensing work."

"Not a problem at all. As a matter of fact—"

"Tina, I was hoping you could help me out Saturday night."

Help him out? Was that how he was going to characterize a second date? And Saturday night? That was only two days away. "I don't know—"

"I promised I'd chaperone the youth group at the movies, but I didn't realize they expected me to bring troops with me."

"Troops?"

"Chaperones," he said. "I think more kids signed up than they expected."

Tina grimaced. Surely there were other people he could turn to. Despite the amount of time that had elapsed, she suspected he hoped to turn this event into another step in the dating game for the two of them. She loved the teens, but she was terribly uncomfortable that any of them might start to see Antony and her as a couple.

She chose her words with care. She didn't want to lie. "Gosh, thanks for thinking of me, Antony, but I don't think that's going to work out." Because she'd rather swim in a pool of ice cubes than go on another date with him—that's the part she didn't say. But that was diplomacy, not lying.

"Ah. Too bad." The silence that followed was short but uncomfortable. Should she try to fill it? "Okay," he said. "Thanks anyway. Give me a call if you change your mind."

Well. That was easier than she expected. He took that surprisingly well.

Come to think of it, Antony hadn't seemed all that disappointed when she avoided giving him anything remotely close to a good night kiss at the end of their date, either. Nor—as he pointed out—had he called her since.

Maybe she was fretting over nothing.

He was still on her mind when her phone rang again. This time she checked the identification. Edie.

"What's up, copper?"

Edie chuckled. "Well, you're in a good mood. What, did you just have an enjoyable session with an imbalanced client?"

"Not funny." Although Edie would have *loved* hearing about Stacy. "No, I think I just realized Antony isn't any more interested in me than I am in him."

"Antony? The sloppy chewer?"

"The very one. He asked me out and didn't sound the slightest bit disappointed when I turned him down."

"Hmm. Why would he bother to ask you out if he didn't care?"

"Well, it wasn't for an official date. He asked me to go with him and the church's youth group to the movies on Saturday night."

"With you and Antony as the only adults?"

"No, it sounded like he was asking several others as well."

"Uh, Tina, I don't think he was asking you on a date. It sounds like he was asking for help."

Tina went silent. So did Edie.

"Oh, goodness, Edie. I think you might be right. That's exactly what he said, that he wondered if I could help him out. I kind of dismissed him the minute he asked. I was so sure he wanted a second date."

"Maybe he does. But it sounds as though he was just looking for volunteers this time."

"And I'm not even doing anything Saturday night."

"But we're still on for tomorrow, right?"

"Oh, Edie, now I feel bad. Let me call him back. You want to come to the movies too?"

"When is it, again? Saturday?"

"Yeah."

"*No puedo, chica*. Rob and I are going out. But are you and I still on for dinner tomorrow or not?"

"Yeah, yeah. My place. Let me call Antony. I'm going to carry guilt around if I don't fix this."

"Sheesh. Doesn't take much to make you feel guilty, does it? Some therapist *you* are."

164

"Hey, some guilt makes sense. And this situation is easily solved. Talk with you later."

She called Antony right away. "Hey, Antony, this is—"

"Tina! Did you change your mind?"

That gave her a moment's pause. He would have known it was her by checking his phone's screen. And his assumption that she'd changed her mind made sense because she was calling back so soon. But the excitement in his voice? That was slightly disconcerting.

"Uh, yeah. It looks like I'll be able to help out with the youth movie trip after all."

"Fantastic! I'm so glad to hear that. How about we get some dinner together beforehand? I could pick you up at, say five o'clock?"

She just about kicked her desk, she was so mad at herself. Or maybe she'd wait and kick Edie tomorrow night instead. He *was* hoping for a date out of this, as she originally suspected. And now it was too late.

"No. No dinner. Thanks anyway. I'll just meet you and the kids at the theater, if you don't mind. I have stuff to get done before then."

Like pulling out her old college psych textbooks and reading up on misplaced guilt.

"Sure, okay." This time there was a distinct note of disappointment in Antony's voice.

Why hadn't he shared that sentiment with her on the last phone call? How dare he sound so nonchalant when she turned him down before and then own up to his real motives now?

She sighed and silently chastised herself. She was making too big a deal out of this. She'd been through worse.

"Okay, then, Antony. Which movie and what showing?"

"The Matt Damon spy thing. Seven thirty."

"Got it. I'll see you there."

She entered the information into her phone and actually stopped to say a little prayer before gathering her things and heading home.

Lord, I really don't want to go out with Antony, but I do love being with the kids. Please help me do what's best for them.

The kids. They would make the evening fun. Most likely someone would attend whose company she'd like to keep.

TWENTY-TWO

Zack arrived at Milly's tea shop a few minutes after four the next day. He hoped Tina wasn't a stickler for time. He had done his best to be punctual for their appointment, but it wasn't easy to leave the farm before the workday was done, especially because they were opening it up to the public tomorrow for the pick-your-own-berries event. Then there was the shower he had to take before heading over. There was no way he was going to show up a mess again. That berry stain on his shirt the other day fulfilled a good month's worth of his doofus quota with this woman, as far as he was concerned. He knew today's Ralph Lauren chinos and deep blue polo shirt were an improvement.

When he walked into the shop, the first person he saw was Milly. She was smiling, as usual, and saying something that obviously tickled her.

And she was saying that something to Tina, who threw her head back and let loose a throaty laugh that gave Zack goose bumps of pleasure. She laughed like a grown woman, not the girlish giggle he had grown accustomed to as a result of Sherry's being the only female in his life these days.

He approached, and both women turned toward him. Tina's expression sobered slightly, but he got the feeling she was happy to see him. She gave him a warmer smile than he would expect from a typical business acquaintance.

"Ah, there's the man himself," Milly said, hugging him gently. "You two pick a table, and I'll bring some tea straight away." She took only a few steps before turning back. "And how about a little between-meal savory? Today I'm making a new kind of finger sandwiches. Chicken curry. They've been quite well received so far."

Tina looked at Zack, her eyebrows raised.

He nodded once. "Sounds delicious, Milly. Thanks."

"Tea for two, then," Milly said. "Coming up."

Tina took charge as soon as Milly left. "Let's have a seat."

He stepped around to a chair at the table she chose and pulled it out for her.

"Oh." She seemed surprised.

This wasn't her office, and his mama raised him to do the little things a gentleman is supposed to do.

"Thank you, Zack."

"My pleasure."

She sat back and observed him as he took a seat. "How have things been with the kids this week?"

He sighed. "We had a new issue come up. Dylan dropped a pipe out of his backpack yesterday."

"A pipe?"

"A pot pipe." He watched a saddened frown mar her pretty face.

"Oh, Zack, I'm sorry. Do you think he's using often?"

He shook his head. "I didn't think he was using at *all,* so I'm probably not a good one to judge how often he's smoking."

She leaned in. "Unfortunately, he's not that unusual. About a third of all students his age use. But there are things you'll want to watch, okay? His eyes, his grades, his concentration, his mood, even the way he smells—"

"Yeah. I just didn't expect this of Dylan. Now that I know, I'll be more likely to notice that stuff. I wasn't the most innocent kid in the world in my youth, either, so I know the signs."

"Well, that should give you some hope, then. Look how well you turned out."

That stopped him. It meant a lot to him that she didn't seem to blame him for Dylan's choice. That she didn't seem to think he was a bad parent.

"How did you handle it?" She leaned down and pulled a small notebook from her purse. "When you saw the pipe, what happened next?"

Milly returned with their tea and sandwiches. Jane followed closely behind with a fresh pitcher of cream and a plate of shortbread cookies.

"For your sweet tooth, Tina." Jane gave Zack a

wink, as if they were teasing Tina together. He returned her smile.

"You bad thing, Jane. Thanks." Tina gestured toward the shortbread, and her playful eyes met Zack's. "My weakness."

He popped one of the buttery cookies into his mouth. "Something we have in common, then." When he looked away from Tina's smile, he caught both Milly and Jane watching them as if they were a television show.

Milly started and pulled Jane away with her. "We'll leave you two to your discussion. Let us know if you need any refills."

They left, and Tina returned to her question. "What did you do when the pipe fell out of Dylan's backpack? Did you confront him?"

"We fought. About the pipe, about his grades. Even about—well, we didn't fight about this, but he yelled at me for not . . ." Hmm. He hadn't planned to talk at great length about Maya with Tina if he could avoid it.

But she sat there, patiently waiting for him to finish his sentence.

"He thinks I should have done more to make his mother stay."

She rested her hands in her lap and sighed. "Zack, you realize, I hope, that he's probably expressing the hurt and anger he feels toward his mother by redirecting it at you."

Zack exhaled. "He's doing a pretty good job of

it, then. It sure sounded like he was mad at me."

"That's because you're safe. You're here. And you've shown him you're going to stick around, even if he fights with you and gets into trouble. He needs to be able to safely vent some of that pain and anger." She put her elbow on the table and rested her chin in her hand. "As a matter of fact, I wonder if Dylan got into any fights after Maya left. That would be pretty typical too."

"Yeah. Not too long after she took off, he was pretty easily rattled. I had to go meet with his principal over some scuffles with classmates. But I thought he was over all that by now. All that hostility."

"He probably learned to hold it in, but he can't be expected to do that forever. I think he'll eventually back off of blaming you. He's thinking like a kid right now. It's important for you to watch for opportunities to get him to identify what he's really feeling. Remember I told you about that before?"

"Yep." He gave her a half smile. "Man, Tina, I was counting on you to handle all the *feeling* stuff with him."

She smiled and spoke in a whisper. "You are learning well, Grasshopper."

He laughed out loud.

"So what else happened regarding the pipe besides the fighting and accusations? How was it left?" Tina leaned forward.

He shrugged. "I took it away from him. Told him we'd talk about it later. He was in the middle of doing homework and, frankly, I wanted to get your advice before I said anything else, especially about Maya. I'm losing confidence in my parenting abilities, to tell you the truth."

"That's understandable. You want to steer your children on the right path, and you start to second-guess every word and action when you see them making mistakes like this."

"Yeah. I don't want to make things worse."

"You won't. You're a conscientious father, Zack."

He sat forward, frustrated. "How can you know that? I say some pretty stupid things to the kids sometimes. Especially when I lose my temper with them."

She gestured toward him as she had toward the plate of cookies. "You're here, aren't you? You've solicited advice on how to be the best parent you can be. A bad parent wouldn't bother. I'm not saying there aren't cases when a parent is simply out of his league, when *nothing* the parent does will make the child stay on the straight and narrow, but some parents give up too soon. And some write off behaviors like pot smoking because they did it themselves when they were young."

"Well." Zack looked down at the table. "Like I said, I wasn't a stellar kid at Dylan's age, either."

"So you have experience you can discuss with him. He wants that more than you realize."

"But what am I going to say? 'I did some of the same things, but I'm all right today'? That's like telling him not to improve. That there's no problem, long term, with skipping school or smoking pot now. Or, in Sherry's case, lying, stealing, and maybe worse."

Tina sipped her tea and shook her head. "Are you still doing those things? No. At some point you straightened out. *That's* why you're all right today. *That's* what you want to share with your kids. What happened to make you straighten out."

He looked into her warm brown eyes, suddenly so full of passion. "Was that a question? Are you asking me what happened to make me straighten out? Or are you saying I should tell the kids about that?"

"Both, actually. You certainly want to reflect, personally, on your past well enough to be certain of why you changed. Something caused you to straighten out. Figure out what that was."

He knew immediately what it was that had caused him to turn around and go in a different direction. But he thought it might be impossible to influence his own kids as he had been influenced.

Tina continued. "And then, yes, you want to communicate on that level with your kids. I don't always advise parents to tell their kids about their own past misdeeds. And I don't think you need to be specific, but both Dylan and Sherry have already shown that anything less involved isn't having an effect on their choices."

"I can't believe they want me to be more involved. Neither one of them seems crazy about what little interaction we have as it is."

She smiled. She really did have a beautiful smile. "They want more." She picked up one of the finger sandwiches. "They just don't know it yet." She took a bite of the sandwich. "Mmm." She pointed to the sandwiches and nodded at him.

"Good?"

She gave him a thumbs-up, which made him laugh. Just as he picked up one of the sandwiches, he heard Dylan's incredulous voice behind him.

"Dad?"

Zack whipped around so quickly his sandwich filling fell from between the slices of bread and into his lap. He stood quickly and faced both of his children. As if punctuating the moment, the creamy dollop of curry-yellow chicken plopped onto the floor between Dylan and him, leaving a thick residue on the front of his light-colored pants.

"Blast!" Zack grabbed a napkin from the table and wiped at his pants, feeling his face go red. He wasn't sure if he was more embarrassed about seeming a slob in front of Tina again or about having his kids catch him talking about them with a counselor.

When he looked up he watched both Dylan and Sherry turn their questioning gazes from him to Tina. Neither said anything.

Tina stood and extended her hand toward Dylan. "You must be Dylan. And Sherry." She shook silent Sherry's hand. "I've heard good things about you both. I'm Tina. Um . . . a friend of your dad's."

Zack realized she had somehow managed to surreptitiously return her notebook to her purse. At least the kids wouldn't see their names in any notes she might have taken.

"What are you two doing here? Shouldn't you be home?" Zack tucked the soiled paper napkin into his back pocket before he remembered it wasn't his handkerchief. He pulled it back out again and then tried to see if he had just spread more stain onto his backside. He heard a snicker and turned back to see Sherry chuckling at him.

She swiftly stopped, but a twinkle remained in her eyes.

Dylan, on the other hand, still looked at Tina as if she were from a distant planet. But he spoke to his father. "Last day of school. Since we don't get to go anywhere tonight, we thought we'd stop by and treat ourselves to some of Milly's little cookie things before going home."

"Her shortbread," Sherry said.

"Oh!" Tina lifted the plate of shortbread from their table. "Have some of ours."

"No, that's okay." Dylan started toward Milly's counter. "We'll leave you two to your . . ." Clearly he didn't know what to call whatever Zack and Tina were doing.

"Actually, I should be going." Tina stood and gave Zack a direct look. She tilted her head ever so slightly toward the kids and used her eyes to signal something to him he couldn't quite make out. Then she smiled at Dylan and Sherry. "I know your dad was hoping you'd fill him in on how the last day of school went." She retrieved her purse and gave Zack a private, conspiratorial raise of her eyebrows. "We can talk later. Give me a call."

"Yeah, okay."

"Nice meeting you, Dylan. Sherry. Maybe I'll see you again sometime."

Sherry suddenly piped up. "Come tomorrow! We're doing pick-your-own berries at the farm! It's lots of fun."

Zack saw a wily smile form on Dylan's face. "Yeah, that's a great idea. Don't you think so, Dad?"

Tina and Zack looked at each other, and Zack didn't know what to say. So he shrugged. "Um, well, yeah, sure. I mean, if you're free you could—"

"Why don't you call me tonight, Zack, and we'll discuss it. You have my cell number."

"Right."

176

She walked out and Zack faced his kids, both of whom wore the grins of proud parents.

"What are you two so tickled about?"

"Dad's got a *girlfriend*." Dylan put his hand out, expecting Zack to give him five.

Milly walked out of the kitchen, saw the change in circumstances, and hesitated. The distraction threw Zack, and he went ahead and gave five to his son. Now he had more or less given credence to Dylan's assumption.

"Daddy, she's really pretty." Sherry looked genuinely pleased. And she hadn't called him "Daddy" in months.

Milly, who had regained her composure, approached. "Two of my favorite teenagers! How are you, kids?"

Sherry said, "Milly, did you know about Dad and Tina?" She turned her smile back on Zack. "Exactly how long have they been having these secret meetings?"

Milly looked at Zack, obviously seeking guidance.

"The kids are asking about Tina being my . . . girlfriend." He swallowed. He knew there was pleading in his face. He didn't want Milly to lie, but she always knew what to say. She'd figure out a noncommittal way of neutralizing the situation.

"Your girlfriend." Milly didn't look quite as shocked as he expected her to. She looked at Dylan and Sherry. "They do look good together, don't they?"

Zack had absolutely nothing in his mouth, but he gasped without thought and then had a choking fit.

Milly grabbed his teacup and handed it to him. She widened her eyes at him. All of this communicating without words was a little beyond his grasp.

Sherry sat in Tina's seat. "Dad, you have to call her and invite her for tomorrow." She popped one of the shortbread cookies in her mouth and spoke around it. "I think she's nice."

Dylan sat in Zack's seat. "Yeah. It's about time, Dad. Maybe a girlfriend is exactly what you need." He picked up a cookie with one hand and a finger sandwich with the other.

Ah, so that was it. The two of them thought a girlfriend would distract him from their shenanigans. Well, fine. If he had to pretend he and Tina were romantically involved in order to get them comfortable talking with her, he'd go along with that. He looked at Milly, whose expression was now completely deadpan. Then he saw a tiny smile light up her face, just for a moment.

Of course, Tina would have to be willing to act out the charade with him. He really would need to call her tonight.

He certainly hadn't planned this course of events when seeking help with his kids. But he had to admit, there were certainly less pleasant ways to go about getting it.

TWENTY-THREE

Tina's cell phone rang just as she rinsed off her dinner dishes. That little nibble of chicken curry at Milly's that afternoon had put her in the mood for more. She decided against takeout and whipped up her own culinary masterpiece. She made a mean Thai curry dish, even if she did say so herself. And she had enough leftovers for another meal. She scooped the remaining chicken into a container, and the thought occurred to her that, were she dating someone, she could have shared this other portion with him.

Her phone rang. She checked the identification and smiled. Was God telling her something, or was she reading too much into a coincidence? She flipped her phone open. "So the web gets thicker, eh, Zack?"

She had obviously caught him off guard. "Uh, pardon?"

"The web—what a tangled web we weave when—"

"Oh. When first we practice to deceive, right?"

She grinned, pleased at the insinuation that he knew about more than farming. Not that there was anything wrong with farming, but she knew now not to make assumptions.

He said, "Who was that? Shakespeare? I can't believe I even remembered that."

"Sir Walter Scott, but I'm impressed anyway."

"Ah. You thought I was a dumb bumpkin."

Oh, goodness, he was a mind reader. "No! I . . . I simply—"

He laughed. The most relaxed, tantalizing laugh she'd heard from him yet. "I'm teasing you, Tina. How could you know anything about me? We've barely gotten to know each other yet."

Yet. A bit of intrigue in that.

"Well, that's true." She walked away from the dishes and relaxed on the couch in the living room. "How did everything go at Milly's after I left? I'm curious to know how you explained our meeting together."

"Yeah, that's kind of what I'm calling about."

"Did you get to chat with the kids about their last day of school? That's why I dashed." She laughed. "That's what all my eye rolling was about—I don't know if you understood that. The time seemed ripe for them to settle in at the table and—"

"Uh, that's not exactly what we talked about after you left."

"Oh. All right. Did you want to chat about it right now?"

"Yeah, but first I thought I should mention the thing tomorrow. The pick-your-own-berry event Sherry invited you to?"

"Right. That was sweet. But I assumed she was just being polite."

"Oh, no. She was dead earnest. They both want you to come."

Tina didn't know what to make of that. How could they have taken to her so quickly?

"Tina, they think . . . well, they saw us together and jumped to the conclusion that we're . . . together."

She was absolutely ashamed at how quickly her stomach flipped, hearing him say that. She really was that young thing Edie teased about—the one writing her crush's name all over her notebook. She stood and paced in front of the couch.

"Ah. Are you . . . are you sure?"

His laugh was soft this time. Just as enticing as the louder one. "They told me they thought it was about time I had a girlfriend."

Tina didn't need to use the mirror on the wall beside her to know a flush had brought the red out in her cheeks. "I see."

"And then Milly told them we made a nice-looking couple."

Tina laughed out loud at that. "She didn't!"

"I think she wasn't sure how to handle it."

"I'll believe that when she *tells* me that," Tina said. "Milly is seldom at a loss for how to handle situations. So did you set the kids straight?"

Silence.

"Zack?"

"Um, I couldn't bring myself to, no. I didn't set them straight at all."

"But—"

"See, I know they were honestly pleased that I might have, you know, moved on after the past four years. But I think a big part of their pleasure was they thought I might become distracted by a . . . by you. I didn't like that so much. That they might be thinking they can get away with mischief more easily if I didn't have such an eagle eye on them."

She fought a small smile. "You thought they were being duplicitous."

"I did."

She sank back onto the couch. "So you thought the most effective way to combat that would be to allow them to believe an untruth about us."

Another silence, and then, "Not your usual method of treatment, I suppose."

She laughed. "No. I can't say I've ever used that approach before. Or read about it in any of my textbooks."

"Look at the situation for a second. I'd really like you to be able to advise the kids, to counsel them. But I've been concerned about how we were going to make that transition. You know, from your counseling me about how to deal with them to your giving them full-on counseling yourself. I mean, you were willing to counsel them directly, right?"

"Yes, that was what I envisioned."

"But this is one way it would make sense for you to be interested in them as people, if you were my . . ."

"Your girlfriend."

"Yeah."

She sighed. Her brain and her emotions were having one doozy of a wrestling match at the moment. "And what happens when we feel the kids no longer need my counseling, Zack? After I've nurtured their trust and then suddenly need to withdraw?"

She could almost hear him shrug. "Maybe they'll always need counseling."

She laughed and heard him do the same.

"Tina, we can figure something out when that time comes. Maybe when we don't need to do this anymore, you could just stop being . . ."

She was *not* going to help him out there. She was curious as all get-out.

"I mean, maybe you could start being annoying or something." He laughed before he even finished the sentence.

She answered him in a prim voice. "Well, I don't know if that's possible, Mr. Cooper."

"No, I didn't suppose so."

He made her grin, that was for sure. "The thing tomorrow—"

"Right," he said. "You don't have to come if you don't want to, of course. But I wanted you to know the invitation really was there. And I wanted you to know what the kids thought our relationship was. All of it is completely in your court."

She ran a finger over her bottom lip. Certainly she wouldn't have been able to pretend such a relationship if she were actually seeing someone. Way too complicated. And, as unorthodox as this approach was, it would enable her to listen to what the kids had to say and give them guidance they might hear, coming from such an unofficial source. She just had to take care that she never lied to them. She would not say she and Zack were dating.

Even though Zack couldn't see her, she nodded in agreement.

"I could use some berries, I suppose."

TWENTY-FOUR

The next morning Tina pulled up at Edie's townhouse. As soon as she got into the little red Mazda, Tina gave her a big smile. "You are absolutely the best friend a woman could have."

"Honey, tell me something I don't know." Edie buckled herself in and slipped off her sandals.

The day couldn't have been prettier. The Virginia humidity wasn't expected to get heavy today, and the sky expanded blue and free of clouds as far as Tina could see.

"I'm serious, Edie." She pulled back onto the road. "This is going to be such a weird way to counsel, and I honestly don't know how I would have handled this morning on my own."

"Nonsense, girl. You would have done fine without me. This isn't so different from what you do with the kids at church. The only weird thing about it is you're not really dating Zack. We'll just downplay that part of it today." Edie gave Tina a quick once over. "You look great, by the way. How'd you get suntanned already?"

Tina lifted her arm and looked at it as if she hadn't noticed it before. "I did a little gardening the other day. Better late than never, getting my zinnias planted."

"Ugh! You and your Italian skin." Every year around this time, Edie verbally lamented her Welsh heritage to Tina. "One day of gardening, and you're a sun-kissed beauty. I spend the entire summer outside and get nothing but freckles."

"Adorable freckles. They make you look like a teenager."

Once they hit the less-populated countryside, Tina handed a sheet of paper to Edie. "You're my navigator. I think I understand where this is, but you know me and directions."

"Mm-hmm." Edie read over the paper. "Yeah, I know where this is. We had a domestic disturbance call there last week."

Tina jerked her head to gape at Edie. "A domestic disturbance?"

"Not at this exact address," Edie said. "Sorry. I meant in the general vicinity. You're a jumpy little berry-picker this morning, aren't you?"

"Be nice to me, Edie. I swear this new layer of complication has me off my game."

"Honestly, relax. The girlfriend thing might actually make circumstances a little easier. You won't have to sneak around to meet with Zack if he needs a private consultation, and you have a perfectly good reason for getting to know the kids."

"I know all that. It's the end of treatment that has me concerned. The last thing I want to do is insinuate myself into the lives of these kids and give them the false hope of a new mother figure in their lives."

Edie remained silent long enough to cause Tina to check that she was listening. "You still with me?"

"Yeah. Just thinking about what you said. You have a valid concern there."

Even though this wasn't news to Tina, her stomach sank to hear Edie confirm her fear. "Oh, Edie, maybe we should just turn around and forget about this thing today."

"Now hold on there, girl." Edie held up her hand. "Let's not retreat just yet. Let's think about this."

Tina kept her eyes on the road. "Okay."

"Let's just imagine you and Zack really are dating each other. Let's say the two of you met under different circumstances and just hit it off and started going out. You are a counselor. So you'd be inclined to counsel your boyfriend's kids, don't you think? I mean, wouldn't it work out that way naturally? You're always counseling me. That's just how you are. And, like I said, you pretty much do that with the youth at church just from hanging around them."

Tina took a deep breath and exhaled. "True."

Edie put out her hands as if she held something between them. She flipped them sideways. "So now let's look at it conversely. Let's say no dating was involved—"

"Which there isn't."

"Right. But say Zack approached you as a therapist and asked you to counsel his kids on this unofficial basis—whether you told them about it or not."

"All right. That's closer to the truth. Or, that *is* the truth."

"Yes, it is. Now, let's also assume the kids didn't jump to the conclusion they did—that you two are dating each other. Originally you planned to casually meet them when they were with Zack, right? Just cross paths on occasion and try to develop enough of a relationship with them so that you could give them some guidance?"

"Mm-hmm. That was the plan."

Edie raised her index finger. "But! Just between you and me and the good Lord, you can't tell me there isn't at least a remote chance you and Zack would have maybe fallen for each other eventually, just from being around each other and your being involved with his kids and both of you being single and apparently very, very, stupid-making attracted to each other. Am I right?"

Tina realized she wore a frown. "I'm sorry. I can't quite figure out the question in all of that."

She watched Edie shrug. "All I'm saying is that neither of you—you or Zack—actually said to the kids that you were dating each other, right? Did Zack tell them you were his girlfriend?"

"No. But he also hasn't denied it."

"Okay, but what I'm saying is, the way the kids think things stand? That might have been how they worked out anyway. So maybe you should just find an opportunity to subtly mention what you do for a living. Just casually work it into the conversation. They're going to wonder pretty soon. I'm sure all they're thinking about right now is themselves, because that's how teens tend to be, but I'm telling you, they're going to want to know what you do. So you tell 'em."

"All right. I'd do that anyway. I wasn't planning on telling them I'm with the circus or something. So?"

"So, if they know you're a counselor, that's half the truth right there. Everyone expects the psychologist to analyze them, even on a social level."

"They do? Do you think I'm analyzing you when we're together?"

"Of course."

Tina laughed. She did analyze everyone, a little. Edie was right.

"And then just don't be slobbering all over their dad when you're around him."

Tina tsked. "Slobbering!"

"You know, looking at him like he's just oh so wonderful. See, that way, not only will they not come to expect too much from you and Zack, they won't be shocked when things don't work out."

Tina frowned again. "You sound so certain it won't work out."

Edie turned to look at her so obviously, Tina took her eyes off the road to glance at her. "What?"

"I'm certain *what* won't work out?" Edie's smile was both teasing and pleased.

Tina thought she was beyond blushing around Edie, but she was wrong. "Right. There's nothing to work out between Zack and me." She mustered a halfhearted laugh. "I'm getting confused with my own game here."

"Or maybe a little more hopeful than you want to admit?"

"All right, all right." Tina waved off Edie's comment. "Who's analyzing *whom* here?"

Edie's voice lost its teasing tone, and Tina heard kind concern. "I don't think the kids are the only ones who could find themselves disappointed when you're done counseling. Maybe not, but be careful."

"I know." Tina agreed. "I'm just involved to counsel the kids."

"Unofficially, remember."

"Yes, unofficially." She blew a little puff of air from her lips. "Mercy, if Zack were actually paying me, I'd have quit by now. Something this touchy is definitely not APA approved."

Edie pointed ahead. "That's the drive coming up on the right. Listen, maybe you'll relax about all of this if you look at it this way. As your friend I could very easily ask for your professional opinion about something personal. I might even ask you to have a chat with Rob and give him advice. That's all you're doing here."

Tina raised a brow and turned a gaze of doubt toward Edie.

"Okay, maybe it's a little different, because I know you and trust you. Just let the kids get comfortable around you, see how cool you are, and then tell them what you do for a living. I'll bet they'll be glad."

The parking area was full of cars, families, wooden baskets, and employees. Tina got out of the car and experienced a moment's peace. It appeared there would be too many people for the kids to be too focused on their dad's new girlfriend. They were working today, so chances were better than she expected that they'd have their hands full.

So she lost her composure in seconds when both Dylan and Sherry approached her from behind.

"Awesome!" Dylan's adorable smile lit up his face. "You came!"

Sherry's excitement showed in the girly handclap she did. She actually gave Tina a quick hug. "Dad will be thrilled!"

Their enthusiasm brought out every bit of concern for their well-being she had within her. She knew panic was in her eyes when she looked at Edie. Edie actually looked concerned at how happy the kids were to see Tina too.

That did it. Without another moment's consideration for consequences, Tina blurted it out. "Kids, I'm a counselor."

TWENTY-FIVE

Zack noticed a few people waiting in line to get baskets for berry picking. Where had Dylan and Sherry run off to? That was one of their jobs today, to keep the customers supplied and moving toward the field.

He grabbed a stack of the diamond-weaved wooden baskets and brought them to the customers. "Here you go, folks." The line dispersed, a few people at a time. "These should keep you busy for a while. There you go." He saw Lorenzo waving for customers to join him at the far end of the bushes. "Head on over to that handsome Italian fellow over there, see? The man in the red shirt? Just bring your pickings back to the stand over here to my right when you're ready to ring out. Have fun."

Then he saw why the kids had taken off. Tina had arrived.

He sighed. Or, rather, his breath was briefly taken away. She looked perfectly casual in a black tank top and denim shorts. He could tell from here she had lovely skin. Like creamy caramel. The warm breeze lifted her dark hair away from her face, and her natural beauty made him smile.

She looked nervous, he thought. The kids were talking with her—

The kids were talking with her! Already? From the look of things, they had approached her when she arrived. He was dying to know what they could have to talk with her about so soon. He hoped this was a good sign. They would never rush so willingly to greet just any woman. It made him feel a little better about allowing them to believe he and Tina were an item.

For an instant he wondered exactly what Tina's personal situation was. He couldn't imagine she wasn't involved with someone.

She responded to whatever Dylan and Sherry had said, and they seemed pleased. They said something else before giving a quick wave to Tina and her friend. Then they headed back to work. Once they left, Zack watched Tina and her friend exchange glances. They were clearly amused about something.

Then Tina suddenly turned and looked directly at him. It happened by accident, he could tell, but she locked eyes with him, and he was sure he saw delight before she put on a less expressive smile. He pulled his handkerchief free and wiped his forehead dry.

She and her friend approached, so he walked toward them as well. Would the kids be watching? Would it look odd for him to *not* embrace her or show affection of some kind?

With disappointment he had to acknowledge that no, they wouldn't find that odd at all.

"That was quite a surprising welcoming committee you got there," he said to her, once she was close enough to hear him.

"So that wasn't your idea, huh?" Tina's eyes sparkled with humor. "I think I'm flattered, then."

"You should be. I'm glad you came." He looked at Tina's friend and put out his hand. "Welcome. I'm Zack."

"Yes, you certainly *are.*" This little spitfire was shorter than Tina and more solid. Not stocky, just athletic looking, as if she had been a high school cheerleader in her day. She gave his hand a firm shake. Somehow, he knew right away he was going to like her.

Tina chuckled. "Zack, this is my flirtatious best friend, Officer Edwina Llewelyn."

"Call me Edie."

"Officer? You're—"

"Yep, I'm a cop. Middleburg police force."

Zack grimaced for just a moment. He wondered if she recognized Dylan from his little field trip to the police station a few weeks ago.

Edie apparently caught the face Zack made. She gave him a crooked smile. "What's the matter? You on the lam?"

"Don't tease the poor man, Edie." Tina rolled her eyes.

Zack tried to smile. "To tell you the truth, I was

hoping you weren't in the police station a few weeks ago when Dylan was brought in. He was skipping school and his friends shoplifted. I didn't see you when I went to pick him up."

Edie looked over her shoulder in Dylan's direction. "That sweet-faced boy? Naw. I would have remembered. What did the arresting officer look like?"

Zack shrugged. "Big. Dark. Serious."

"Mm-hmm, that's what I figured. Sounds like Tina's old boyfriend was probably the one who brought them in. Bucky Reynolds."

Tina's face flushed a rosy red. Now Zack tried to remember more clearly how that officer looked. What he acted like. All he remembered was bulk, as in gym workouts. And stern. He didn't want to think about that guy dating Tina.

He cleared his throat. "So what were the kids so eager to talk with you about when you got here? They both looked to be bending your ear when I saw them."

He watched relief relax Tina's face, probably because he changed the subject. And then he saw amusement light her eyes again. She and Edie gave each other that same look he saw them share after Dylan and Sherry walked away from them.

Edie spoke first. "Well, our resident counselor here had a turn of conscience when she saw your teens. She saw fit to announce her profession to them the second she got out of the car. Maybe even before she set a foot on the ground. I just know it was as sudden as gunfire."

Zack's eyes widened. "You told them you were a psychologist?"

Now it was Tina's turn to grimace. "I couldn't help it." She shrugged. "I don't do well with pretense, Zack. It goes against my grain. I'm sorry."

"But their reaction was the best part." Edie said. She looked at Tina. "Tell him."

Tina smiled and glanced up at Zack from under her dark lashes. He found it a truly beguiling look on her.

"They were thrilled."

"Thrilled?" He scratched his head.

She nodded. "They asked if you knew what I did for a living."

Zack laughed out loud.

"And that's not all," Edie said.

"They asked if I could maybe watch what went on between you and them without making it terribly obvious. They asked if I wouldn't mind subtly giving you advice. You know, about how to be more fair as a parent. Not so strict. I think they figured I was someone you'd be willing to listen to."

"Seeing that she's your girlfriend and all." Edie rested her hand on her hip, a smile dimpling her cheek.

Zack looked from Edie to Tina. "So, essentially,

they've secretly asked you to do exactly what I secretly asked you to do."

"Pretty much."

He glanced toward the teens. They were busy with customers and seemed to have forgotten about Tina. "So *I* think they need the counseling, and they think *I* need it, more or less."

Tina chuckled. "That's a fairly standard attitude when loved ones come to me for help. It's always the *other* person who needs guidance."

"And my involving you in a supposedly romantic relationship with me—that wasn't really necessary."

Edie muttered something just quiet enough that he was unable to hear distinctly. Tina obviously heard her and gave her a look that had "zip it!" written all over it.

He wasn't sure, but he *thought* he might have heard something about icing on the cake. Yep. He liked this Edie person.

Tina stepped back into the take-charge mode he'd seen her use before. "Why don't Edie and I get involved over there, maybe helping out or something, so I have an opportunity to chat some with Dylan and Sherry?"

Zack shook his head. "Too obvious. We haven't been dating long enough for me to put you to work."

Both of the women laughed.

"You go on and pick some berries," Zack said,

"with my compliments, of course. As soon as I can do it subtly, I'll encourage them to join you and direct you to some of the bushes that haven't been hit much yet. That should give you time together."

He had a harder time than he expected convincing Dylan and Sherry to join Tina and Edie. He was sure they would appreciate the break from work, but now that he knew they wanted Tina to set him straight with regard to his parenting skills, he understood. They wanted Tina chatting with *him,* not them.

"I would like all of you to get to know each other. And I want her to feel welcome. Now, go on."

A short while later he looked up from the cash register and spotted them from afar. He smiled when he saw very little berry picking and quite a lot of talking going on. And he saw all of them laugh together. There was always the chance that some of that laughter was at his expense, but that was fine if it helped Tina to communicate with his children. Heaven knows, he wasn't doing a terrific job of doing that himself. And there was no way Tina would denigrate his role as a father. He instinctively felt he could trust her to strengthen his relationship with Dylan and Sherry.

"Excuse me? Sir?"

With a quick shake of his head, Zack stopped

gazing into the field and looked at his customer. Or customers. A buxom brunette stood in front of a heavy-set blonde and two teenage girls. They weren't in line to weigh their pickings. They looked as if they had just arrived.

"Good morning, ladies." He laughed softly. "Sorry about the daydreaming. Did you need baskets for—"

"Hunky produce guy!" With a gasp the brunette stared at him as if he were world famous. She squeezed the arm of her friend, who had her head turned toward the teens.

She, too, looked at him and gasped. "Why, it's you!" And then she immediately censored herself and acted as if she had said nothing odd at all. She busied herself giving orders to the teens. "All right, Faye, Heather. Each of you take a basket from the nice hunky—I mean, take a produce from the gentleman. I mean, a basket. Take a basket. Come on, stop dawdling."

The teens barely reacted to the inaccurate accusation and took baskets from Zack.

"Thanks." The more bubbly of the two girls smiled at Zack and then linked arms with her chunky friend and stepped away. "Come on, Heather, this is going to—" She stopped still and gasped.

This was one gaspy set of females.

"Heather, it's him!" She pointed toward the field. "That's Dylan. The boy I told you about from my English class. It's him! Look, do you see how adorable he is? Didn't I tell you?" This last was said as if she were describing kittens dressed in cute little bunny suits. Another gasp. "Oh my goodness! And that's *Tina!* Do you *see* who he talking to? *Tina!* From church!"

The two adult women turned their heads at that, and they stepped away from Zack to join the teens.

Zack found himself unable to look away from them. He was a grown man with a business to run, but they had just shown extreme interest in two people who mattered to him. And they had dubbed him Hunky Produce Guy, which was, in itself, enough to stir his curiosity.

"Well, doggone if it *isn't* Tina," the brunette said. "Somehow I didn't picture her as the pick-your-own-fruit kinda gal." She swiftly looked around and caught Zack eavesdropping.

He stepped back abruptly. He tried to act as if he hadn't been tailing them, but the smirk on the woman's face indicated he'd been pegged. She stepped toward him and put out her hand.

"I'm sorry," she said. "We've been rude. I'm Gerry, and my friend here is Carmella. We've seen you making deliveries to Milly's tea shop a few times."

"Ah. I see. Well, nice to meet you, Gerry. Carmella." He shook hands with Gerry and nodded briefly at the other woman as Gerry talked on.

"We're in a women's . . . discussion group that meets at the shop once a week." She crooked her thumb over her shoulder. "Our friend Tina runs it." She turned and pointed in Tina's direction. "She's the beautiful Italian-looking one over there, you see?"

Zack swallowed. "Yes. Yes, I see."

"Mm-hmm." Gerry crossed her arms and rested them against her waist. "I hope you don't mind my prying, but I noticed you don't wear a ring. Are you single, by any chance?"

"Gerry!" Carmella's full cheeks blushed, and she chose to step away and join the girls, who were headed toward Zack's son.

Zack raised his eyebrows at Gerry before he could stop himself. He had to wonder what Tina was treating *this* one for. Debilitating pushiness, maybe?

She continued. "I mean, I only ask your marital status because if you're single, you could do a whole lot worse than Tina Milano." She raised her hands as if she were giving up. "I'm just saying."

With a tilt of the head, she walked several steps away. Then she stopped, turned, and said, "And don't think *she* hasn't noticed you, either. Because she has. And, personally, I've never seen the point in wasting time."

She didn't wait for a response, which was a good thing. Zack was dumbstruck. What an in-your-face woman! He was shocked. Yes, that's what he was. Tina had told him to try to pinpoint his emotions. Well, he was shocked. Was that an emotion?

And the woman's daughter—or maybe she was the *other* woman's daughter. Whoever she was, she had eyes for Dylan. Zack considered how he felt about that. He felt . . . wary. Was *that* an emotion?

But the pushy woman had also stated frankly that Tina had noticed him, as a woman notices a man. So, despite everything else, one emotion stood out and overrode all others. And this one he recognized for sure.

He was happy.

TWENTY-SIX

That evening Tina ate her dinner of leftover curried chicken and rice while catching up with her mother on the phone.

"I'm sorry to munch in your ear, Mom. I'd eat later, but I have plans. And I don't want to let you go. I'm afraid you'll fly off to Fiji or something if I don't catch you while I can."

"Not a problem, sweetheart. I shouldn't have called at dinnertime. And I don't have any more trips scheduled for another month."

"A whole month, huh?" Tina loved the way her mother had reinvented herself once she retired. Tina had worried that her father's death would rob her mother of her will to live, but over the past five years her mother had finished her long career as a sales engineer and explored areas of life and the world she had never experienced before.

"How about you, honey? What are your plans tonight? A date?"

Tina swallowed a long drink of water. "Nope. Well, a guy will be there—I went on one date with him a few weeks ago, but I'm not interested in him at *all*. It's a group thing. With the youth group from church. Just a movie."

Because of her plans to join Antony and the kids, she had taken another quick shower after she got home from Zack's farm. She wore her comfy terrycloth gym pants and a T-shirt, meaning to change into nicer clothes later for the movie. At the moment, however, comfort was key.

"Well, I'm glad to hear you're getting out there, at least. You work too hard."

Tina laughed. "Gee, I wonder where I learned that. To tell you the truth, I was out most of the day with Edie at one of those pick-your-own-fruit places. So I'm a little sleepy to be going back out. You know how that is."

"Oh, come on. You sound like an old woman."

"Honestly, Mom. I'd just as soon get comfy on the couch and watch something less action packed tonight. We're going to that new Matt Damon thriller."

"Oh, I like that Matt Damon. He's a cutie."

Tina shook her head. Her sixty-year-old mother thought Matt Damon was a cutie.

"Yeah, I suppose so. But I'm not in a Matt Damon mood. I have this funny romance novel I started earlier this week—"

"Okay, what's going on?"

"Hmm? What are you talking about?" She took her last bite of chicken and stood up to clean her dishes.

"Tina, you're not a party girl. I get that, and I'm glad. But you're only thirty-four, and you're vivacious and fun loving. What's so wrong with this evening's plans?"

Tina shrugged. "It's not a big deal. It's just that I hate having to be 'on' for the kids and 'off' toward Antony."

"The guy you went out with?"

"Yeah. I only agreed to go tonight because I thought he wasn't interested in me. But then I found out he has a sliver of hope. Ugh." She glanced at the clock. "And I have to go get ready, Mom. I'm sorry."

"Don't be silly. And don't worry. You're a good communicator. You'll set that Antony fellow straight. Call me tomorrow. I love you, honey."

Tina sighed after closing the phone. That was another thing she'd rather do than go out tonight—have a nice, long conversation with her mom.

In an energetic burst of bad attitude, she decided to emphatically *not* doll herself up for tonight. Certainly the kids couldn't care less. They wouldn't even notice.

By the time she forced herself out of the house, she decided not to even bother changing. Terrycloth gym pants, a simple T-shirt, and sneakers. She grabbed a hoodie on the way out the door. The air-conditioning in theaters never failed to overdo, and she didn't want Antony to have any excuse to put his arm around her and warm her up. Maybe she was getting too paranoid about him, but she wasn't going to take any chances.

She had to laugh to herself after she arrived at the theater, went through the ticket line, and waited in line for popcorn (dinner or no dinner, there was no sitting through a movie without popcorn). Here she was, about as dowdy as she could possibly be, yet she had noticeably turned quite a few heads. The first time it happened, she thought she must have imagined it, but two more times she saw, in her peripheral vision, guys turn back and look at her has she passed. She started to feel like the vivacious young woman her mother had called her. Yeah, she still had it.

"Tina!"

She turned to see young Faye dashing toward her. She had her school friend Heather with her. And this time she didn't have to pull Heather along as she had that first time at the youth group meeting at church. It looked as if Faye's liveliness might be rubbing off. Tina had noticed the effect earlier that afternoon, too, when Carmella and Gerry had shown up at Zack's farm along with the two teens. Faye had a way of waking people up.

"Well, Faye, I'm starting to feel like I'm your mom or something, spending so much time with you today."

Faye laughed. "You're way cooler than my mom."

"She *is* cool, isn't she?" That was Antony, and Tina had to work hard to keep her expression from changing. She popped a piece of popcorn in her mouth. "Hi, Antony. How's the turnout tonight?"

He gestured behind himself, and Tina realized the large group of people in line to enter Theater 12 was composed mostly of the church youth. "Pretty good-sized group of kids," Antony said. "Pastor Vince said to tell you thanks for helping out. He and his wife are at the front of the group there. You ready to go on in?"

Oh, mercy. It sounded as if he expected her to sit with him. She looked toward the concession stand. "Uh, you go on in with the kids. I'll be right there. I forgot I wanted to get—"

But she didn't finish her sentence before she saw Zack. And Dylan. And Sherry. All of them were looking at her with varying degrees of disappointment in their expressions.

She jerked her head back toward Antony and realized that Faye and Heather were no longer nearby. Nor were most of the kids in their group. So for all appearances, she was alone with Antony. As in, on a date.

On top of that, she knew she looked as if she had arrived in her pajamas.

Zack and the kids approached her. Zack no longer looked disappointed. His expression was pleasant and almost businesslike. But Dylan and Sherry looked at her as if they were toddlers and she had just told them there was no such thing as Santa.

"Ha! Zack!" She tried her best not to sound

guilty. She had done nothing wrong, after all. She stepped toward them. "Hey, kids! Ha! After all that time together earlier, here we are again. Ha!" Why did she keep saying "ha"? She sounded as though she had a nervous disorder. She could only shoot up a quick prayer that Antony had stepped away to join the youth group.

"Hey, I'm Antony. Nice to meet you."

Nope. He had dug his heels into the sand, looked directly at Zack, and seemed to be staking a claim. If he put a proprietary arm across her shoulders, Tina was going to gnaw it off.

"Zack." He shook Antony's hand and seemed to be sizing him up. "Hi. And these are my kids, Dylan and Sherry."

Both kids gave a quick nod to Antony and then looked back at Tina, as if awaiting an explanation. And she was dying to give them one. Dying to explain to Zack that she wasn't actually dating Antony.

But then she had to ask herself: Why? She and Zack owed nothing to each other on the romantic front. It would be odd for her to take him aside and assure him she was available.

Certainly she didn't want the kids to think that Dad's so-called girlfriend was two-timing him, but what was she going to do, insult Antony right in front of everyone? *Oh, don't mind him. He's nobody to me. And he eats with his mouth open too.*

Antony put an end to any chance of explanation. "We should get in there, Tina. The movie was supposed to start a few minutes ago."

"Yeah, ours too." Zack gestured for Tina and Antony to walk ahead of them and then shot a look at Dylan and Sherry, both of whom looked as if they wanted to confront Tina.

They all had to wait in line a moment before giving their tickets to the young theater employee. Antony was briefly ahead of Tina, so she managed to glance furtively behind herself, at Zack. She spoke softly. "Sorry."

His smile was warm and set off a twinkle in his eyes. "Don't let it worry you." And then he glanced down, ever so quickly and back up again.

Tina was floored. He had given her the same once-over she had received from several other men tonight. She felt a thrill pass through her.

"That's a new look for you," he said. He seemed positively tickled.

Tina turned to follow his gaze and gasped. "Oh, for crying out loud!" Now she had *two* things to explain to him. And no wonder men kept giving her second glances tonight. Her terrycloth pants were too long when she was home, barefoot. She had been so annoyed at stepping on them that she had grabbed two big safety pins and pinned the backs all the way up to her calves. They were still pinned that way, leaving her socks and sneakers fully exposed.

Here she thought she was one hot mama, when in fact she had simply added to her already thrown-together, bag lady appearance. Why hadn't anyone told her?

The line suddenly moved forward and she struggled to unpin her pants without holding up the people waiting behind her. She heard Zack's attempt to suppress a laugh. Despite her embarrassment she started laughing too.

"Stop," she said. "It's not funny."

Zack pulled her out of the line. "Here. Stand still and I'll fix it."

There was something so sweet in the gesture that she could have hugged him. In seconds he stood and handed her the two pins. Now her pants hung normally down over her sneakers.

"My hero." She smiled up at him. "Thanks."

He smiled back and she felt all was well between them. "My pleasure." He rejoined his kids. "Good night."

"Night."

Once she broke her gaze away from his, she noticed Antony, who studied Zack with narrowed eyes.

And she noticed Dylan and Sherry, neither of whom had anything remotely close to a smile for her.

TWENTY-SEVEN

Halfway into their movie both Dylan and Sherry laughed out loud at the humor of a scene. Zack smiled, pleased that the Matt Damon movie had sold out. The kids needed these laughs. They had both been rather sullen when they walked in, and he had been relieved that the previews were already showing. It kept them from being able to discuss what they thought they had just witnessed—Dad's girlfriend stepping out on him.

So his hopes were high afterward, when they went for ice cream at the shop near the theater. They got as far as placing their order before Sherry cracked the nice facade of peace Zack had erected.

"So *she's* a major disappointment and a half." She plopped onto the wrought-iron chair, a gloomy ragdoll.

Dylan looked at Sherry and then at Zack. "I'm sorry about that, Dad." He and Zack both joined Sherry at the table. "Just shows that you never really know about a person."

"Now, hold on, kids. You're not being fair to Tina."

"Not fair?" Sherry let her jaw drop open. "Dad.

She paraded that goon around in your face like you didn't matter at all."

"That's not true, honey. If you had paid attention, you would have noticed how uncomfortable that entire situation made her."

Dylan sniffed. "Well, *good!* She *should* be uncomfortable."

"No, she shouldn't." Zack sighed. He couldn't have them thinking poorly of Tina, but he didn't want to tell them now, while they were so disillusioned, that he had merely asked her to counsel them. They would surely read that as his thinking they were problems in his life. "Look, Tina and I aren't . . . that is, we don't—"

"You aren't exclusive?" Dylan asked. "Is that what you're trying to say?"

Zack seized upon that. "That's it, yes. She and I never agreed to date each other exclusively."

They never agreed to date each other at *all,* but this would do for now.

"Well, that's just stupid." Sherry looked at him as if that's exactly what she thought he was. "I mean, are you dating any other women we don't know about?"

"Dad has a secret harem." Dylan said. "He needs to keep his options open."

Zack rolled his eyes. "This doesn't have anything to do with keeping options open—"

"Tina seems to have *her* options open." Sherry wasn't lightening up as Dylan had. "That doofus she was with looked at her like she was his property. And he looked at you like you'd better think twice about trespassing."

Dylan laughed. "I don't think it was all that heated, Sher." He glanced at Zack. "But you could tell he liked her a lot, right?"

Zack tried to keep his expression neutral when he nodded. He hated to admit it, but he rather enjoyed hearing Antony called a goon and a doofus. And the kids were right. Other than the moment Antony turned his back on Tina in the ticket line, he had seemed a little like a hunter guarding his prey. Zack knew he was being biased, but he wouldn't have figured Tina to choose that particular guy for a boyfriend.

Their ice cream was ready, but when he stood to get it, both kids stopped him.

"I'll get yours, Daddy." Sherry said it as if he were a little boy rather than her father.

"Yeah, sit, Dad." Dylan went to the counter with his sister.

Zack almost laughed. Suddenly he was their invalid old dad, shunned by the Jezebel with the doofus goon of a boyfriend. He had to make this right if he had any hope of getting Tina's help. Or seeing her again.

"Look, kids." He spoke the moment they returned, ice cream and napkins in tow. "Tina and I don't know each other all that well yet. It's way too soon for us to be making demands on, or

214

promises to, each other. We're really still at the getting-to-know-you stage. Nothing more."

"But you called her your girlfriend." Sherry's voice carried a whiff of whine.

Zack shook his head. "Nope. I never called her that. I believe your brother here may have done that."

Dylan leaned in. "But you do like her, right? You *are* interested in her?"

Zack took a huge bite of ice cream, large enough to buy time and certainly large enough to bring on a rapid case of brain freeze. He pressed his fingers against the pain in his forehead and tried to think straight. Not only did he want to be as honest as he could be with his kids, it was time to be honest with himself.

"Dad?" Sherry's obvious concern was probably half about his brain freeze and half about his feelings for Tina.

He nodded. "Yes. Yes, I do like her."

Dylan repeated his more pointed question. "You're interested in her?"

He wasn't about to come right out and lie, so he nodded again. "I am." He looked at the table and chuckled, relieved about his admission. "I'm definitely interested in her."

When he looked back up, both kids studied him as if they'd only just met this man. In a way, that was the case. Surely they both remembered the tense relationship he had with their mother before

Maya ran off four years ago. And he hadn't mentioned an interest in any other women since. Now he was acknowledging to them—to himself—that he had hopes. He had to admit to feeling a subtle wave of fear rippling deep within his heart.

"Well, then. I guess we have to give her a second chance." Sherry sighed and ate another scoop of her strawberry sundae.

"I'd rather you give her a *first* chance, sweetheart." Zack tried to smile at Sherry enough to bring one out on her face. "She truly hasn't done anything to blow a first chance. To be honest, we haven't even gone out on an official date, okay? She owes me nothing. I just . . . like her." Again, he felt that trace of concern, but he also enjoyed a wave of anticipation. For all he knew, she'd dump the doofus.

"All right, Dad." Dylan sat back in his chair, resigned. "We won't make trouble. Right, Sherry? We'll be the perfect kids around her. No problems, no worries."

Oh. Now that might not be the best approach. If they clammed up about their troubles, problems, and worries, how was Tina going to counsel them?

"No, no." Zack shook his head and hand simultaneously, negating Dylan's suggestion as graphically as possible. "Don't be perfect kids. Be yourselves."

Both Sherry and Dylan laughed at that.

"Well, thank you very much." Sherry finally had a smile on her face, albeit a sarcastic one.

"It's a promise," Dylan said. "She'll see us at our worst."

TWENTY-EIGHT

The next morning Tina crossed paths with Edie in the church fellowship hall between Sunday services.

"Hey, I missed you at the nine o'clock." She draped her arm across Edie's shoulders. "You look a little groggy, lady. Did you sleep in?"

"You bet I did. I had to. I didn't get home 'til way beyond my bedtime. Late, late night with Rob. The boy is going to be the death of me."

"Was this a romantic late night? A little too much kissy face?"

Edie snorted. "If only. No, I made a deal with him that I'd help him get his new sound system set up if he'd come with me to church today. He's skipped too many Sundays. I don't like to see that becoming a habit."

Tina made a show of looking around the fellowship hall. "And? Where is that heathen?"

"I heard that."

Tina turned and fended off Rob's attempt to bonk her on the head. She liked him nearly as much as she did Edie. She'd be amazed if they didn't marry at some point. She tilted her head and studied him.

"Hmm. You look familiar, but I can't quite place the face. Are you famous?"

"Infamous, is more like," Edie said.

"Were you at the first service, Tina?" He made a mock pleading face. "Please tell me I didn't come on the day Pastor Henry talks about tithing."

Tina patted him on the shoulder. "No, don't you worry your pretty little head over that. He addressed the consequences of backsliding and spotty church attendance."

Edie laughed. "Are you working in the youth room today?"

"Yeah." Tina nodded. "I'm thinking about doing some groundwork for inviting Dylan and Sherry to come to next week's youth service. I think they know some of the kids in the group already."

The worship music started and filtered out to the hall. Ushers started closing the doors to the sanctuary.

"Gotta go." Edie took Rob by the arm. "Come on, sweetie. I don't want you to miss the collection."

Over his shoulder, Rob threw an exaggerated grimace of despair to Tina, who laughed.

"Have fun, you two."

Her smile remained in place well after she walked away from them. By the time she reached the youth room, however, she experienced the mildest twinge of sadness. She really wanted what Edie and Rob had together. Granted, they waffled about commitment from time to time, but they were right for each other in so many ways.

Tina knew her faith and focus were healthy. She had decided long ago to rest in God's plan—whatever it was—with regard to her love life. But at thirty-four she often found it difficult to maintain that peace of mind and heart. Sometimes she feared she leaned too heavily on the waiting part of God's plan. Did He want her to step forward? Be more proactive?

Could You make that more clear, Lord? Show me the right approach? The right person, if he's out there?

Of course, Zack came to mind, as he had so often this weekend, but she knew better than to assume he came to mind because God brought him there. Zack just happened to be the man of the hour. He wasn't necessarily the man for her.

"Tina's here!"

Tina readied her smile and then experienced genuine pleasure when she realized shy Heather was the person announcing her arrival with such enthusiasm.

"Good morning, Heather! You're sure in a good mood. You should be a door greeter today."

Heather hooked her arm with Tina's, as her bubbly friend Faye had often done, and spoke just above a whisper. "Today's my day."

"Your day?" Tina's voice lowered, equally intimate in tone.

"I'm accepting Christ today."

Tina gasped. "That's awesome, Heather!" She

gave the girl's arm a squeeze before releasing her. What she found especially dear was Heather's desire to announce her decision in front of her peers. It suggested she had probably already accepted Christ in her heart.

"Yeah, it is awesome. Faye and the other kids really made me feel welcome here. I never had that before. And everything Pastor Vince teaches about Christ fits so well with what's going on in my life right now." She looked at the other kids, many of whom were already taking seats, ready to begin the service. "I want what they all have."

This was exactly the reason Tina wanted to invite Dylan and Sherry here. This was a great youth group—the kids were good kids, but they weren't what many teens envisioned when they thought of Christian teens. These kids were funny and cool and had plenty of life struggles, just as most kids had.

The worship music started, so Heather joined Faye and the other teens while Tina migrated to the back of the room with a couple of other adults.

Antony's absence this morning brought her an extra measure of joy. Last night he had hedged about whether or not he would be here in the youth room this morning. She had the distinct impression he was awaiting her encouragement, which she didn't give.

The guy was nice enough, and he was the perfect gentleman last night, but Tina tried diligently to spend enough time ignoring him and focusing on the teens to give him the message that she wasn't interested. She even made sure to let a couple of the kids sit between Antony and her. She knew she'd never be able to concentrate on the film or anything else if Antony started chomping, open-mouthed, on a big bucket of popcorn.

When Pastor Vince asked if anyone had anything to announce, she raised her hand.

"Tina." Vince waved her up front. "Come up here so everyone can see you."

She spoke as she walked to the front of the room. "I want to commend you guys on being so welcoming and Christlike when we have new people come join us. I hope you realize your kindness can have an everlasting effect on a person." She and Heather exchanged smiles. "And that's what I wanted to mention. I'm planning to invite a family I recently met to Middleburg Bible for next week's service. I'm not sure where they stand, belief-wise, but if they agree to come, the teens will probably be in here. I think they need to be welcomed enthusiastically and shown what a loving and fun group we are." She grinned.

One of the more lighthearted boys said, "But we're always like that. What, are these people gangsta or something, that you're warning us ahead of time?"

Tina laughed. "No. Not gangsta. Just important. To me. And . . . to Christ."

Pastor Vince stepped up. "Yeah, it never hurts to be reminded, guys. We don't want to ever give anyone the impression that we're cliquish or judgmental or any of that stuff, right?"

When the service had wrapped up and the kids were socializing, Faye and a beaming Heather approached Tina. During the service Heather had done as she said—she had publicly professed her faith in Christ and His promises.

Tina gave Heather a hug. "I loved seeing you up there, young lady."

Heather glanced at Faye before speaking. "Um, we wanted to ask you something. About the people you mentioned—"

"Is it Dylan and his family?" Faye broke in as if the question had been ready to burst forth ever since Tina's announcement.

Tina chuckled. "Yes, as a matter of fact—"

"Yes!" Faye just about jumped up and down with glee.

"Now, you behave yourself, Faye." Tina gave her a crooked smile. "I happened to notice you took every raspberry from the bushes in that boy's general vicinity yesterday."

Faye rolled her eyes. "Yeah, *you* noticed. He was oblivious."

Tina laughed. "Just a sample of the world of men and women, sweetheart."

• • •

When she arrived home from church, Tina put in a call to Zack. The call went immediately to his voice mail. Maybe he was working in the field and not picking up.

"Hi, Zack. It's Tina Milano." Now why did she give her last name? Surely he knew who just plain Tina was. She sounded so formal.

"I have an idea I want to discuss with you. I don't know what your schedule is like, and I know this is rather last minute, but since you were available to meet me at Milly's shop at eleven a few Mondays ago, I thought that might be a good time and place for you. Maybe you're making deliveries in town again tomorrow? I'm blocking the time off for then, and if you could just give me a call one way or the other, I'd appreciate it."

She closed her phone and felt just the slightest bit guilty. She had to sit there and think for a while to figure out why.

Granted, she felt better with the idea of chatting with Zack before suggesting to him that he and the kids go back to church. He had mentioned his wife in passing when they briefly discussed Middleburg Bible Church before. Tina wasn't sure what the story was there, but it probably mattered in the grand scheme of Zack's faith. So sitting in the comfort of Milly's shop was better than coldly hashing out the idea over the phone.

But—ah, there it was, the source of her guilt—she knew there was another, less professional, reason she didn't simply ask him to call her to chat about her idea.

She wanted to see him again.

TWENTY-NINE

Shortly before eleven the next morning, Tina arrived at Milly's. She stepped in, sighed, and broke into a smile. It was like a little piece of heaven. The June humidity had finally begun to settle in, but the air in the tea shop was comfortably cool. A gentle cello solo filtered out from the CD player. And the fragrance of whatever amazing pastry was baking in the oven completed a most welcome setting.

"Good morning, Tina! Just stopping in on your own today, then?" Milly's ever-present cheer always lifted Tina's mood, even when she was already content. And she definitely had room for improvement in her disposition today. Although she was excited about inviting Zack and the kids to church, anxiety lingered about the impression she probably gave Dylan and Sherry when they saw her at the movies with Antony Saturday night. She and Zack would have to address that.

The shop was busy for a Monday morning. All but one of the tables was occupied, but Jane and Milly managed to keep business smooth, regardless of how crowded the little tea shop became. Every customer in the place looked rclaxed and pleased.

"No, I won't be alone today. I'm meeting with Zack again." Tina pulled a chair out. "Is it all right for us to take this last table?"

"Please. I saw him earlier today when he dropped off this morning's delivery. Now I understand why he said he'd see me later as he left." She lightly clasped her hands together. "And is this meeting business or pleasure?" She smiled again. "Or should I mind my own business?"

"Milly, you could never be nosy as far as I'm concerned."

"Well, that's quite flattering. I don't know if everyone would agree with you there."

"The meeting is purely business. I hope that doesn't disappoint you?" Tina gave her a quick grin.

Milly shook her head. "It doesn't disappoint me if it doesn't disappoint you." And then she looked steadily at Tina for maybe two seconds. The moment of scrutiny felt far longer to Tina, who glanced down at the table before responding.

"Oh. Well. I'm not sure if I'm disappointed or not, to tell you the truth. He's an awfully nice guy."

"He is that. And did you two ever clear up the little misunderstanding Dylan and Sherry had about your relationship?"

"You mean their thinking we were dating each other?" Tina grimaced.

"Yes, that would be the misunderstanding I had in mind."

Tina shrugged. "Not in so many words, no. Neither of us has confirmed or denied it."

"Oh my. You sound like a politician."

"Zack thought they might be more open to spending time with me if . . . well, it made it easier . . . it gave us a reason to be meeting if they walked in on us again, as they did here."

"I understand. They certainly seemed to warm up to the idea quickly. I think they miss having a woman around."

Jane approached. "Some tea, Tina? Crumpets? Scones?"

"Um . . ." Tina glanced behind herself. No Zack yet. "Maybe just tea for now, Jane, thanks. We'll see what Zack wants when he gets here. Maybe he'll prefer something more substantial."

Jane tilted her head. "I'd say you're about as substantial as he's going to find."

Tina and Milly both gasped and laughed at the same time.

Milly tsked at Jane. "Back to the galley with you, young lady."

Jane gave them a saucy smile before making her way back to the kitchen.

"As you can see," Milly said, "Jane's pulling for something beyond a purely business relationship for you and our man Zack." She put her finger to her chin and looked skyward. "I believe I'm inclined to lean in that direction myself."

"Hmm." Tina crossed her arms. "Maybe you *could* be nosy, Milly."

The tea shop owner chuckled and then became more serious. "Honestly, though, my initial reason for suggesting he call you was because I see and hear such good things about your counseling. You know that, don't you?"

"Yes, I know. And I don't mind the teasing. I do want to help Zack and the kids. That's what I'm hoping for. But I have to admit, one reason I'm fairly comfortable with the whole pretense at romance is—"

"Because you're actually attracted to him?"

Tina smiled and peered into Milly's eyes. "Have you ever thought about going into counseling?"

Milly rested her hand on the table and leaned forward. "I'm a bit like a bartender in that regard, dear. People often seem eager to confess their concerns to me." She straightened. "To tell you the truth, I rather like that."

The bell over the front door mixed with the classical music, and Milly and Tina turned.

Zack walked in, looked at both women, and hesitated. "Am I late?"

"No, no, come on in." Tina waved him over. "I was early."

"Jane's gone back to get some tea for the two of you." Milly lifted her chin toward Tina. "But Tina wanted to wait for you before ordering anything to eat. Shall I bring you something?"

Zack grinned, and Tina was struck again by how attractive he was, especially when he smiled. She hadn't seen a lot of that when they shared those few moments at the movies.

He looked at Tina. "I know the kids ate most of those little chicken curry sandwiches when we were here last time—other than the one I wore home, that is. Did you want to get some more of those?"

"Do you have those today, Milly?" Tina gave Zack a wink. "I'm definitely interested, and I think Zack's feeling daring, ordering those while wearing such clean pants."

Zack's grin dimpled and he glanced down at the hems of her pants. "And you've reverted to a more traditional look. No safety pins today?"

She reached over and gave his shoulder a little shove. They both chuckled.

When Tina looked back at Milly, she was studying them as if they were a couple of children at play. Tina supposed that was how they were acting, actually. She cleared her throat, and Milly grinned.

"Chicken curry sandwiches, then?" Milly looked at Zack. "I have some lovely cucumber sandwiches as well made with cucumbers from Zack's farm. They would go nicely with the curry."

"Those sound perfect." Tina nodded.

The moment Milly left, Tina launched into the explanation she had previously insisted she didn't need to provide. "I'm so sorry about that mess at the movie theater."

"Mess?" He stuck out his bottom lip and shook his head. "Nah. You might not have looked your absolute best, but you were still cute as a button. The pinned-up pants weren't *that* bad looking."

"Not my pants! I'm talking about Antony—" She caught his smile. "Oh. You knew what I was talking about." She wanted to give him another shove, but she didn't want to get any more casual than they already were.

"Yeah, I knew." He nodded. "You don't need to apologize. Your love life is your own business. Please don't think you have to—"

"But that's just it. Antony isn't my . . . I mean, I went out with him one time, and only one. I wasn't on a date with him Saturday night. We were chaperones for the youth group, that's all. He's not my boyfriend."

"Ah. And have you told him that yet?" He had a twinkle in his eyes.

She had to laugh. "You can tell, huh?"

"Oh yes."

"And did Dylan and Sherry think he was my boyfriend? I'm so sorry—"

Zack lifted his hand to stop her. "Tina, stop apologizing."

Jane and Milly brought their tea and sandwiches to them. Zack paused so he and Tina could thank them.

"Enjoy." Milly smiled at them and then joined Jane in tending to other tables.

Zack leaned in. "I understand you have a life to live. Your involvement with me and the kids is only one small part of that. They will be fine."

"But did you have to explain anything to them?"

A small shrug. "Once I took their Tina voodoo dolls away from them, they calmed down considerably."

"Oh, stop. Do they hate me, though?"

He looked at her more seriously. "Honestly? They were disappointed. It might have been easier to pacify them if I had known you and . . . Antony?"

She nodded.

"Yes, if I had known you two weren't a couple. But I wasn't about to assume anything like that, so I just told them you and I were too new an item to expect exclusivity from one another yet."

As often as they had discussed this charade, she still felt a frisson of excitement hearing him call the two of them an item. She felt so childish in that.

"I mean, I managed to imply that without officially lying to them." He glanced down before continuing. "They were already pretty down-hearted. I didn't think the time was right to tell them our romantic relationship was a pretense just so you could counsel them. I think they would have been pretty hurt hearing that."

So much for her frisson. He had just stomped all over that. Pretense. Yes, that was what the romantic feelings were. Time for her to grow up and treat this arrangement more professionally.

"I agree. It sounds as if you handled it well, Zack. I just hope the misunderstanding hasn't killed any chance that they would be open to an idea I got this weekend."

He gingerly picked up one of the chicken sandwiches, still leaning over the table to eat it. Tina almost laughed at the care he took with such a small piece of food. Finger sandwiches simply looked out of place in big masculine hands like his.

Zack swallowed the bite in no time and smiled back at her, as if he knew what she thought and agreed with her. "So what's your idea?"

She sat back and clasped her hands in her lap. "What do you think about the idea of the kids coming to the youth group at church next Sunday?"

Zack hesitated as he lifted his cup to his lips, so Tina kept selling the idea.

"They're a great group of kids, and I know they would make Dylan and Sherry feel welcome. And they're cool too. I think your kids would like them. They would be a better peer group than the ones you've described to me so far—the shoplifters, the partiers. You know."

He nodded and replaced his teacup in the saucer.

"But I don't know if I could convince them to go back to church without me."

Tina laughed without thinking, and he looked up swiftly.

"Oh." He smiled. "You want me to go too."

"That would be the plan, yes."

She watched the vacillation play out in his features. "Zack, what happened with you and church? You said you used to go to Middleburg Bible before."

He rubbed the back of his neck. "Yeah. A long time ago. When my wife was still around."

"Were you believers?"

"I was. A fairly new one when I met Maya. I didn't think it would matter all that much, her not believing in God yet. I figured she'd catch on once she started attending church with me regularly." He looked at Tina and chuckled about that. "Let's just say she wasn't a fan."

"And the kids?"

"They were pretty young when she stopped coming with me. And we fought about it. I'm sorry to say that we fought about it in front of them. I think they probably came to hate Sundays. I know I did." He took another drink of tea. "After a while it was just easier to not bother trying to get any of them to come with me. Then I stopped going too. I didn't make a conscious decision about that. I just realized one day that I'd had an excuse for every Sunday for as long as I could remember."

"Would you be willing to give it another try this Sunday? For the kids' sake? We could all go to the first church service together. The music is pretty modern, and the teaching is really vibrant. And then you could join me at the back of the youth room and the kids could mingle with the other teens."

"Sounds good to me. I don't know how the kids are going to feel about it, though."

Tina picked up one of the cucumber sandwiches. "I think I might have a good way to lay the groundwork before we ask them. A few kids in the youth group are especially outgoing. I'd like to ask them to invite Sherry and Dylan first, in the fellowship hall, and then we could talk with them about it too. Nothing secretive. I'll fess up to setting the kids on them when we talk with Dylan and Sherry, but the idea might carry more weight coming from their peers than from you or me."

He smiled. "Yeah, we might not want the idea looking like yours at all. I think they might still be suspicious that you're dating old Antony behind my back."

She rested her forehead against her fingertips. "Eesh." She looked up, an idea flashing in her mind. "Oh, but this could be good in that respect too. If Antony comes to the youth service this Sunday, Dylan and Sherry will see that his connection to me really is that we're both chaperones."

"Antony will be there?" Zack arched one eyebrow. "In the youth group room?"

Tina shrugged. "It's likely, yeah."

The look that crossed his face was downright mischievous. "This idea is sounding better and better."

"Hmm." Tina gave him a sideways glance. "I don't know if I like the look in your eyes, Zack."

But that wasn't quite the truth. She did know. She liked it just fine.

THIRTY

Tina's next tea shop meeting with her women's group exhibited all the decorum of a teenage slumber party. She nearly had to raise her voice to bring everyone to order. Her client Sally, a buyer for a local department store, traveled so often she seldom attended meetings, but she had made it today.

"Oh, Sally, you don't know what you've been missing," Gerry said before popping a bite of chocolate-pecan scone into her mouth and smiling around it.

Sally tucked her long auburn curls behind her ears and surveyed all of the women—Gerry, Carmella, and Meredith—before she guessed. "Meredith left her job?"

"No way!" Meredith gasped. "I might be on the verge of getting that raise. I'm not going to mess that up."

Sally tried again. "Carmella followed through on swearing off sugar—"

They all stopped midaction, including Carmella, who held a cream-covered scone in front of her open mouth.

Carmella set down the pastry. "It's pretty much a guaranteed no on that unless we start meeting at a weight-loss clinic instead of this divine tea shop."

Tina managed to interject, "I've offered to change venues—"

"No!" This simultaneous vote came from all of them, including Carmella.

Sally turned to Gerry. "I guess that leaves you, then. What did you do, shoot someone?"

Although she was sitting, Gerry propped her hand on her hip and arched her eyebrow, pretending both offense and threat. "Not *yet,* no."

"So who's left?" Sally looked to Tina, who finally felt she could take charge.

"Sally, I'm afraid these lovely ladies are pulling your leg. What they're insinuating—"

"Tina's dating the hunky produce guy!" Carmella's voice blurted far too loudly for Tina's comfort.

"Shhh!" Tina looked around in embarrassment before frowning at Carmella. "That's not true, Carmella, and even if it were, I'd rather you all show me the same courtesy I show you with regard to your personal business."

Sally stared at Tina. "Who's the hunky—"

"His name is Zack," Gerry said, her voice low. She gave Tina a glance. "Better?"

"Thank you, yes." Tina repositioned herself in the chair. "But we're not here to discuss whether or not I'm dating anyone, all right, ladies? This is our time for your concerns. Let's focus on that. Agreed?"

The women seemed properly chastened and exchanged glances with one another before nodding like schoolgirls.

Carmella raised her hand, which was not part of their usual protocol.

Tina chuckled. "Carmella. What's happening with you this week?"

"I'm concerned about . . . well, my daughter Faye—"

"*Love* Faye," Sally said.

"Yeah, well she's of the impression . . ." Carmella looked to Tina, confusion all over her face.

"What is it, Carmella? Remember, this is a safe place."

"Okay. Well, she's of the impression that this boy she's interested in . . . well, she suddenly thinks she has a chance with him. She's getting her hopes up, which always worries me about her, you know. But she thinks she has a chance—"

"You already said that." Gerry softly drummed her fingers on the table.

"I know. It's just that she thinks Tina's dating the boy's father."

"Ha!" Gerry held her hands open, as if presenting Carmella as evidence. "And there you go." She looked at Tina. "See, we have to talk about him. About Zack."

Tina sighed. "Carmella, I assume you're talking about Dylan. I understand Faye has taken notice of him lately."

"Yeah, and this weekend? When they were picking berries? She heard him talking with his sister about you. You and his father."

That caught Tina's attention, but she played it cool. "Why do you think Faye got the impression that my relationship with Dylan's father would help her with regard to Dylan?"

Carmella shrugged. "She knows you like her . . . you *do* like her, don't you?"

"Very much."

"Okay. And she said you asked her to make him feel welcome in the youth group next Sunday—"

"Next Sunday?" Meredith leaned in.

Carmella nodded, and a hint of the gossipy air resurfaced. "Tina's bringing them to church."

Tina ignored the raised eyebrows around her. "I actually asked all of the kids in the youth group to make Dylan and Sherry feel welcome. And, Carmella, I have to tell you my role there isn't to play matchmaker. Faye knows that already. If anything, I encourage the kids to make *friends* rather than trying to develop romantic entanglements. But let's get back to your original concern." She opened her mouth for her next comment, but then drew her brows together. "I'm sorry. What *was* your initial concern?"

Another shrug from Carmella, and Tina began to suspect the entire "concern" was merely a vehicle to share a bit more news about Tina and Zack.

Carmella said, "I guess I just don't want Faye to get hurt. I know the boy has been in trouble in the past, for shoplifting and fighting and things like that."

Tina raised her hands. "No, no, no. We're not going to do this, ladies. Carmella, this is a safe place, and I hope you will all hold sacred our promise to each other that what is shared here stays here, but please refrain from introducing information about people that isn't corroborated. Dylan did not shoplift. I know the incident you mean, and that was a mistake."

"So just the fighting, then." Carmella nodded, as if making note for future gossip.

Tina frowned. "Carmella—"

"That was quite a while ago." Carmella jerked her thumb over her shoulder. "Back after his mother left, I think."

Milly stopped by the table with a warm pot of tea and removed the empty one. She topped off everyone's teacups. "Do we need to replenish any of the pastries, ladies? Or would you care for some sandwiches? I have some egg-and-watercress finger sandwiches I've just made."

Sally sat up. "Yes, please, Milly! Who knows when I'll get back here again." She eyed the group. "I'll pay for those myself, girls, since I'll probably eat most of them."

"You've been missed, Sally." Milly grinned at her. "I'd love to hear about your latest travels. You come by after hours sometime, and I'll ply you with a late lunch just to hear your stories."

"It's a deal." Sally took a cautious sip of hot tea. "Mmm, jasmine. My favorite."

Tina put her hands on the table after Milly left. "All right. I think we need to move away— again—from the subject of Zack and his children." She looked at Carmella. "You and I are both going to chat with Faye, all right? It's important that she stays focused on her grades, friendships, and preparing for college. And I'll talk with her about the fact that my job doesn't include finding love matches for Dylan, Sherry, or—"

"Zack." Sally said the name, not necessarily in context with Tina's comment, but almost with the uplift of a question. She repeated herself. "Zack? Isn't that what you said his name was?"

Meredith nodded. "That's him."

"That's the hunky produce guy? Zack?" Sally leaned in, more animated than before.

Tina's stomach acids bubbled ever so slightly. Now what?

"Why?" Gerry had perked up, her eyes narrowing at Sally. "A light bulb just clicked on, didn't it?"

At once Sally seemed aware of the eyes of the women on her. She glanced at Tina and waved off the comment. "Ignore me. Jet lag. Too many trips this month. Actually, that's what I'd like to talk about, if no one minds my going next. My father needs me to spend more time with him here in town, but I've met a fascinating man who lives two states away."

Sally deftly launched into the description of a dilemma interesting enough to steer everyone clear of all discussion of Zack and his children. Tina encouraged dialog and then advised Sally before moving across the group and discussing the concerns of others.

As the group disbanded, Sally quietly said, "Could I talk with you privately for just a second, Tina?"

When they were alone, they stepped out of the shop together. Tina slipped her satchel's strap over her shoulder as she asked, "What can I do for you, Sally?"

Sally wasn't the type to hesitate over uncomfortable conversations. "It's about that Zack fellow."

Tina swallowed. So the curious look in Sally's eyes earlier had been about more than jet lag, as Tina suspected. "Yes?"

"I just wanted to give you a warning. You don't have to tell me anything about whether or not you're involved with the guy. But I have a friend—well, she's more of an acquaintance than a friend, really. I'm not particularly fond of her, but she seems to enjoy sharing some of her more intimate secrets with me."

Tina gently clenched her jaw. She would remain poker-faced, regardless of what Sally told her.

"She tells me she's been developing a . . . special friendship with the guy who delivers produce to—" She obviously caught herself before saying anything too specific. "To her place of business. I haven't talked with her lately because I've been traveling so much. And, frankly, I've avoided her recently when I've been in town. But she's mentioned his name before, and I remember it was Zack. How many hot produce guys named Zack do you think there are in our little town?"

Special friendship. Even on the surface that sounded deeper than anything Tina might have developed with Zack so far. Well, that was all right. She and Zack hadn't said or done anything she had to regret if he was already getting involved elsewhere. She sent up a quick prayer of gratitude for that.

But how was he fitting a special friendship into their charade before the kids? Something wasn't right with this story.

"I appreciate the heads up, Sally. But you needn't worry. Zack and I aren't romantically involved. There's nothing wrong with his seeing your acquaintance."

"I beg to differ." Sally pursed her lips. "My acquaintance is married."

THIRTY-ONE

At church the following Sunday, Tina heard the entire sermon through the ears of her teenage guests, and she couldn't have been more pleased with Pastor Henry's choice of topic.

The June morning sun washed over him as he stood under the church's skylight. Tina smiled. He looked downright beatific. In his comfortable, folksy voice, Henry referred to Matthew 9:13. "Look with me at the latter half of the verse. Jesus says, 'For I have not come to call the righteous, but sinners.'" Henry looked out on the congregation. "You hear that? He came to call the sinners. That's *all* of us, friends. No one is too far outside to be welcomed inside."

Henry gave an inclusive and welcoming talk directed at those who either knew little about true Christian love or who were suspicious of it. Tina kept taking cautious glimpses of Dylan and Sherry. She wanted to make sure they didn't feel pressured to be here for her sake—for Dad's "girlfriend." Zack might have given them a pep talk beforehand or he may have demanded that they be on their best behavior. Or maybe he didn't try to influence their decision to attend at all.

Regardless, both of them appeared focused on what the pastor said.

Tina also stole a glance at Zack. His attention was so captured by Henry's words that he looked as if he were using his intense blue eyes to listen. He abruptly turned those eyes on Tina. She was so taken aback, she froze.

She watched the steely blue concentration soften with his smile.

There was no way this man would dishonor another man's wife, she was sure of it. She couldn't claim unfaltering success with regard to character judgment—she had certainly been wrong before on both a personal and professional level. But Zack would have to be truly devious or disturbed to behave as she had experienced him so far if he were carrying on with a married woman.

Still, Sally wasn't one for idle gossip. Tina felt obliged to unearth whatever led to this talk about Zack and a married woman. But she would do it directly with Zack and give him all the respect he deserved. She just wasn't sure when she'd be comfortable asking.

The following hour, spent with the youth group, went even better than the general service had. Tina fought a smile every time she saw young Faye temper her behavior toward Dylan. Carmella and Tina had spoken with Faye and encouraged her to exercise her usual friendly behavior toward both Dylan and Sherry.

"But I'd avoid any flirtation with Dylan," Tina had said. "What he needs right now are good Christian *friends*. You might intimidate him if he thinks life will become more complicated by his getting involved with the Middleburg Bible youth."

So this morning Faye was the picture of platonic friendship right up until the moment both Dylan and Sherry looked elsewhere. Then her eyes became dewy and calflike, and she studied Dylan as if she would never see him again.

Tina shook her head and spoke softly to herself. "It's a start, anyway."

"Hmm?" Zack stood nearer to her than she realized.

"Nothing." She smiled. "I just think Dylan and Sherry are a hit. Don't you?"

He watched the teens for a few moments. "Not sure. At least they're both acting comfortable. I think it was a good idea to have some of the kids approach them in the fellowship hall. And it looks like it helps, their knowing some of the kids already." He smiled at her. "We'll ask them about it over lunch. We're still on, right?"

"Sure." She lowered her voice. "I get the impression they've forgiven me about Antony enough to socialize with me—oh, my."

In her peripheral vision she watched Zack turn to see what had stopped her.

Antony had just walked in. Tina had assumed he decided not to attend today.

Both she and Zack immediately sought Dylan and Sherry, so they both saw Dylan glance away from the group of boys he was talking with. His gaze landed squarely on Antony, who stood in the doorway, surveying the room.

Next to Tina, Zack sighed as if he were about to take on a daunting task. "Well, a man's got to do what a man's got to do." He rested his hand on her shoulder. The casual observer would think the gesture involved no thought whatsoever, but the proprietary body language would be clear to Antony.

Zack barely moved his lips when he spoke. "Please excuse my familiarity, ma'am. Can't be helped."

Tina knew she should caution Zack not to be too obvious. After all, she wasn't eager to suggest to the entire youth group and their chaperones that she was in a dating relationship she wasn't actually in.

Yes, she'd caution him. In a minute. Or two.

Finally she turned her head toward him. "Okay, I think he probably got the message—"

But Zack had turned to speak to her too. Obviously neither of them intended to look so keenly into the other's eyes, but that's how it worked out.

He seemed so close to her, and his hand on her shoulder took on an intimacy she hadn't expected. The simple act of his one nervous swallow made her face flush with heat.

Dylan's voice behind them caused them both to jump. "So you were telling the truth, eh, Tina?" A grin lit across his face at their sheepish expressions. "What?" he said. "Did I interrupt a *moment?*"

"Never mind that." Zack almost put his hands in his pockets before he switched gears and crossed them over his chest.

Tina smiled. He looked as if he had been busted at something. And *this* guy was supposed to be running around with a married woman?

A mild frown pressed at Zack's brows. "What do you mean Tina was telling the truth?"

"About that guy at the movie theater. He does work here."

Tina nodded. "Of course he does." She glanced over in Antony's direction. He was surrounded by a group of teens, but he glanced at her for a second before taking in Zack. To her profound relief he eyed her again and then gave her a quick nod of understanding and a resigned smile. She smiled back and spoke again to Dylan.

"You know, Antony's really popular with the rest of the guys in the group. Very athletic and all that. You might actually like him if you decide to come back another Sunday or if you get involved in any of the youth activities during the week."

Sherry interrupted any further Antony discussion by inserting herself between Zack and Tina. She put a hand on each of their shoulders, and Tina nearly gasped at the gesture. Yes, it was easy enough to touch someone's shoulder, but this was such an endearing action, considering how disappointed Sherry had been about Antony. Sherry's comfort with Tina brought back hope. Not only might she be able to help Sherry on a professional level, she melted just a little at Sherry's obvious acceptance of her as a . . . as a . . . what? Girlfriend for Dad? Mother figure?

Tina made a mental note. They needed to spend some time together soon to make headway before the dating charade went too far, if it hadn't already.

"We're still going to lunch, right?" Sherry looked from Zack to Tina.

Her dad nodded. "Yep. As a matter of fact, we should get going, if that's okay, Tina."

"All right if I bring a new friend?" Sherry asked.

Zack and Tina shot looks at each other and smiled. This trip to church had been an excellent idea.

Still, Tina was unable to avoid rolling her eyes when Sherry ran to grab her new friend. She laughed when Sherry returned, arm in arm with Faye. "Girl, I should have known."

The kids pressed for Italian, so they made their way to Ciro Ristorante in Aldie, one town over.

Tina hadn't expected they would go this fancy. Pizza would have been fine with her, and she said so.

"I'm about pizza'd out." Zack bumped against Sherry. "This one has been on a kick."

Sherry shrugged. "Yeah, I have. I'm a little burned out too. But I'd love some pasta."

"Mmm, ravioli!" Faye said. "And it smells awesome in here, like garlic bread."

None of them had any trouble finding plenty to order.

Tina relaxed her concerns about the possibility of Faye's spending the entire lunch hour batting her lashes at Dylan. One would never guess Faye's attraction to Dylan based on her behavior. She acted the same toward him as she did toward Sherry.

"You two should totally come to summer camp with us this year, shouldn't they, Tina? We go to this awesome place in the Pennsylvania woods—"

"Ick. Bugs." Sherry scratched at her arms as if something were already crawling on her.

"Don't you come across bugs working in the field at home?" Tina asked.

Dylan smirked. "She's pretty creeped out by those too."

"But it's not like that at camp. Really." Faye's enthusiasm would have drawn Tina in, were she a potential camper. "We sleep in cabins, not tents. Air-conditioned, even. And there are all these cool things like zip lines and team competitions, and a huge trampoline in the middle of the lake—"

"That does sound kind of cool." Dylan sat back and played with the paper on his soda straw.

"And a band. Always a great band." Faye tapped her fingertips on the table edge as if she heard the band right there and then.

Tina nodded. "The music is terrific. They always hire professional musicians for the week."

"You go too?" Zack smiled at Tina.

"Wouldn't miss it."

"Oh no." The dread in Dylan's voice was so genuine, Tina knew at once he wasn't teasing her about her going to camp. When she looked at him, his focus went beyond her and toward the restaurant's front door. He sunk down in his seat and reached his hand up to fuss with his hair. He looked like a criminal attempting to elude police detection.

And so it was, in a way.

"Well, if it isn't my girl Tina."

Tina knew the voice before she even saw the face. She turned and tried to hide her annoyance.

"Bucky. How are you?"

She didn't care how he was. *His* girl. Please. But clearly his presence made Dylan uncomfortable, no doubt because of the shoplifting incident several weeks ago. So she would try to be more pleasant with him than she had been when he crashed her girls' night out with Edie.

Officer Bucky Reynolds stood in full uniform, oozing swagger and condescension. He surveyed Tina's group and rested his gaze on Dylan before turning his eyes to Zack. He gave Zack a curt nod.

If Zack felt any discomfort by the man towering over him, he didn't show it. "Good to see you again."

"Yes, sir." Bucky glanced quickly at Dylan, who met his eyes only briefly before concentrating intently on the straw in his hands. Bucky's lips pursed for a second before he spoke to Zack again. "Everything going all right for you these days?"

Tina's eyes widened when Zack smiled directly at *her*. "Everything is going just great." He looked back at Bucky. "Thanks for asking."

Bucky was unable to keep his features in check quickly enough to hide his surprise and anger about Zack's insinuated involvement with Tina, but he threw a smile on like an ill-fitting hat.

Edie strode up behind him, also in uniform, interrupting anything Bucky might have planned to say in response. She broke into a grin when she saw Tina and her gang. "Hey! My favorite people!" She leaned over to give Tina a quick hug before addressing Zack and the kids. "I was thinking about you all this morning. I'm ready whenever you are for another of those pick-your-own events. My berry supply is gone already."

Tina smiled up at her. "No wonder I didn't see you in church this morning. I didn't think you were working until later today."

"I switched shifts with another officer. He had an emergency thing come up." She looked over at Bucky. "It's me and the Buckster today."

The Buckster appeared increasingly uncomfortable with the chummy group. "Edie, I'm going to go pick up our order." He gave Zack another nod before he left. "Be seeing you."

"You bet." Zack smiled with confidence, but Tina saw a subtle narrowing of his eyes as he watched Bucky walk away, as if he were sizing him up. Then, with ease, he refocused on Edie. "We'll probably have another pick-your-own event in a couple of weeks. We'd love to have you come by again."

"It's a plan." Edie tugged at the waist of her slacks. "Well, I'd better get back to Bucky there. We're still on for tomorrow night, right, Tina?"

"Still on. You're on popcorn duty. The DVR's already set to record tonight's show." She smiled at the group around the table. "We're *Amazing Race* freaks."

Edie nodded and pointed at Tina. "Don't let anyone tell you who wins before we watch it." With a wink of assurance aimed directly at Dylan, she turned to leave. "Great seeing you, kids."

"Sheesh." Faye spoke softly, as if Bucky could

hear her from across the restaurant. "What's he got against you, Dylan? Those were some skunky looks he gave you."

Under the table Tina gave a nudge to Faye. She didn't know if Faye would understand why, but she spoke right back up before Dylan had a chance to respond.

"Of course, he gave those skunky looks to all of us. He's like that sometimes, isn't he, Tina?" She looked Tina in the eye. She had understood. She chuckled. "Of course he doesn't like you, Mr. Cooper, because he still likes Tina."

Another nudge under the table, and Faye was off and running again.

"I mean, who *doesn't* like Tina, right?" Her nervous laugh did nothing to distract the kids from what she had just said.

Sherry frowned and leaned forward to look at Tina. "You dated him too?"

Mercy. Why did Tina feel she should have worn red taffeta and fishnet stockings today?

"Never mind that." Zack raised an eyebrow at Sherry, who looked as troubled now as she had upon seeing Antony and Tina at the movies. "Tina's dating life is none of our business."

Still, Tina hated to leave Sherry with the wrong impression. "I've been single for . . . about fourteen years, Sherry. And I haven't really dated much during that time. You just happened to meet two of the few."

Faye spoke in a deep, male-sounding voice. "The few. The proud. The—"

She stopped as soon as Tina managed to direct a fish eye at her. What had gotten into the girl?

Dylan's snigger turned their heads. He looked at Faye, and the shake of his head communicated that he found her both entertaining and ridiculous. Everything a teenage boy looks for in a friend, especially after the tension of Bucky's scrutiny.

To Tina's delight, Dylan's subdued laugh was contagious and caused them all to relax.

It wasn't until they were well into their ravioli and manicotti that Tina realized Faye had embraced the idea that Zack and Tina were an item. Of course, so had Antony and Bucky. And who else? Her pretense with Zack was taking on believers, and she had yet to truly counsel either Sherry or Dylan.

Zack didn't seem to be in any hurry.

Maybe, like her, he had started to blur the lines between simulation and reality, between an awkward alliance and a bond that gained strength every day.

THIRTY-TWO

Several nights later Zack stepped out of his shower and toweled off. On dusty, harried days like today, a second shower in the evening was a must and a pleasure. Back before Maya left, he never got into their bed with the day's grime lingering. To this day, even though he slept alone, the habit had stuck.

He shut off the fan and heard a gentle knocking at his bedroom door.

"Dad?"

Dylan.

"Hang on." Zack put on a T-shirt and boxers and opened the door. He was struck by the seriousness in Dylan's expression. "You all right, son?"

Dylan nodded, but his frown remained. "I need to talk with you."

Oh no. What now? A failed exam? A detention notice? More pot escapades? Not for the first time, Zack wished he and Tina had been more assertive in arranging time for her to be alone with the kids. Things just hadn't worked out that way yet.

Zack opened the door all the way. "Come on in." He heard a trace of impatience in his tone and kept from voicing his next thought. But he glanced at the clock on his nightstand and knew he needed to get to sleep soon. Early day tomorrow. He sat on the end of his bed, and Dylan joined him there.

He took so long to start talking that Zack's mild concern deepened. "What is it, Dylan?"

Despite Zack's past requests that he look him in the eye when he spoke, Dylan kept his head lowered. "I've been thinking a lot about Sunday."

"This coming Sunday?"

"No. Last Sunday."

Zack waited. This reminded him of Dylan's first steps as a toddler, each one taken after great thought and followed by a frustratingly long pause. Zack finally prompted him.

"Last Sunday. Which part of it?" The looming glare of that puffed-up cop, no doubt.

"At Tina's church. What the guy said. The pastor. About . . . you know, the part about everyone being welcome there."

Zack's heartbeat picked up. He was ill prepared for any talk about church and faith. He was still a Christian—still believed Jesus was the world's Savior—but church? The Bible? Why hadn't he kept up?

Uh . . . a little help here, please, God? Could sure use some wisdom right about now.

Zack turned to face Dylan more squarely. "Yeah. I remember that part."

Dylan nodded. "Right. And then Vince, in the room for teens?"

"The youth pastor?"

"Yeah. He was, you know, so cool. It was like he'd known me forever. And he didn't know anything about me. I could tell it didn't matter. And the kids. I mean, some of them, they know who I've been hanging with."

"You mean people like Tim and Piker?"

Dylan nodded without a hint of defensiveness. "Yeah. People like them. But those kids at the church didn't act like they thought they were better than me. More good, I mean. You know?"

Zack smiled. Now that Dylan mentioned it, Zack realized he was right. "You're saying they accepted you. Is that it?"

"Yeah."

"Didn't judge you."

Enthusiasm lightened Dylan's voice, and now he looked Zack in the eye. "That's it. No judging. I couldn't tell what I liked about that group —that church—but I think that was it."

"That *was* a pretty cool group of kids." Zack recalled his own surprise, probably felt because he hadn't had experience with Christian teen groups before.

Dylan broke a moment of silence with a soft guffaw. "Well, they weren't *all* cool. There were a few nerds in there."

Zack gave his son a soft punch on the arm. "Now who's being judgmental?"

"I know." Dylan laughed. His smile softened as

he furrowed his brows again. "Anyway. Their whole thing about Jesus?"

Please, God. No hard questions?

"Yes?"

"They make such a big deal about Him. Different than I've heard before."

Dylan blushed before speaking again, and Zack's heart melted for a moment. His boy looked so young.

"Dad, I think I want to know more about Him."

Well, that was easy.

"Me too." Zack ran his hand through his damp hair. "It's been a while for me too. So we'll go back. See what else we can learn. How about that?"

"There was a thing this evening. I think the youth group gets together on Wednesday nights."

"I'm sorry, Dylan. I didn't know."

"No, that's okay. I wasn't sure about going." He stood. "But I wouldn't mind going again Sunday. We're not having a pick-your-own event then, right?"

"Not for another week. And we'll work out something on that when we do."

Dylan nodded and headed for the door.

Zack said, "I'll let Tina know her church was a hit."

"Yeah." Dylan smiled. "She's pretty cool, I guess. Except for all the dating."

"Come on, now. Something tells me hers wasn't

exactly a wild past. And I thought we were avoiding the whole judging thing."

"Yeah, well, I just hope she's done with all of that now that you two are hanging out."

Zack knew no appropriate comment to make without throwing some fashion of lying in there. So he just smiled at his boy. "Night, son."

Dylan left and Zack turned off the lights. He settled into bed and considered how smart Tina had been to invite Dylan and Sherry to church. And him, of course. He had appreciated the inclusive sermon as much as Dylan had. Now he realized Middleburg Bible had always been that way. He had been the one to leave, but not because the church gave him any reason to do so.

He suddenly bolted upright with his next thought. It dawned on him that Pastor Henry hadn't been talking about Middleburg Bible Church welcoming sinners. And in that Bible verse, Jesus certainly hadn't been talking about Middleburg Bible Church. He had been talking about Himself. No one was too far gone to be loved by *Him*.

That point was, as Dylan called it, a big deal. Why hadn't he caught that when Dylan talked about Henry's sermon? Should he go talk with Dylan about that now?

He padded down the hall but heard Dylan's light snore before he even reached his room. He smiled. He remembered those days when he dropped off to sleep seconds after his head met the pillow at night.

They would talk in the morning.

He shook his head. He missed that opportunity with Dylan because he didn't think about Jesus the way he used to. How far he had strayed from the young man who recognized the protective hand of Christ after a drunk-driving accident so many years ago. He had never stopped believing. He had simply stopped thinking about faith. About Him. But, as Pastor Henry said, he wasn't so far outside that he couldn't get inside again.

God had answered his quick prayer for help when he listened to Dylan this evening. Now Zack realized the help wasn't for Dylan alone.

THIRTY-THREE

Tina missed Zack's call to her office the next day. He phoned just as she was finishing up her session with Brandy. The session was free of the young mom-to-be's occasional drama.

"Pregnancy definitely agrees with you," Tina said. "And I'm so proud of you and Mike. Not every couple manages to iron out their different approaches to things. I think you two are getting in sync with your baby preparations now."

Brandy stood and slung her purse straps over her shoulder. "Well, I have to admit he's giving in to me more than I am to him." She sighed. "I have a good husband."

"Yes, you do. You be nice to that boy, you hear?"

Brandy giggled and then abruptly turned her back to Tina and pointed at her own backside. "Oh! I almost forgot. Look!"

Tina glanced at Brandy's rear end in some confusion. "What am I looking at?"

"My rear end, of course!" Brandy was positively ecstatic.

Tina laughed. "Pardon me?"

Brandy faced her again. "I'm *showing!* Don't you see how big I'm getting?"

There was no way Tina was going to concur on this one. "Um, Brandy? You *do* know the baby's up front, right? That's where you'll start showing."

"Uh-uh." Brandy shook her head with lip-jutting confidence. "Not in my family. My mother tells me she could always tell she was pregnant before she had any other signs, just by how big her tush suddenly got. So for *my* family? I'm showing. I already can't zip up my pants all the way!"

Tina laughed again as she escorted Brandy to the door. "I have to say I've never known anyone to be so thrilled with growth in that particular area. I'm . . . happy for you?"

"Thanks, Tina!" Brandy walked out and called over her shoulder. "I know. I'm crazy, right?"

A hint of Tina's smile remained as she walked back to her desk to check her messages. Then her smile broadened at the rich sound of Zack's voice flowing from the machine.

"I hoped I might catch you free, Tina. This is Zack. I'm making a few deliveries in town this afternoon, and I wanted to talk with you. I thought I'd do that in person if you happened to be available—"

Tina dialed his number before his message even finished.

Zack arrived at her office dressed in jeans and a teal polo shirt that couldn't have flattered his eyes and suntan better. But he addressed her with a distracted air she hadn't heard when they talked on the phone. His open schedule had apparently become full.

"I'm so sorry, Tina. I just got a call from Dylan. He uses my old Jeep to get around. He and Sherry are stuck on the other side of town. It sounds like the battery died while they were at some tennis matches going on at the high school. I need to swing over there and give them a jump-start."

She hid her disappointment. She had actually combed her hair and applied lipstick. She was ridiculous.

"Ah. I understand. I hope the problem isn't too pricey."

Zack shook his head. "I'm sure it's nothing. But I really did want to talk with you. Could I give you a call later?"

"Sure." She thought her demeanor was friendly and light, but he suddenly looked at her so seriously. If she didn't know better, she'd even say the look was . . . passionate. Right out of the blue like that. As if maybe the thought had occurred to him to kiss her goodbye. He caught her so off guard, her breath emptied right out of her in something like a closed-mouth sigh.

He gave her a quick nod and walked out.

She picked up a brochure from her desk and fanned herself. Had the air-conditioning suddenly broken?

She was still fanning herself a second later when Zack dashed back in. Tina started.

"Hey," he said. "You want to come with me?" The serious face had transformed into that of an eager, fun-loving adventurer. "It would give you a chance to talk with the kids. And you and I will have some time together on the way. To talk, I mean."

She had absolutely nothing else on her calendar today. With only the slightest bit of shame, she knew it wouldn't have mattered even if she had. She grabbed her purse and her keys. "Let's go."

"So the church idea was a good one!" Tina's mood lifted even further. Despite her seat belt, she sat turned in Zack's direction as they drove toward the high school. The warm air breezed in through the truck windows and tossed his blond hair as if he were a male model in a cologne commercial. "Do you think Sherry got as much out of it as Dylan did?"

Zack shrugged. "She definitely enjoyed Faye, I know that. Nice girl. But Sherry hasn't come to me the way Dylan did, asking to go back again. She tends to be the sociable one of the two, so I wouldn't be surprised if she was more sold on that part of the group."

"Hey, that's a huge draw for kids. It's usually important for them to feel accepted before they can understand what accepting Christ is all about. You really might want to consider letting them go to the youth camp this summer. The church has scholarships if you're interested."

He smiled but gave her a little frown. "You must think I'm pretty broke, huh?"

"Oh! No, I'm sorry." She grimaced. "It's just—"

"I know." He nodded. "Of course you'd think that if I asked for you to help me for free."

He was right, of course. That's exactly why she figured he struggled financially.

Zack took a deep breath and released it before speaking again. "I'm kind of in recovery mode right now."

"You don't have to explain anything to me, Zack." Tina hated having caused the conversation to turn to money.

But the smile he gave her wasn't awkward or uncomfortable at all. "No, I want to. I'm not sure if I want to tell you this because you're a counselor or because I like you so much."

Well, now. She rolled her window down just a little more to let the breeze cool the back of her neck. She swallowed. "Go on."

He chuckled softly, and so did she.

"When Maya took off, she really caught me by surprise."

"So I gathered."

"I mean, I *really* didn't see it coming. We had a pretty sour relationship by then, but I didn't expect her to suddenly leave with someone else. And it never occurred to me to take any kind of financial precautions."

"Oh." Tina sucked air in between her teeth. "So she—"

"Cleaned me out. Took every cent she could."

"Mercy." Tina wondered what Zack saw in this woman in the first place. She'd love to know more about her. She thought it would help her know Zack better. And the kids.

Zack slowed to make a turn. "To her credit, she never tried to take half the value of the farm or the house, which she could have. And she wasn't able to get to my retirement account. I think she just wanted out as fast as she could." He breathed out another deep breath. "So I've been building everything back up over the past four years." He looked in her eyes for a moment before turning back to the road. "I guess that's a lot to dump on you—"

"No—"

"I didn't want you thinking I was financially lazy. Or stupid. Or inept."

"Zack, I think I know you well enough to see you're none of those things. Anyway, I've been meaning to ask you more about your . . . your marriage and divorce."

He glanced at her again. "To help you counsel the kids."

"Uh . . ." She wasn't sure how to answer that

one. "Well, the more I know, the better I can counsel them, definitely."

She watched his brows furrow, and he rubbed at his forehead. She chose to let her silence prompt him to be forthcoming.

He sighed. "I didn't go after her." The frown remained. "That's stayed with me to this day."

"You're disappointed in yourself?"

"I knew for sure after she left that she had been enthusiastically unfaithful during our last year or so of marriage. But I also knew that Bible story— the one about the guy who went after his unfaithful wife and showed her God's love. Brought her back and accepted her."

"Hosea."

He nodded. "Right. But I just couldn't do it. I was too angry with her. Too hurt." He shot a glance at her. "I hurt for the kids, you know?"

Hmm. "Not for yourself? It can hurt a lot, don't you think, to have your spouse abandon the life you had together?"

She suddenly thought of Phil. After all of these years, her ex-husband seldom managed to break through her current-day thoughts anymore. At the moment, however, he almost managed to make her miss Zack's next comment.

"I could tell she was disappointed in me, but I just couldn't seem to figure out how to make her happy."

The memory of Phil colored Tina's response,

but she also knew she spoke the truth. "Maybe she was one of those people who don't know how to be happy."

Zack regarded her for a moment. "Depressed, you mean?"

"Maybe." She shrugged. "Or maybe just too lazy or spoiled to find happiness on her own."

Zack snorted. "Not Maya. She worked really hard on finding happiness on her own."

"You mean on her own with other men."

"Exactly."

Tina shook her head. "No, I'm talking about starting within. Finding happiness—or I should probably call it peace—within oneself." She smiled at him. "It certainly helps to know Jesus."

Zack pulled into the parking lot of Loudoun Valley High School. Tina immediately looked around for Dylan and Sherry, but he had stopped the car. He looked at her, a twinkle of amusement in his eyes. Despite a flush up her neck, she most definitely liked what she saw in his expression—unabashed admiration.

She smiled. "What?"

"That's what it is." He nodded. "That's what I noticed about you, right from the start. There in the rain that first day in front of Milly's shop. You've always been a woman at peace with herself."

Well, she didn't know what to say to that. Even after he looked away, spotted the kids, and then drove in their direction, she still struggled to process what he said.

Because "always" was a pretty big word. And now she wanted very much to tell him just how far from peaceful she used to be.

THIRTY-FOUR

A nd that's Matt." Sherry pointed in her yearbook to the picture of a sullen-looking boy with hair long enough to hide behind.

"A friend?" Tina kept her voice neutral. She remembered Zack's mentioning Matt with concern. "Boyfriend?"

The two of them sat alone at the kitchen table while Zack and Dylan replaced the Jeep's battery outside.

They had asked Tina to stay for dinner. She made a salad and homemade mustard-vinaigrette dressing they all enjoyed. Her efforts made her feel more a part of the family this time than on her last visit, although she wasn't sure that was a good way for her to feel, considering her true relationship with Zack, Dylan, and Sherry.

Sherry shrugged in response to Tina's question. "Matt's not really a boyfriend. We haven't gone on any dates yet. But—" She glanced toward the door. Zack, visible through the panes, was showing Dylan something under the Jeep's hood. "But he really likes me." She spoke softly, despite the closed door between her voice and her father's ears.

This approach to openness from Sherry was

what Tina and Zack had hoped for tonight. Tina leaned back in her chair. "How can girls tell these days? I mean, has he come right out and told you he likes you, or does his behavior tell you something?"

A shy smile spread across Sherry's face. She pulled one of her legs up and hugged it. "Both. He already told me he liked me. He said I was hot. And he could be dating older girls from his own year—he's a junior, like Dylan. Or, I guess now they're seniors, aren't they? Anyway, he's been trying to get *me* to go out with him. I would go, too, but I keep getting on restriction."

"Would your father allow you to go on a date with Matt if you weren't on restriction? What does he think of him?"

Her sudden sullenness matched Matt's expression in the yearbook. "I'm not officially grounded anymore, but Dad's kind of clueless." She looked up suddenly, her eyes wide. "Please don't tell him I said that. But he is."

"Clueless how?"

Another shrug. "Oh, you know. He still thinks I'm a little girl. And he thinks all boys are—" She made air quotes and spoke in a melodramatic tone. "After the same thing!"

Tina gave her a noncommittal smile. Good golly, what did the girl think "hot" referred to? She made her next comments softly, but she decided Sherry needed a frank question. "Your dad probably thinks that because he's *been* a boy of Matt's age. Boys are wired a bit differently than girls are, but you probably know that. What is it about Matt's behavior that shows you he's not after sex?"

Sherry's eyes widened and color rushed to her cheeks. "He hasn't . . . he hasn't tried anything, you know?"

"Hmm. That's good to hear. I remember when I was your age." She lifted her eyebrows. "It was a while ago, but not *too* long ago."

Sherry giggled.

Tina counted off on her fingers. "I always noted three things in a boy—how he spoke to me, where his eyes went, and where his hands went. It's pretty hard for a guy to give the wrong impression if he shows you respect in those three areas, you know?"

She got up to refill her water glass and to give Sherry a chance to process that. She knew Zack had already called Sherry's attention to Matt's roaming hands at the movie theater. And the "hot" comment wasn't too far from Sherry's memory yet. No doubt Matt's eyes had accompanied such a comment, roaming over those parts of Sherry's cute little figure he considered most attractive.

"Yeah." That was all Sherry said, and it was said with a slow, distant tone, as if she had left the kitchen and transported back to the movie theater

274

to review Matt's behavior. Or maybe another time with Matt Zack hadn't heard about.

Tina sat back down and continued in her off-the-cuff manner. "Let me ask you something I ask a lot of the teens I counsel. Only answer if you want to."

Sherry returned her attention to the here and now. She looked Tina in the eye. "Okay."

Tina leaned back and clasped her hands behind her head. "If there were one thing you could change about your relationship with your dad, what would that be?"

Sherry tsked out a quick breath. "Easy. Time."

"Time?"

"Maybe not so much now. I'm getting older, right? So I want to spend more time with my friends." Sherry slipped away from the table and stood looking out the window at Zack and Dylan. "But the last few years? He hasn't had any spare time. He works constantly. I haven't signed up for anything like sports or drama, which I'd really like to do, 'cause I don't think he'd ever be able to come to any of my games or shows." She gave Tina a sad smile before looking back out the window. "That's pretty lame, huh? I should do those things anyway, for me, shouldn't I?"

"No, that's not lame at all. That must make you feel a little lonely. Have you talked with him about it?"

"Not really. Sometimes I think he's had a life's

worth of complaining from females already."

Ah. Sherry's turning her back on Tina—on any woman with the potential to hurt her and her father—had been no accident. "Did your mother complain to him a lot before she left?"

"I can't remember her *not* complaining to him. Or about him." She turned and faced Tina again. "They're coming back in. Let's change the subject, okay?" She strode to the refrigerator and pulled out a liter of soda.

Both Dylan and Zack were laughing about something as they entered. It was the first time Tina noticed how much they looked like each other. Although they were both blond, Dylan must have taken after his mother in facial features—brown eyes and a less angular face than his father's. But he had the same full lips, and when he laughed, he became a younger, smaller Zack.

"Sorry, girls." Zack smiled first at Tina and then joined Sherry at the counter. "The job took a little longer than I expected." He pulled down a glass from the cabinet. "Anyone else want water or soda?"

"No, thanks." Dylan headed out of the kitchen. "I'm going to take a shower. Are you going to stick around, Tina?"

She stood. "Uh, no, actually. I should be getting home."

"Okay. I'll scc you later. Sunday, I guess. Did

Dad tell you we were going to your church again?"

"Are we?" Sherry sounded upbeat about the idea. On the heels of hearing she was still interested in busy-hands Matt, Tina nearly pumped the air with her fist. It wasn't too late to reach her.

Zack nodded and gave Sherry a smile. "Yep."

"I'm so glad," Tina said to Zack before she spoke to Dylan. "No, I didn't know that, but I think it's great."

"Yeah. See you there." Dylan gave her a small wave and bounded up the stairs.

"I was hoping you'd be up for sitting with us again this Sunday, Tina." Zack downed his water and obviously didn't notice Sherry frowning at him.

She crossed her arms. "Why wouldn't she want to sit with us? You two are . . . you know, *together*."

Zack and Tina looked at each other, and neither answered Sherry at first.

"Well, a gentleman never assumes, Sherry." Zack got very busy washing his hands at the sink.

"Sheesh, I would think we'd even pick her up from home and ride there together at this point." Sherry had yet to unfold her arms. She looked quite the authoritarian. She made Tina smile.

"Speaking of rides, I think you'd better get me back to my car, Zack."

"Right! We'll take the Jeep so the battery gets a good charge." He dried his hands and gave Sherry a kiss on the top of her head. "I'll be back in a while, sweetie. You two be good."

Sherry kissed him on the cheek and gave Tina an impish grin. "*You* two be good."

Tina suddenly didn't know where to look. If Sherry had meant to get back at her, bringing color to *her* cheeks, she had definitely scored a win.

Tina half expected Zack to make a casual apology on Sherry's behalf once they were out of earshot. So she looked twice at the grin on his face.

"What are you so tickled about?"

He shook his head and tried to work his features into a more serious expression. "She's obviously getting comfortable around you to make a crack like that." He opened the passenger door of the Jeep for her and waited until she was settled before closing the door and walking around to his side of the car.

Tina knew she shouldn't enjoy the fact that they seemed like a couple. Yes, that was the setup here, but she was trying to be careful to interject her professional status in the relationship whenever possible. The fact that people sensed chemistry between Zack and her? Her pleasure in that was definitely immature. But that didn't make it any less real.

She struggled to keep from letting the moment turn into something flirtatious. As soon as they drove away from the house, she put her counselor's hat back on and got to work.

"Yeah, she was comfortable enough that I think I can give you some advice you'll find helpful."

His smile faltered subtly. The man was quick to notice a change in tone.

"Ah. Good. What have you got for me?"

"Sherry opened up some while you guys were outside. Faye and a few other girls from the youth group have gone out of their way, it seems, to befriend her. They'll be good peers for her. Most of those girls have a good handle on self-respect and long-term goals in their lives. Those are important characteristics for Sherry to adopt."

"That's fantastic. I've tried to talk with her about that kind of thing, but I can tell she doesn't think I know what I'm talking about."

Tina smiled. "Lots of teens think their parents are clueless. She'll catch on about you when she's older. But we can't lean on Faye and the other girls to be Sherry's only influence. She showed me pictures of some of her other friends at school in her yearbook. Some of them didn't . . . well, I shouldn't make assumptions based on photographs, but none of them were involved with anything at school. Obviously that's not always a bad sign, but—"

"Right. Sherry's not really involved in anything else, either, but she's a good kid at heart."

"Yes, she is. Zack, did you know Sherry is interested in drama? And possibly in going out for some of the sports teams?"

He frowned. "She is?" He glanced at Tina. "She told you that?"

"Mm-hmm."

"But, why wouldn't she tell me? Why hasn't she tried out for anything?"

"There are probably a number of reasons—fear of not being chosen for a part or making the team, for one. She'd consider those outcomes rejections, and she already feels rejected because her mother abandoned her."

She heard the softest groan of sadness from Zack.

"But she also has a lack of confidence with regard to your priorities. She thinks you couldn't take time from your work schedule to support her at performances or games."

"But I would!"

"She needs to see that. I don't know if it's too late for her to try out for next year's teams, but start asking her questions about things like that. Show an interest. Maybe find a time to mention she might be good at acting. The next time you watch a movie together, talk about the skill of the actors first—that would work."

"She's going to know I'm doing this because of you."

"So what?"

He shrugged. "Do you think she'll think my interest is genuine?"

"Isn't it?"

He looked at her again, and she tried to look more kind than demanding. He responded with a soft chuckle.

"You're a little more direct than I expected you to be."

She smiled. "I'll take that as a compliment."

He grinned as he watched the road. "All right. I'll do those things."

"And there's something else you need to know, to keep in mind while you talk with her."

He turned onto Washington Street and drove toward Tina's office. "Okay."

She sighed. "This isn't unusual at all with broken marriages. But she's very protective of you, Zack."

"Protective?" He frowned. "What do you mean?"

Tina pointed toward her car. "The little red Mazda there. Sherry carries a burden of hurt for you because of the way your marriage ended. She identifies with your pain, and she doesn't want anyone to hurt either of you like that again. The fact that she's been as welcoming to me as she has is a real testament to her efforts to move on. But that concern for you—her desire that your life not involve any more hardship—that keeps her from coming to you with her own needs."

He pulled up behind Tina's car and turned off his engine. "But the girl about made me crazy with lying about where she was spending the night last month. And when she took Lorenzo's car—how was that protecting me from hardship?"

"Yeah, I know. Her behavior won't always be consistent. I think both of those incidents were misguided attempts on her part to be independent. In her fifteen-year-old mind, she thought you'd never know about those bad decisions on her part."

"Well, what kind of needs is she holding back from me? Female things? I mean, Lorenzo—you remember you met my assistant?"

She nodded.

"Yeah, his wife Ilsa stepped in and helped Sherry through . . . well, Maya left when Sherry was going through, you know, puberty. Right when a young girl needs her mother's guidance."

Tina sighed again. "Well, thank God for Ilsa. Sherry definitely needed that. She'll always need women who can act as mother figures for her." She surprised herself when she considered her own role in Sherry's life being finite. She hadn't expected the thought to make her throat catch as it did.

"Tina?" Zack had seen it reflected in her expression. "Are you all right?"

She nodded and opened her door. Zack hurried to get out and come around to meet her. She clenched her teeth and accepted his strong, calloused hand. She stepped out of the Jeep and started talking again to get away from the vulnerable feeling enveloping her. His touch, his concern, his family. Fleeting things for her. She knew better than to expect she'd have those blessings in her life for long.

"Zack, she's probably not going to complain to you if she feels that she doesn't get enough affection or time from you. She may not even realize it herself. She'll just naturally look for affection and time from other men. Do you understand what I'm saying?"

They reached her car, parked beyond the glare of a streetlamp. In the muted light, before she dug through her purse for her keys, Tina saw Zack's brows knit together.

"Yeah. You're talking about guys like that kid Matt."

"Exactly." She couldn't find her keys and tsked with annoyance. "Stupid keys."

Zack supported her purse with his hands. "Here. I'll hold it so you can dive in there two fisted."

"Thanks." As she dug, both of them seemed to lean in, as if she were about to unearth ancient treasure. "I love these roomy purses *except* when I need to find my keys. Makes me feel like such a ditzy female. Ah!"

She looked up a second before he did. When she

jingled her keys, he smiled at her, mere inches from her face.

"Eureka." But his voice barely spoke the last syllable.

Neither of them pulled away, which would have been the proper thing for a counselor and a client to do. Tina wished his eyes were less blue. Less kind.

Would it really be so awful if I kissed him?

The power of that thought scared sense into her, and she straightened like a soldier at attention. Her movement had the effect of making Zack do exactly the same thing. What a pair they must have looked.

She held her purse and keys in front of herself as if she were a little old lady. "Well. I'll, um, we'll chat about church. Or we'll see each other in church. Or . . . something."

He let out his breath as if he had been holding it. He placed both of his hands over hers. "Tina."

Oh no. She would *not* be able to stop herself if he said or did anything more. One more word, one more movement, and she was going to throw her purse to the sidewalk and grab that handsome face and kiss it. Her breath picked up to match her heartbeat, and she looked down at the ground. "I've got to go, Zack."

He held on a moment longer before he gave her hands a gentle squeeze and released them. "Okay. I'll give you a call about Sunday."

She nodded without looking back up at him. She scurried to get in her car and pull away. Her hands didn't stop shaking until long after they drove their separate ways.

And it was the shaking that troubled her most. Yes, she wanted to behave as a professional should. Yes, he was attractive enough to make her shake in her boots. But she wasn't shaking with passion. She was shaking with fear.

What was she afraid of?

THIRTY-FIVE

The following night Zack spent several hours sorting through boxes he hadn't touched since Maya left. Something had prompted him to dust them off and carry them up from the basement. Three boxes packed in haste and anger four years ago. Now he had them spread out on the living room floor. It was time he got rid of some of these mementos or set them aside to see if the kids wanted any of them. He'd have to ask Tina if he should wait a few more years before even asking the kids what they wanted.

Friday night. The first one since Dylan and Sherry finished up their respective restrictions. So he was on his own. Assuming the kids ever shaped up enough to avoid regular restriction, he figured he'd better get used to spending weekend evenings alone.

He stopped his thoughts and laughed at his sorry self. Good thing he had put on some upbeat Motown to keep his mood from dipping to the poor-pitiful-me level. Martha Reeves and the Vandellas made it pretty hard to mope in the middle of "Heat Wave."

Faye had invited Sherry for a sleepover tonight with a couple of other girls from the youth group.

Despite Faye's clean reputation, Zack called her parents earlier and chatted with them to make sure the girls truly planned to be there all night. Faye's mother, Carmella, reminded Zack they had met at an event at his farm not long ago. Nice woman. Awfully talkative, but nice. The father managed to slip away from the phone conversation at some point during Carmella's monologue, but Zack was unable to do the same.

Dylan was due home soon from a concert at the community center. So Zack loosely taped two of the boxes shut again and made ready to close the other if necessary, just in case these memories would open old wounds for his boy. A few local rock bands were performing in town to raise funds for the American Cancer Society. Dylan planned to come home directly from the show. Zack wasn't naive, but he felt pretty confident that Dylan preferred to stay out of trouble now. Yes, Piker and Tim would probably be at the concert, but Dylan had already said he wouldn't go anywhere with them afterward.

Still, Zack had turned to prayer several times during the evening on behalf of both of his kids. He didn't know why he had fallen so out of the habit of regular prayer. Then he pulled another item from one of the boxes, and he remembered one reason why.

He and Maya looked so young in the silver-framed photo. And so they were. He was twenty-one on their wedding day, and she was barely twenty. She had her rich, dark hair in a fancy updo with tiny white flowers stuck in it. Frilly white dress. Bouquet of roses in her hand. And she smiled at him in the picture, not at the photographer. She looked so hopeful.

He, on the other hand, was all smiles for the photographer, who had been his good friend Jess.

Several years later, when Jess told Zack that Maya had come on to him, Zack had refused to believe him. Their friendship didn't survive the conflict.

Now Zack sat alone on his couch, wishing he could track down Jess to apologize. Not every man had been so quick to tell Zack the truth. Ultimately, he lost his cheating wife and his loyal friend.

He closed his eyes.

And I blamed You some for that, Lord. I did. You didn't answer my prayers the way I wanted.

He heard the kitchen door open and slipped the photo back in the box. When the door slammed shut, he stood to see what was wrong.

Dylan stormed into the living room and nearly ran into him before he stopped abruptly. Zack watched Dylan fight to wipe his expression clean, but there was no mistaking the anger in his eyes.

"What's the matter, son? You okay?"

Dylan walked around Zack as if he hadn't spoken.

"Dylan." Zack tried not to let his own anger rise. "Stop right there and tell me what's wrong. Are you in some kind of trouble?"

The anger washed all over Dylan's features again. "Of course you'd think that. It's all *my* fault, isn't it?"

"What's your fault?"

"Nothing!" Dylan paced as if he couldn't wait to run upstairs.

"Okay, come on, sit down and talk to me. I'm not going to blame you for anything if you aren't to blame. I promise. Come on. Sit." Zack tried to calm Dylan by being the first to take a seat.

Dylan hesitated and finally perched on the arm of the couch across from his father. "It's that stupid cop. That *jerk* cop!"

Not the police again. But at least tonight didn't end with a call from the police station. So it couldn't have been as bad as before.

He knew how difficult it could be to calm down when someone ordered you to do so. Taking a deep breath, he tried to speak to Dylan in a calm voice. Maybe it would help him to relax.

"What happened with the police? Try to just tell me without letting it rile you up again. You're home now. You're all right."

"I'm *not* all right. I'm . . ."

He sighed, and Zack waited.

"The concert ended and some of the kids came with me to the Mini-Mart. Just for sodas and stuff, you know? We were just going to have a snack or something before heading home."

"Okay."

"I was with some kids I met at the youth group at Tina's church. There were a bunch of them at the concert. And I guess Piker and Tim were at the concert too, because they were at the Mini-Mart. They asked me if I wanted to hang out with them, and I said I had to get home."

Excellent. Zack wanted to give his boy a hug.

"And they were cool with that, and the kids of the youth group seemed cool with Piker and Tim, you know. They acted like they did with me at church, like I said before."

"Right, got it."

Anger marred Dylan's features again. "Then that stupid cop drives up, just as me and some of the kids walk out of the store."

"Are you talking about Officer Reynolds?"

Dylan nodded. "Tina's old boyfriend. That one."

"What happened?"

"So he gets out—" Dylan stood and mimicked Bucky's behavior. He hitched his pants up and jutted out his jaw, slowly surveying everything before him. Zack considered asking him to show more respect for authority, but the kid had the guy down pat. Zack was intrigued.

"He looks at everyone all normal like. Even Piker and Tim, who walked back to their car like they were going to leave. But then he sees me, and it's like after he looks past me, he remembers who I am."

Zack tried to stay calm, but if this story was going in the direction he thought it was, he was going to be in for a struggle.

"He walks up to me and says, 'You behaving yourself tonight?' Just to me. No one else. And I said, 'Yes, sir.'"

"Good for you."

Dylan carried on as if Zack hadn't spoken. "He looks at my soda and goes, 'You got a receipt for that?'"

"For a *soda?*" Zack's blood felt hot in his veins.

"Yeah. So I told him I didn't ask for a receipt, and he looks at me like he knows something really bad about me. Then he looks at my friends—the kids from church—and makes this face at them—" Dylan lifted his eyebrows and smirked. "—like he and they all know I'm a lying thief. And then he walks into the store without saying anything else."

"And that was it?"

"*Yeah,* that was it. But, Dad, it was so embarrassing."

"I know. I'm not minimizing—"

"I didn't do anything wrong, and he made me look like . . . it was like . . . what are those kids going to think of me with this cop singling me out like that?"

"How did they react, once Officer Reynolds went into the store?"

Dylan shrugged. "They looked embarrassed too. For me, I mean. One of them said something about what a jerk the guy was. Another said, 'What was *that* about?'"

"So they sympathized with you, from the sound of it. That's good."

Dylan still didn't seem to hear him. "I had to tell them I had a run-in with him before, when I was hanging out with Piker and Tim, even though I didn't do anything wrong. Aside from skipping school, I mean." His jaw clenched. "Even to *me* it sounded like I was lying about not having shoplifted. Especially after he walks right past Piker and Tim and doesn't even look twice at them."

Zack's jaw did some clenching of its own. He took a deep breath and released it before he stood and rested his hands on Dylan's shoulders. "I'm not going to tell you that wasn't a mean-spirited thing he did to you, son, because it was. And you're going to get more chances to show those kids you're a good person. You said yourself they weren't the type to judge, and it sounds like they're still that way."

He hesitated to make his next comment, but Dylan was old enough to hear it. "From what I've seen of this guy so far, his reason for picking on you personally was because you're my son, and I'm . . . well, he's jealous that Tina is spending time with me. With us."

Zack didn't mention the fact that his status with Tina would eventually change and probably prompt Bucky to back off.

"Just don't let him bait you into acting on any anger if you come across him in the future. And I'll get some advice from Tina about this."

Dylan shook his head. "I don't want your girlfriend fighting my battles. Your battles. That's so wimpy."

Zack didn't feel much humor when he tried to give Dylan a reassuring smile. "No battles. She's a counselor. I'm going to ask for her advice as a counselor." Zack chose his next words with care. Dylan was right. If Tina were his girlfriend, he probably would have acted without involving her. To be honest, he wasn't sure that would have been the best approach—he felt like punching the guy right in his smug face. "We don't want this to get any more tense than it already is, right?"

"Uh, Dad? You're kind of squeezing—"

"Oh!" Zack released Dylan's shoulders. "Sorry. I didn't notice." Tense. Yes, this situation could get extremely intense. In the past he had managed to keep his anger from erupting physically, even over the men Maya "entertained."

But messing with his kids? He did need Tina's advice—needed to hear her voice—because he was struggling to stay home right now rather than driving into town in search of a certain bully too full of his own power.

It wasn't until Dylan headed off to bed and Zack picked up the phone that he realized the time. If he called Tina now, he'd surely wake her up. He closed his phone, sank back down onto the couch, and rested his head in his hands.

He needed to calm down. He needed counsel. He needed some kind of assurance.

A strange peace settled over him, and he realized, not for the first time, that his heart was slowly changing. This time he only took half as long to recognize that what he really needed was prayer.

THIRTY-SIX

Tina hadn't planned to go into the office the next morning. She didn't often get the chance to sleep in, even on Saturdays, but she had aimed for that today.

However, two birds—they sounded like mockingbirds with an amazing repertoire—decided to launch into a lively competition just outside her bedroom window. By the time she got up and encouraged them to sing elsewhere, she found herself energized by the brilliant morning sun pouring in through her open blinds.

She lifted up the window, discovered a balmy breeze, and got the yen to get in a little jogging before the day grew too warm.

Her townhouse sat only a few blocks from Washington Street, the main road through Middleburg. And her office was several blocks farther down Washington. As she jogged it occurred to her again how much more exercise she would get if she didn't drive to work every day.

Yet, by the time she neared her office, the sweat she had broken reminded her why she usually drove. She made her living listening to the problems of her clients. She didn't want one of those problems to be their having a sweaty, stinky therapist.

She stopped at her office to grab a bottle of water from her mini-fridge. The flashing light on her answering machine caught her eye the moment she entered.

"Tina, it's Stacy. Stacy Sumner? Look, I know I don't have an appointment set up, but I need to talk with you as soon as possible."

Ugh. The self-obsessed "all of this is natural" actress wannabe needed to talk with her. Talk *at* her was more like it. Why did this woman come to her when she had no intention of getting more psychologically healthy? Tina was ever hopeful for her clients, but Stacy was so hard to take.

Tina spoke to the answering machine. "After the holiday, Mrs. Sumner." Stacy had obviously called after hours on Friday. She'd have to deal with life until the Fourth of July passed. Tina grabbed her bottle of water and left the office.

She absolutely loved Middleburg at this time of day, especially on Saturday. Everything and everyone was just starting to stir, although the Farmers' Market was probably already open in the opposite direction down the street.

Hmm. Maybe Zack and the kids were down there now. She could turn around, go check—

No. She couldn't just inject herself into their lives for personal gratification. If Zack needed advice, he'd ask for it. If he needed companionship, he'd . . . he'd look elsewhere. That wasn't her role.

I'm not a girlfriend. I just play one on TV.

Along with a slight diminishing of her Saturday morning jog buzz, she experienced a sudden craving for something from Milly's tea shop, which was fine, because she would reach it in about ten more minutes. Scones? Shortbread? Macaroons?

With a shake of her head, Tina admitted she was a terrible excuse for a health nut. She was jogging on her way to eat pastry. It was like pinching pennies so you could flush them down the toilet.

She slowed down as she neared the shop and smiled at the "Open" sign already out front. It wasn't really yummy pastry she craved. She was hungry for a visit with Milly.

She walked in and found her friend bustling about, on her own, while heavenly fragrances—butter, vanilla, cinnamon, fruit, chocolate—drifted through the air. Maybe Tina *did* crave something yummy after all.

Milly's genuine smile lit up as soon as she saw Tina. "What a lovely surprise. I didn't know you had started running again."

"I haven't, really." Tina took a long drink from her water bottle. "I woke up earlier than I planned and just had to get out in that fresh morning air. I figured I might as well get a little running in." She smiled. "And now I'm thinking I might as well get a little tea and crumpets in."

Milly laughed. She continued to lay fresh lace cloths on the tables. "I don't have any crumpets for you this morning—"

"I was kidding, Milly. What I—"

"But I do have something new and chocolaty for you to try. I'd love your honest opinion."

That shut Tina up for a second.

"Oh. I was going to say I really just wanted to visit with you, but I wouldn't want to let you down if you desperately need my feedback. I am, after all, a professional."

Milly pulled out a chair at the table she had finished setting up. She presented the seat with dramatic flair. "Then we must do this up right. I'll bring you some Earl Grey, if you don't mind. It's the best accompaniment with this bit of dessert, I think."

Tina grinned and checked her watch as she took a seat. "Dessert at nine in the morning." She sighed and lifted her eyebrows, giving Milly her most supercilious expression. "I wonder what the *little* people are doing today."

The "bit of dessert" Milly brought out made Tina laugh. The crust of the pie-shaped wedge looked to be buttery cookies of some kind and was topped with chocolate mousse, topped again with whipped cream, and finished off with some kind of crumbled chocolate.

"I call this my Malted Chocolate Mousse Cake," Milly said. She set it before Tina and then set down a rose-covered cup and saucer and a small pot of tea.

"Mercy! Does it come with an insulin drip?"

Milly poured Tina's tea. "Nowwww, it's not nearly as sweet as it looks. At least I don't think so. You tell me."

She was right. The dish was creamy and rich and, yes, sweet. But Tina didn't know many people who would consider it too sweet.

"You've outdone yourself, Milly. And I can tell you right now that I will not be jogging home. More like a slow saunter."

Milly rested her hands on her hips. "I'll take that as a positive vote, then."

"Without doubt. It's a big fat yes from me. And I stress the 'big fat' part."

A call came in on Tina's cell. Milly pointed to the small phone holder banded around Tina's arm and said, "Ah. Your arm is ringing. I'll be back." She stepped away and headed for the kitchen.

Tina grinned when she saw Zack's name on the screen. If he was calling from the Farmers' Market, maybe she'd end up strolling over there after all, despite her relatively sweaty appearance.

"Good morning, Zack. Are you calling from the open-air market?"

Hesitation preceded his answer. "Um, no. I'm home. Lorenzo's at the market for me this morning. Say, Tina, do you have a minute? I need your advice about something."

He didn't sound as if he were in a jovial mood.

"What's up?"

"Something happened to Dylan last night. And I think it has less to do with the trouble he got into awhile ago with his shoplifting buddies and more to do with . . . with you and me." He lowered his voice. "With our pretending to be dating."

She frowned. "Is he all right?"

"Yeah, he's fine. He was pretty upset last night, and he hasn't gotten up yet today, but—"

"Zack, what happened?"

By the time he finished telling her, she was certain smoke was shooting out of her ears. "That worm!"

"He didn't do anything illegal. Bucky, I mean." Zack's voice was calm, yet she knew him well enough to hear stress. "But if he repeats this kind of behavior toward Dylan, I think I'm going to talk with someone who has authority over him. I can't have some thug harassing my son."

She didn't realize until now that she had stood at some point during Zack's account. "Of course you can't. We're not going to let that happen again. Thank you so much for telling me about this."

"Well . . . I thought you might have some advice for me. As a counselor, I mean, not as the guy's ex-girlfriend."

She winced. There were a few parts of that comment she didn't enjoy hearing. She hoped Zack wasn't regretting his entire association with her, thanks to Bucky's interference. And, although she knew she was Zack's counselor and not his girlfriend, it stung a little to be reminded, especially under these circumstances. She'd like to smack Bucky for bringing this bad blood into her friendship with Zack.

"Let me look into a couple of things and get back to you later today. I promise you we're not going to let Dylan be embarrassed like that again."

"No, we're not."

Again, there was a slight distance there. If she couldn't call off the hound, Zack would.

A couple walked into the tea shop as Tina closed her phone. Otherwise she would have growled out loud in frustration and anger. When Milly walked out to see to her new customers, she eyed Tina. Concern descended over her features. "Problem?"

Tina glanced over her shoulder at the people who had just entered. "Yeah." She sighed. "You go ahead with your customers, Milly. I'll talk with you later." She pulled money from her little armband when she replaced her phone. She left it on the table and headed for the door.

She should probably be thankful she'd have to walk the distance between Milly's shop and the police station rather than making a quick drive in her car. She was going to need that time to calm down.

Unfortunately, Tina's anxiety grew as a result of her inability to get to the station as fast as she wanted. It was all she could do to respond calmly to the clerk at the front desk.

A good old country gal, C.J. put a friendly face on the police department for newcomers, and even for some of the jail's more benign regular "guests." "Hey, Tina! Where have you been keeping yourself, young lady?"

"Hi, C.J." Unprepared for this detour in her morning jog, Tina had to mop the perspiration from her forehead with the back of her hand. "Listen, I'm sorry, but I have kind of an emergency. I don't suppose you could tell me when Bucky is scheduled today?"

C.J. reached into the desk drawer and passed a couple of paper napkins to Tina. She pointed toward the back of the station. "Sure, honey. As a matter of fact, he's—"

"Well, if it isn't my girl Tina!"

Tina cringed at Bucky's voice. She tried to take a calming breath or two as she blotted her forehead and the back of her neck.

He walked out from the back rooms as if the president of his fan club had just asked for him. He stepped past C.J.'s desk to get nearer to Tina.

"To what do I owe this honor?" He cast a sly eye at her before lowering his voice. "I see you ran here. Decided you needed a little bit more Bucky time in your life, didya?"

She drew in her breath to keep from yelling at him. With determination, she spoke, her teeth clenched. "May I speak to you in private, please?"

He straightened and actually looked surprised by her attitude. Could he really be that unaware of how obnoxious he was? She remembered their dating days and realized that yes, he could be that unaware.

"Sure. Come on back. I'm just filling out reports. It'll be like old times having you hang out with me back there."

Tina glanced at C.J. as she walked past her. From the frown C.J. directed at Bucky's back, it appeared she was in Tina's camp. She looked at Tina and shook her head.

By the time they were alone, Tina had managed to calm herself enough to unclench her teeth. Bucky's style was so weird, and sometimes Tina couldn't tell if he was being sarcastic or just dense. The uncertainty tended to throw her off balance in dealing with him.

The room was cold and full of pale gray desks and filing cabinets. Edie's touch was evident at one of the desks, with photos and dried flowers decoratively placed there. As Bucky said, Tina had been back here before, when the two of them dated. She wasn't sure if that's why she associated the room with bad feelings now, or if those feelings were all about Bucky's behavior toward Dylan last night.

"Now, what's troubling my little lady?"

Tina actually groaned. "Listen, Bucky. You and I both know I am not your lady. I never really was, okay? Let's get that straight right off the bat."

He crossed his arms over his chest. "I don't know how you can say you were never my girl. We dated for two months and twenty days. Twenty-one, if you count the day you broke up with me."

"Good grief, Bucky. You logged how long we dated? That doesn't strike you as odd?"

He jutted out his jaw. "Not really. It's the way I'm wired. I'm organized. And I remember everything up here." He tapped his temple as if the secrets of the universe knocked about in there.

She sighed. "Okay, whatever. The reason I'm here is to tell you to back off with the bad attitude toward Zack and his son."

Guilt immediately flashed through his eyes before he caught himself. Then he frowned and tilted his head like a bad actor in a soap opera. "Who?"

"Oh, don't even try that with me, Barney Fife." She called him that just because she knew he hated it. "You've singled Dylan out because of my . . . my relationship with his father. You went out of your way last night to embarrass him in front of his friends. He's just a kid."

Bucky stood up taller. "You think you know everything? That *kid* was brought in for shoplifting a few weeks ago. I had good reason to suspect—"

"You know Dylan wasn't involved with the shoplifting, Bucky. Don't think I haven't heard about that." She couldn't seem to stop talking now. "You're just jealous of Zack. That's all this is, and it's not professional. You need to focus on your job, not my personal business."

She suddenly realized she was right up in his face. Or, rather, he was considerably taller than she, so she was up in his Adam's apple. She backed off, which he apparently took as fear on her part. She knew Bucky wouldn't hurt her, but she was afraid he might kiss her. The thought made her shudder, which he also seemed to read as fear.

He leaned forward, and she had no choice but to take another step back. "Listen, Tina, I've been patient with your pushiness because of our history together."

She laughed, but it was a bit of a bluff. She knew better than to let him think she was intimidated. This had to be settled once and for all. She repeated the word with disdain. *"History."*

"Yeah, that's right. And for all you know, that farmer of yours is up to no good at that place of his. Growing something he shouldn't. Employing people he shouldn't. I might have to start checking into some of those things, and you'd better keep your nose out of it."

The nerve! "Listen, Gomer, *you'd* better keep *your* nose out of Zack's business. He's a good man. He's a *real* man. And you won't get away with harassing *him*. I know attorneys." Before she knew what she was doing, she had poked her finger into his chest. He was, after all, standing too close to her, and she wasn't about to step back again.

His brows knit together like a couple of warring caterpillars. "Don't . . . poke . . . me. *Girly*."

Girly? What was he, a pirate? She lifted her index finger without another moment's thought. "What are you going to do, you big bully? *Arrest* me?"

THIRTY-SEVEN

H e *arrested* you?"

Tina jerked her cell phone away from her ear. Edie's reaction was so loud, Tina feared Bucky would hear and come confiscate the phone. She had put the ringer on vibrate immediately after texting Edie, but she wasn't sure if she could talk quietly enough to keep from alerting Bucky that she was calling in the cavalry.

She whispered and cupped her hand over the phone. "I can't talk, Edie. Just get here as soon as—"

"I'm right around the corner in the squad car. I'll be there in two minutes."

Tina heard Edie utter the words "stupid Bucky" before she ended the call.

True to her word, Edie stormed into the station within minutes. Tina couldn't see her, but she could hear her as she moved past C.J. (who clearly wanted to stay out of the argument) and charged through the office in search of Bucky.

"Bucky!" Edie sounded like somebody's mother. She must have found him. "What in the wide world of nut jobs are you *doing?* I'm on duty, man! I don't have time to undo your temper tantrums! Do you realize the mess you've created? This is false arrest, dude!"

"She assaulted a police officer."

Tina could hear the stubbornness, but there was so little certainty behind it, she knew she'd be released within moments. Especially with Edie on the attack.

"She assaulted you. *Really,* Bucky? That's what you're going with? Assault? I have to tell you, I'm considering assaulting you myself. The woman is maybe a hundred pounds dripping wet. What did she do, pull a shiv on you?"

After a moment's silence, Bucky's petulant voice finally answered. "She poked me."

Another short stretch of silence. Finally, Tina heard Edie's tired voice. "Give me the keys."

Tina heard the jangle of keys, which drowned out something Bucky said. But she was able to hear Edie as she walked out of the office and headed toward Tina's cell. "You are one piece of work, Bucky boy, I'm telling you. Do me a favor and call Rob. He's over at my place working on the deck. Tell him I said he should take you out tonight. With my blessings. Talk some sense into you."

Edie rolled her eyes when she saw Tina. "You okay, jailbird?"

"I can't say this is how I envisioned the day unfolding when I got up this morning, but I'm fine. Thanks for coming so fast."

Edie lowered her voice. "He didn't really arrest you, you know."

Tina frowned. "But he said that's what he was doing. He even read me my rights."

Edie smiled. "That goof. No, he just told me." Edie cocked her head in his direction. "He knew as soon as he lost his temper that he'd gone too far. But he didn't know how to back out of it."

"I want to talk with him."

Edie sighed, her expression pained. "Come on, Tina. No more drama this morning, okay?"

"I'm not after drama. I want to apologize for poking him. But I also want to clear up this conflict. That's why I came here in the first place. I was just too angry to make any headway with him."

"Want me to stick around?"

Tina nodded. "We'll probably behave better if you do. I promise I'll make it quick."

They found Bucky staring at one of his reports, not writing a word. He looked up, saw them both, and dropped his head right back down, hound-dog-style. He made an attempt to busy himself with his paperwork.

Tina approached him and sat in the chair next to his desk. She took a deep breath and sighed. "Bucky, I'm sorry I poked you. And I'm sorry I called you Barney Fife."

Edie snorted, and they both looked at her. She shrugged. "At least she didn't call you Gomer again."

"And I'm sorry I called you Gomer." Although she apologized to Bucky, she said it, deadpan, to Edie.

Bucky spoke without looking at either of them. "Gomer wasn't even a cop."

Edie didn't bother trying to hide her amusement.

Bucky rolled his pen back and forth on the desk. He mumbled a comment Tina couldn't understand.

"I'm sorry? What?"

"I said, I'm sorry I arrested you."

She nodded. "I forgive you. But, Bucky, it's time you and I spelled out what our relationship is, just so there's no more confusion. You and I had a nice two months together—"

"Two months and twenty-one days."

"Right. And twenty-one days." She shot a glance at Edie, who stared at Bucky as if he had two heads. "But we are definitely *not* suited for each other. Okay? Can we agree on that, please? We are not going to go out on another date. Ever. You need to move on, and I need to move on, and we need to be kind to each other in passing—"

"Well, you're not very kind to me in passing, you know."

"But that's just because you come on to me whenever you see me. You call me your girl and tell me I'm super hot."

He shrugged. "Lots of women consider that stuff complimentary."

"Not me. Okay?"

"Okay." His sigh was full of resignation and defeat.

Tina hated to press further, but she was here and might as well clear things up all away. "And you need to back off of Zack's son."

He sat up. "Hey, I've got to do my job."

Tina lifted her hand to still him. "I honestly don't think Dylan will give you any reason to trouble yourself. And neither will Zack. Or his daughter." She leaned forward and waited for Bucky to look at her. "They're good people, Bucky."

He studied her seriously for a moment before he lifted a shoulder and pulled a face. "Yeah, okay. No hassles unless they cross me."

Tina put her hand out to shake. He hesitated, but then he took it and shook.

Edie rubbed her hands together. "Annnnnd, my work here is done. Tina? You want a ride home?"

"That would be great." She stood. "Thanks."

"Hey," Bucky said, catching her before she walked out the door.

She turned back. "Yes?"

"What's so great about that guy, anyway?"

Without moving her head, Edie eyed Tina.

Tina swallowed. How could she build up Zack as a good boyfriend, knowing this was a temporary, platonic relationship? Then she realized there was nothing wrong with telling

Bucky—with telling anyone, really—what she liked about Zack, even if she wasn't truly dating him.

"He's kind and humble but strong at the same time. He really loves his kids. And I can tell, just by the way he opens doors for me, and by the way he listens when I speak, and by the way he trusts me with his concerns, that he has a lot of respect for me."

Edie said, "And he's about as easy on the eyes as a man's going to get. That doesn't hurt."

Tina stared at her, eyes wide. Bucky probably didn't need to hear *that*.

Edie spoke as soon as they walked out of the station. "The squad car's at the corner there. Poor old Bucky. This isn't a good weekend for him socially, I'm afraid. Losing his best friend *and* his girl in the same day. Quite a breakup extravaganza for the Buckster."

"I'm *not* his girl."

Edie said nothing. When Tina looked at her, Edie wore a subtle Mona Lisa smile.

"What?" Tina asked. "What's so funny?"

Still silent, Edie melodramatically brushed her hair away from her face. Then Tina replayed what Edie had just said.

Tina stopped at the car. "Hang on. Did you say Bucky lost his best friend today?"

Edie's smile grew, and Tina thought out loud.

"But I thought Rob was his best friend." She gasped as Edie fussed with her hair again. Tina grabbed Edie's wrist to still it. "You *didn't!*"

Edie laughed and wiggled her fingers, flashing a dazzling engagement ring. "I did."

Tina emitted an understated shriek and hugged Edie up. "Congratulations! Why didn't you say something earlier?"

Edie shrugged. "He asked me again last night, I decided to say yes, and you went out and got yourself busted. Same old, same old."

On the way to Tina's, Edie shared her change of heart about marrying Rob. "I said yes, but it's going to be a longish engagement while he gets a better foothold financially. And so we can do premarital classes at the church and stuff." She described the simple ceremony both she and Rob wanted. "He's going to ask Bucky to be his best man, so I hope you don't mind being my maid of honor."

Tina shouldn't have been surprised by the request, but she was. Her eyes felt a quick sting of tears before she got control of her emotions. "I'm honored, silly. Is that why you told Bucky to get together with Rob tonight? So he could tell him?"

"Yeah. I was kidding about Bucky losing his best friend, but you know how it is. Once guys get married they often do less guy stuff. I'd just as soon they still get together. I'm still planning to get together with you."

"Glad to hear it." But her thoughts swiftly leaped to memories of Phil. When they got married, he did less guy stuff. But eventually he did less in general. If she had had the training then that she did now, she would have recognized his depression for how dangerous it was.

She shook herself away from thoughts of Phil. It was better to think of today. Of people today. Events today.

"You think Bucky will honor his word about Zack and the kids?"

"Oh, sure," Edie said. "I can't say he won't ever flirt with you again, as bad as he is at it. I think he can't quite help himself there."

They pulled up at Tina's townhouse, and Edie said, "You know, you're probably going to have to give up one of them."

"One of whom?"

"Not whom. *What*. One of your relationships with Zack."

"What do you mean? I only have one relationship with him." She got out of the car and looked in at Edie. "I'm his counselor."

Eddie nodded. "Uh-huh. Listen, lady. You were about as frank with Bucky just now as I've ever seen you. I think it's time you were at least as frank with yourself."

No words, clever or otherwise, came to mind for Tina.

"Now let me get back to work." Edie shifted the

police car into gear. "I'll see you in church tomorrow."

Tina watched Edie drive away while too many thoughts vied for her attention. She had promised Zack she'd get back to him today about the conflict with Bucky. She took the jogging band off her arm and removed her phone. She might as well get that call taken care of now. She'd report just the facts, ma'am. No need to tell Zack about the "arrest." She'd just let him know Bucky had agreed to back off.

And then she needed to shower, fix a cup of coffee, and have a serious debate with herself.

THIRTY-EIGHT

The next day Tina sat on one of the benches outside the church and watched the teens play pickup basketball in the parking lot. Dylan walked away from the game and approached the Gatorade tub on the table next to her.

The youth group stayed after the final Sunday service for a cookout to celebrate the Fourth of July. The holiday wasn't until tomorrow, but the church deliberately avoided organized activities that day, encouraging families to celebrate together. While Dylan shot hoops with the other boys, Zack and Sherry helped at the grills, flipping burgers.

As one of the people who set up everything earlier in the day, Tina had a moment's break, which she spent relaxing and enjoying the teens' fun. Even though she and Dylan seemed to be bonding well, she was surprised when he chose to sit with her while he drank his Gatorade.

"You decided to give someone else a chance to score some baskets, huh?" She shared a smile with him.

"Right." He chuckled. "I'm pretty bad, actually." He lifted his cup to indicate one of the taller boys. "But everyone's pretty bad except for

Erik. He got a scholarship to UVA, did you know that?"

"Yes. I'm really happy for him. That's a great school."

She was about to ask him whether he had considered where he would apply when he switched subjects on her.

"I wanted to thank you for talking with that cop for me. Dad told me you did."

"Oh. My pleasure."

Dylan laughed and made her smile. "Yeah. I'm sure it was a real pleasure."

"Well, maybe not a pleasure, no. But I thought it was the least I could do."

"I think that was gutsy, your confronting a cop, even if he was an old boyfriend."

As planned, she hadn't told Zack about the "arrest." She wasn't sure what kind of reaction that might provoke in him, but she knew it wouldn't be a positive one, so she simply sidestepped any mention of it.

Dylan spoke to her while he watched the others shoot the ball. "I think that's the angriest I've seen my dad in a long time, when I told him what happened at the Mini-Mart. You probably helped him avoid getting into some trouble of his own."

Tina hesitated to keep Dylan sitting there with her. He had finished his drink. But she didn't know when she might have another moment alone with him. She hadn't had enough private time with him yet. So she dove in.

"Dylan, if there were one thing you could change about your relationship with your dad, what would it be?"

He looked at her, his expression a mix of amusement and puzzlement.

She smiled back. "Humor me?"

He stood, and she thought she had lost him. But he scanned the gathering, stopped when he noted where his father was, refilled his cup, and returned to Tina. A very good sign.

"If you had asked me that four years ago—or even a month ago—I would have told you the one thing I wanted to change would be how he was about my mom."

"How do you mean?"

"He didn't do a thing to get her to come back—at least as far as we could tell. For Sherry and me, there was lots of fighting, then one day she left us, and that was it. He never went after her."

"And she never came back." Tina wanted Dylan to consider both sides of that circumstance.

"No. She never came back. And I used to think that was all his fault. His fault she left. His fault she stayed away. Like he didn't care. Like he was glad she was gone." He took a long drink. "Even when I heard some of the farm employees talk and knew she had boyfriends and left with one of them."

He stopped, took a deep breath, and let it go, possibly in an effort to release the pain accompanying his words.

"I still blamed Dad. I thought he should have fought for her."

No wonder the boy had begun to sail as if he had no rudder. He didn't realize his own father was a worthy role model. Still, Dylan and Zack's relationship seemed on the upswing now.

"And now? What's your take on things now?"

He sighed. "She would have left no matter what."

Tina waited. He had more to say.

"The other night, when I came home all ticked off about that cop? Officer Reynolds?"

"Yes."

"It took me awhile to notice, because I was so angry. But the next day I remembered. When I came home, Dad was sitting there all alone, going through her things."

"Whose things?"

"My mom's. The stuff she left behind. Stuff from when they were together."

Oh, poor Zack.

"I think he doesn't realize Sherry and I know that stuff's there. He keeps it in the basement, but we've seen it. I think he tries to protect us from remembering too much. Not because he didn't care about my mom, but because he cares about us."

He glanced over his shoulder in the direction of the grills. Tina did the same. Zack and Sherry were hard at work, but she said something that made him laugh so hard he turned and faced her, sharing the moment with her.

Tina smiled as if she were over there with them. When she turned back to Dylan, he was watching her. She felt her face flush.

"I think he brought those boxes out the other night because of you," Dylan said.

"Me?"

He nodded. "I don't know if he's opened any of them before, but he opened them the other night for sure. I think he's finally moving on, you know?"

Oh no. What had she done, to set up such a situation? What were the kids going to think of her when she was no longer in the picture?

"But—"

"So in answer to your question," Dylan said, "if I could change one thing, I would get him to talk with me about all that stuff. About my mother and why she left. How she left. About how she *never,* not once, tried to visit me or Sherry all these years."

"What do you feel when you say that?"

She was surprised he didn't have tears in his eyes when he looked at her. He looked sad, but he smiled through it. "You're being a shrink right now, huh?"

She just lifted her eyebrows and waited.

He shrugged. "I didn't always notice this, but I feel angry. I've been angry for a while now. The only difference, really, is that I'm not angry at Dad anymore."

Tina sighed. It was a start. A good start. Maybe she'd have time to help him work through his anger at his mother too. And maybe at God. Even—

"And I'm not angry at myself anymore, either."

Well. She struggled to hide her shock at his insight. She usually had to counsel the children of divorce about their innocence in the failure of their parents' marriage. She decided to credit Dylan with enough awareness to look headlong at that self-anger. "So you figured out that's why you were getting self-destructive, huh? The skipping school? Hanging with—"

"Yeah. Hanging with trouble." He shook his head, his sad smile possibly for someone other than himself now. "They just keep, like, sinking, Piker and Tim."

Erik, the UVA-bound player, called out from under the basketball hoop. "Hey, Dylan, want to fill in for Alex?"

"Yeah." Dylan looked at Tina, his sweet brown eyes seeking her consent.

She waved him away. "Go play. Thanks for the chat."

He walked backward toward Erik and spoke to

her. "You coming over for Fourth of July stuff at our place tomorrow?"

Zack hadn't said anything to her about this, so she was slightly taken aback. "I . . . I can't, no. I already promised my mother I'd visit her in Virginia Beach. I'm driving down as soon as I leave here."

He just nodded and threw her a final wave before he pivoted, his blond hair flopping about, and tried unsuccessfully to steal the ball from Erik.

She arose and walked toward the grills. She was eager to talk to Zack about how he could strengthen his bond with his son.

Before she reached Zack and Sherry, they both smiled at her. Their pleasure clinched it—this afternoon was one of her very favorite of all time.

"There she is," Sherry said to Zack. "You can ask her now."

Thanks to Dylan, Tina could guess what was coming. Zack was going to invite her to whatever they had planned by way of a Fourth of July celebration at the farm. They both looked so upbeat, she hated the fact that she'd have to turn them down.

She was eager to visit with her mom, who was scheduled for another trip overseas in less than two weeks. But she didn't want to leave Zack and the kids.

She didn't want to leave them. She sighed.

Ever.

THIRTY-NINE

That evening Zack and the teens joined Lorenzo, Ilsa, and their twins for an impromptu dinner at Dobbins Inn and Tavern, just west of town. They had made an event of buying the perfect fireworks for their little Independence Day celebration the next day, and no one felt like going home to cook.

It wasn't until Zack went to the Inn's restroom that the idea turned out to be a bad one.

It all unfolded in a matter of seconds. He walked out of the men's room and felt a sudden grab at his arm, fingernails digging into his flesh. Before he could move beyond the corner of the darkened alcove, he was pushed against the wall. Disoriented and acting on instinct, he raised his fists and very nearly struck out to defend himself.

Stacy Sumner's excited face and playfully fearful voice stopped him. "Steady there, bruiser. Put away the fisticuffs."

Now disorientation of a different kind enveloped him. His kids were right around the corner. His friends. Maybe other people he knew. Any of them could walk in on this scene at any moment. Regardless of the vantage point, this wouldn't look good. Stacy was a customer, a voluptuous flirt, and a married woman. And she was way too close to him. She was also way stronger than she looked when she caught a man by surprise.

"You shouldn't jump out at a man like that, Mrs. Sumner. I might have hurt you."

She stuck out her bottom lip, as if she were five years old. "Mrs. Sumner? *That* hurts me, Zack. I've told you about that before. I want you to call me Stacy."

He gently removed her hand from his arm and tried to move her back without being forceful enough to seem rude. "Stacy, then. Excuse me, but I have to be getting back to my family now."

She didn't move any farther than he had placed her. He was still somewhat cornered, unless he moved her again or was willing to brush up against her to get away, which was *not* going to happen.

"Oh, don't worry about them." She flipped her hand in the general direction of the dining area. "I checked before following you. They're up to their elbows in ribs and chicken. I can't believe our luck, your coming here when George and I are also here."

He widened his eyes. "Your husband?" One more person who could misconstrue this moment. And Zack knew George; he was likely armed.

That did it. Rude or not, Zack had to take charge. He took hold of both of her shoulders and turned her so they had switched places. Stacy giggled, as if he were making a romantic move, which was exactly why he had hesitated to touch her in the first place. "Look, Mrs. Sumner—"

"Stacy!" This time there was a trace of anger in her slightly raised voice. She quickly adjusted her smile, as if she wasn't as tense as she sounded.

"Stacy. Look, I don't know what made you think I would welcome your doing this, but I don't." He had always considered this woman false and, frankly, sad, but he made a point of being friendly with all of his clients regardless of their personalities.

"What are you talking about?" Her expression faltered, but she continued to look at him as if he had given her cause to smile. "What about all those romantic chats we had when you made your deliveries to our inn?"

"Romantic chats?"

She arched one brow and went to touch his chest, as if he hadn't said a word of discouragement to her. "I can always tell when a man is smitten, Zack, so don't even try to deny it."

Suddenly Zack realized he had broken into the most nervous sweat he'd ever experienced. He grabbed her wrist to keep her from touching him. "Mrs. Sumner, Stacy, I didn't talk with you differently than I do any of my other customers, male or female." He took a step backward. "I'm sorry if you misunderstood my friendliness as anything other than good business. You're just a customer to me. That's all." He took another step backward. "Now, I really need to get back to my family."

Her lips drew into a tight, ugly line across her face, and her eyes blazed at him. She cursed at him before saying anything else, so he turned his back on her and left. Behind him she spat out her words. "You ignorant farm boy. You wouldn't know how to act with a real woman if she came with a set of instructions."

Zack stopped and turned. He took a step back toward her. Although he kept his expression neutral, she suddenly looked frightened, so he spoke as calmly as possible.

"Mrs. Sumner, you will need to find a different produce supplier for your inn. I won't be making deliveries to your place of business from here on out."

Another curse bounced off his back as he left the darkened area and returned to his table.

Stacy had been right about one thing—his kids and friends were all up to their elbows in ribs and chicken, laughing and talking energetically. Still, when Lorenzo caught Zack's eye, he gave him a second look.

"Everything okay?"

They all stopped talking and turned in his direction. He fought to remove any hint of trouble from his expression. He forced a smile.

"I'm fine, as long as there's still a plate for me in there somewhere." He squeezed back into his spot between Dylan and Sherry.

"Wow, Dad." Sherry studied his face. "You're all sweaty. What did you do, run all the way back to the table?" She grinned at him.

Zack pulled his collar away from his neck. "Just a little warm in here, I guess." He looked at his dinner and tried to concentrate. He lifted his knife and fork.

"Zack. Lorenzo."

Zack looked up into the eyes of George Sumner, Stacy's husband. The clatter of his knife dropping onto his plate turned heads all around them.

Lorenzo spoke first. "George! You just getting here, man?" He wiggled his fingers, sloppy with barbeque sauce from his spareribs. "I'd shake your hand, but . . ."

"Relax. No problem." George looked at Zack, who had yet to speak.

Zack lifted halfway from his seat and extended his hand to the man he had just dropped as a customer for reasons he hoped never to share. "George, good to see you, sir."

They shook hands, and all Zack could think was, *Please don't ask about the business. Please don't ask about the business.*

And then Stacy Sumner joined her husband, and matters far more immediate than the business stepped front and center. She looked at Zack as if he had stolen her car and then linked her arm through George's.

"Come on, honey. I want a drink."

Zack got busy with his meal the moment they left, but Lorenzo was watching him when he looked up. The question in Lorenzo's eyes assured Zack he would have to give him some kind of explanation for his odd behavior. But for now, he gave Lorenzo a slight shake of the head, and they eventually settled back into a normal evening.

Still, as the two families parted in the parking lot, Lorenzo managed to share a few private words with Zack.

"What happened in there?"

Zack shook his head. Lorenzo was his closest friend, and he'd be the one Zack would confide in, if anyone. But he wasn't sure if he should tell anyone what happened with Stacy. "Maybe later, Lorenzo."

"It's that wife of George's, isn't it?"

Zack snapped his head upright before he knew what he was doing.

Lorenzo sighed. "That's what I was afraid of. I saw her checking our table earlier, and she obviously didn't see what she was looking for. I guess that was you."

"Lorenzo, man, you know I'd never—"

"Dad, can we please go?" Dylan wasn't close enough to hear, but he quickly approached.

Lorenzo put his hand on Zack's shoulder. "We'll talk later."

Well, that decided that. He couldn't avoid telling Lorenzo, and it sounded as if he'd figured out things already.

Zack spoke little on the drive home and was relieved both kids had brought their iPods with them. So many thoughts crowded his mind.

He wanted to make sure Lorenzo knew he hadn't fallen prey to Stacy's come-on.

He fought against Stacy's angry accusation that he wouldn't know how to treat a real woman. That kind of accusation had been Maya's defense when she ran after other men. Her straying had been his fault, she said.

Was any of that true?

Even if he could remove his ego from tonight's scuffle, the parallel to his own failed marriage made him feel for George. Should he tell George his wife had made a pass at him?

The one person who would give him advice was the last person he could go to about this. Tina had such great insight about how he could relate better with Dylan and Sherry. She was a good counselor. But she had agreed to counsel him about the kids. This was something altogether different.

And if he was completely honest with himself, he knew his hesitation to share this incident with Tina had very little to do with her role as his counselor.

He didn't know if he and Tina would ever spend time together after Dylan and Sherry reached the emotional balance they seemed to be approaching. Regardless, he'd just as soon the subject of Stacy Sumner stayed as far from Tina's attention as possible. She didn't need to hear about this dirty little secret. No good could come from that.

FORTY

The moment Stacy sat on the loveseat in Tina's office, she crossed her legs and jiggled her stiletto-clad foot as if she were keeping time to an unheard version of "Flight of the Bumblebee."

Tina was furious with her, but she labored to keep her voice calm. Stacy had left several messages over the holiday weekend demanding an audience. Tina knew Stacy and her "emergencies" well enough that she didn't rush home from her brief weekend visit with her mother. But she did cancel lunch plans with Edie today to squeeze Stacy into her schedule. And now she learned Stacy had yet to fulfill Tina's previous requirements before seeking further counsel from her.

"Stacy, I made it clear you weren't to come back here without having at least made an appointment for an acting audition or an interview with a local theater company. Why did you think lying to me about that would be all right?"

"Look, I'm sorry. I was desperate to get you to schedule me. Please don't kick me out, okay? I *did* make a couple of phone calls, but I haven't actually followed through on them yet. It's a start, right?"

Well. That was as close to humble as Tina had ever heard from Stacy.

"But I swear I almost walked right out on George Friday night. I would have come here to see you right then if you had been here."

Tina made a mental note to lock her office door and turn off all unnecessary lighting when she stayed after hours from now on.

"George is the most boring man ever, and now he's asked me to start budgeting. Budgeting! And then this *thing* happened Sunday night, and I . . . well, my Fourth of July was just horrible yesterday. The timing couldn't have been better for me to see you this afternoon. And now I don't know *what* to do."

"So you called me in a state of panic Friday night because George asked you to start watching your spending? Is that what you're telling me?" She hated that she let sarcasm seep into her tone, but she happened to know those stilettos alone cost nearly three hundred dollars. She kept up with such things, even if she wasn't fool enough to spend that kind of money on shoes.

"Okay, so maybe I let him get to me a little more than usual the other night." Stacy closed her eyes and shook her head as if she were trying to force the memory away. "It's just a culmination of so many things about George that add up to my overall frustration, you know? And then this thing happened Sunday night—"

"All right. What happened Sunday night?"

Stacy uncrossed her legs and shifted into a forward lean, as if she were about to tell the juiciest story in the world.

"Okay, George and I are out at a restaurant, right? And I see this guy there who I have kind of a . . . a special friendship with."

Special friendship. Tina had heard that phrase somewhere before.

"What do you mean by that, Stacy? Are you saying you're intimately involved with this man?"

Stacy waved her hands, as if she could erase the image from Tina's mind.

"Not intimately, no. But romantically? Yeah, it's been going in that direction. We have reason to meet regularly for business, and it's been kind of a mutual lust fest, even though we haven't acted on it." She lifted her eyebrows and said, "You're my therapist, now, so don't you go judging me."

Tina sighed. "Stacy, I'm not judging you. At least I'm trying not to. On a spiritual level it's not my place to pass judgment. That's between you and God. But as your therapist I have an obligation to give you guidance. And while I'm not judging *you,* I can tell you right now that your *actions* in this situation are morally . . . reprehensible. Your decision to go behind your husband's back and even talk with another man about an affair is a bad decision. There is *no* gray area here. It's a bad decision." She sat back and knew she probably had zero impact on the woman's conscience. "But tell me what happened Sunday. At the restaurant?"

Stacy hesitated, her lips tight.

As far as Tina was concerned, she could just take her tight lips and march on out of here for all the good Tina's counsel was going to do. But Stacy wouldn't leave. She had that need to throw every complaint about her life at Tina. She wouldn't go until she had given Tina her story and found a way to blame someone else for whatever happened.

"Okay. So there I was, all upset with George for being so cheap on top of boring and I don't know *what* else. I saw my special friend there at the restaurant, and I couldn't help myself."

"Go on."

"I'm telling you, Tina. The guy has had eyes for me right from the start. And we accidentally run into each other in the restroom area, and he's flirting with me like always. But this time I follow through. I take him up on his interest. But what does he do? The creep gets all scared. Practically pushes me out of the way. Totally rejects me and tells me to find someone else to get my produce from."

Tina didn't realize she had gasped until Stacy stopped and stared at her.

"What," Stacy asked. "What did I say?"

That was where Tina had heard that term. Stacy

was the woman Sally warned her about. The one who had a "special friendship" with someone named Zack.

Tina had to collect her wits quickly. She loved this little town, but sometimes it was simply too small for her comfort.

Had she misread Zack all this time? Had he fallen prey to this woman, despite his devotion to his kids? Despite his . . . well, he had always seemed to think *Tina* was something special. Or had she misread him the way Stacy had?

The very idea of crediting Stacy with being in the right was simply too hard to consider.

But Zack had to have taken some hard knocks to his self-worth as a husband when his wife left him for another man. Had he tried to heal through the attentions of someone like Stacy? By carrying on a flirtation that put him on the opposite side of the very thing that destroyed his marriage? That didn't sound like the Zack she knew.

And she couldn't even talk with him about this. Stacy was her client. This was privileged information.

Lord, please help me here. Please help.

All of these thoughts zapped through Tina's mind within seconds. She breathed out and heard her voice shake when she first started talking.

"Stacy, what exactly do you want from me? Why have you shared this information with me?"

Stacy lifted up her hands and shrugged. "What should I do? Should I call this guy—"

"Oh, for the love of—" Tina caught herself. She ran her hands through her hair. "No, Stacy. You do *not* call him. He has severed ties with you. You have, perhaps, dodged a bullet we like to call divorce."

"But maybe I *need* a divorce."

"Well, you're not going to get my help with it." Her voice had a harsh bite to it. She stopped to breathe. "As a matter of fact, the next time I see you, I want you to bring George with you. I think I need to meet George, and the two of you should consider couples counseling."

Stacy's eyes widened. "You're going to tell George about my friend?"

"No. That's private, between you as my client and me as your therapist." What Tina wouldn't give for a chance to sever the relationship. But the ethical thing for her to do was to help Stacy figure out why she was such a mess. Tina worked to speak peacefully, to suggest an understanding, open tone to her voice. She knew her emotions were interfering with her ability to act professionally.

"Stacy, you sound as if you're deliberately sabotaging your marriage. Talk to me about your early days with George. Tell me why you wanted to marry him in the first place."

She focused on Stacy's answers for the

remainder of their session. But, as she always did after counseling Stacy, she felt powerless. The woman didn't seem to embrace any of the healthy counsel Tina had to offer. And today's revelation about Zack—whatever that revelation was—had dealt a heavy blow to Tina's willingness to keep investing wasted time in this client's therapy.

It was just past four o'clock by the time Stacy left and Tina checked her schedule. She had no further appointments today and would normally use the time to put her session notes in order. But right now she felt in need of a little counseling herself.

It was definitely time for a spot of tea.

FORTY-ONE

That afternoon Zack watched Sherry maneuver the John Deere tractor across the field like a pro. She pulled the trailer alongside the hay bales, shut down the engine, and turned with a proud grin to her father.

"See? I'm an awesome driver." She jumped down from her seat and dusted off her hands.

"Must be all that practice you got in Lorenzo's car."

Sherry's smile turned sheepish. "No more practicing without you, I promise." She stood before him and swayed back and forth for a moment, like a little girl. "But I'm old enough to start logging behind-the-wheel hours now, you know. You think maybe you could help me get some driving time in?"

"Sure." He lifted a bale of hay onto the trailer. "Just as long as we don't have to drive anywhere but on the farm property."

Sherry gasped. "What! Of course we have to drive off the prop—" She stopped and smacked his arm. "Oh, Dad."

"Yeah, I'll go with you." He reached for another bale. "We can go for a drive after dinner if you want."

"Wow, thanks. But I need my learner's permit first. Maybe we could go get that tomorrow, you think?"

"I don't see why not."

"Thanks, Dad!" She jumped toward him and gave him a hug.

He hugged her back. He wished they always related like this. "I'm glad you want to do this the right way. I'm proud of you for that."

Two of the farmhands pulled up in one of Zack's pickups, starting the dust flying again.

Zack waved to them. "You two want to take over here for me?"

"Yep," the driver said. He handed the truck keys to Zack. "That's what Lorenzo sent us over for."

The other worker grabbed a hay bale and grunted out a few words. "He and your boy are already back at your house."

Zack gave the driver a friendly slap on the back before joining Sherry, who had already hopped into the passenger side of the truck.

"Great, then. Thanks, Tommy." He tipped his hat at the other worker before he and Sherry drove away. "Thanks, Ned."

They hadn't quite reached the house before Zack turned their casual conversation toward more serious matters. "So how are things going with Matt? You going to bring him by the house soon? I should get to know him if—"

"I'm not going out with Matt anymore."

"Were you going out with him?" Zack kept his eyes dead ahead and his voice light, but he was getting frustrated by how little he knew of his girl's personal life. He *tried* to ask the right questions, but she wasn't always that forthcoming. When had she managed to go out with Matt without his knowing?

Sherry waved at the air. "No, that doesn't mean the same for us as it does for old—" She paused. "For parents. We don't actually *go out,* it just means we're, you know—"

"Going steady?" Zack figured he'd give it a shot.

Sherry giggled. "Okay, Dad."

"But you're not . . . going out with him anymore?" Again, he kept his voice relaxed and hid his elation. Tina would be so proud of him for his levelheaded behavior in this conversation. His thoughts lingered on her then, until he realized Sherry had said something that raised a red flag in his distracted mind.

"Sorry, babe, what did you say?" He glanced at her, and she looked uncomfortable.

"I, um, I said he was macking on me at the fireworks thing."

He was afraid to ask. But he did. "What, exactly, is macking?"

She shrugged, clearly more comfortable with the slang than any explanation. "You know, he tried—"

"He made a move on you?"

"Yeah."

Zack couldn't help the frown that news caused. He had to exercise all kinds of effort to *merely* frown. He had hesitated to let Sherry go out with friends after the early fireworks they had at home on the Fourth. But she had promised she would only go for the Leesburg fireworks show and come home. Judging by how short a time she was gone, she had been true to her word. Yet that grabby kid had found time to make a move on her.

"Don't worry, Dad." Sherry turned in her seat to face him better. "Nothing happened. I did what Tina said. I listened to how he talked to me and noticed where his hands and eyes went. He didn't get far before I figured him out. I mean, he didn't get anywhere."

"Do I need to have a talk with him or his parents?" He pulled into the driveway and parked the truck.

"No!" Sherry laughed after she blurted out that word with amazed disbelief at the very idea. "Wow, Dad, you might as well make me go to school in a nun's costume."

He laughed. "Habit."

"What? No, it's not a habit. He only really tried the one time."

"No, I mean—"

"I smacked his hand away, and he was all insulted. Faye said if he apologized for trying, it might have said something good about him. But he swore about it and everything."

"Faye was there?"

She nodded. "Yeah. Her whole family was there."

"Her whole family?" He sighed. When Sherry asked to go to the fireworks, he had wondered if he should try to join her and bring Dylan along. He wanted to adhere to Tina's counsel that Sherry needed his attention. "I should have gone with you. I just didn't want to interfere with your fun with your girlfriends."

"Well, *yeah*. No offense, but that would have been weird, having my dad come along."

"But we could have gone as a family."

She opened her door. "I know. But for something like that, Dylan would probably have run off with some friends, and then I'd just be there with my dad. Kind of lame. At least Faye had her mother there."

She stopped abruptly, and he wasn't sure if she felt bad for him or for herself, at the mention of mothers and the possible association with Maya. Females could be so confusing. He'd like to fix this, but how could he, if he didn't know what was broken?

"Sorry, Dad." She looked at her lap.

"What are you sorry about?"

She shook her head as if she weren't going to answer, but then she said, "I know you don't like to talk about her. About Mom."

Until she said the name, he didn't realize how long it had been since he heard Sherry mention Maya. Had that been for his benefit?

"Is that how I seem, Sherry? Like I don't want you to mention her?"

She didn't lift her head. With a shrug she answered in a quiet voice that threatened to shut him out. "I don't know."

"Oh, Sherry." He had to stop to swallow against the tightness suddenly in his throat. "Please forgive me, sweetie. I've been so busy thinking about what I lost that I didn't consider you. I mean, I did, but not enough, obviously." He cupped his hand gently over the back of her lowered head, as he used to do when she was a trusting little tomboy. "You can talk about Mom as much as you want."

Poor kid hadn't said a kind word about Maya all these years for fear of hurting his feelings.

She raised her head, her eyes glistening with tears. Zack was shocked at the pain and anger in her eyes. "How could she leave us like that?"

That caught him off guard. He couldn't keep up with Sherry's thought processes. He had expected reminiscing. "Uh, she, well, she didn't leave you and Dylan, honey. She left me."

"Yeah? Well, *I* don't see her around here, either. If she didn't leave me, why isn't she a part of my life? She left me the same day she left you. How unimportant must a kid be for her mother to walk out and never come back? Never call. Never write. *Nothing.* She's not even on Facebook or Twitter or anywhere I post. She doesn't come up when I Google her name. She doesn't want me to find her."

Where in the world had his head been all this time? Had Sherry been especially private about this, or had he been too busy with his own grief to notice hers?

"Sherry, you've been trying to find her?"

He clenched his jaw, fighting anger with Maya all over again and feeling the sting of tears for his girl. He scooted across the bench seat so he could envelope Sherry in his arms. As soon as he hugged her up, she rested her head against his chest and cried more freely. For a moment he remembered her at six, when her best friend rejected her and bonded with someone new. He had hugged her exactly this way then. She really wasn't all that much bigger now. Still a petite little thing. And more fragile than she typically let on.

He was able to handle the few tears that threatened to spill from his eyes. Just a few. He wiped them away easily enough.

"If you want to find her, sweetie, we'll try to find her, okay? But I don't want you to believe that she left because you weren't worth staying for."

"Then why?" She sniffed, but she already

sounded better, just for his talking with her and holding her.

He gently rubbed his chin across the crown of her head. "Sometimes people are so unhappy they think they're in the most unhappy place they can be. They figure anywhere else would be better. They're so sure of that, they're willing to walk away, even from people who love them. People they love."

"Why was she so unhappy?"

He shook his head. "I'm not sure, honey. Your mom was unhappy with her home life—with her parents—when I met her. And I don't think I turned out to be the rescuing hero she expected." He wondered how many "heroes" she'd been through over the past four years. But he also wondered where he had truly let her down. He had certainly been far from perfect.

He pulled back and gently tipped Sherry's chin up so she'd look him in the eyes. "Your mom was confused. I can say that because I know how much she loved you and Dylan. *Loves* you and Dylan. One day she's going to remember that, and I hope you'll be able to forgive her when she does."

Sherry actually smiled. A sad smile, but a genuine one.

"In the meantime," he said, "I want to make sure you know you can talk to me anytime about stuff like Faye's mom being there and how you felt without having your mom there. Or if you want to remember good stuff about Mom too." He smiled. "Right? I'm a big tough man. I can handle it."

"Thanks, Dad." She was no longer crying, and she wiped her face dry. "You actually helped. I feel better."

He grinned. "I guess I should credit Tina for that. She really knows her stuff about—" He stopped himself. Did he really want to talk about Tina's counseling efforts on their behalf? If Sherry knew that he had sought counseling about his troubles with Dylan and her, would she slip back into thinking there was something wrong with her?

But he may have stopped talking too late. Sherry stepped out of the truck, but she looked in at him, her mental wheels clearly turning.

"I don't think you ever told us, Dad. How did you and Tina meet, anyway?"

FORTY-TWO

Tina finally found herself alone with Milly an hour after she arrived at the tea shop. Before that, while the shop still bustled, she kept her nose buried in a book of devotions and tried to concentrate on any guidance that might pop out at her. She periodically sat back and listened to Milly's CD player. Maybe the peaceful sonatas and concertos would wash over her and still her concerns.

Once the last customer left, she set the book next to her plate of tea sandwiches and hoped Milly wasn't in too great a hurry to close up and leave.

The fact that Tina chose to linger apparently wasn't lost on Milly. After she stepped to the front door and brought her "Open" sign inside, she picked up a tray and stopped at Tina's table. "I like to see you relaxing once in awhile, young lady. Can I bring you a fresh pot of tea?"

"Goodness, no. Thanks, Milly. I've had so much already, I'll probably cry tea instead of tears next time I'm so moved."

Milly said nothing for a moment, and Tina saw that look in her eyes. The search for something more than what had been said. It was one of

Milly's gifts, this knowing how and when to delve deeper. She set the tray on the next table and pulled out a chair for herself.

"Do you think you might be so moved sometime soon, then?"

Tina smiled and reached over to give her friend's hand a quick squeeze. "You're the best, Milly." She sat back and tried to retrieve the words she planned to use. She had to be careful with Stacy's privacy, but she wanted to find peace about Zack. "I'm a little confused right now, and I wondered if . . . well, I think you know Zack better than I do."

Milly's eyebrows raised ever so slightly. "Probably so. Unless the two of you have had a good number of in-depth conversations about his past, it's likely I know him better." She smiled. "But with regard to the last month or so, you probably know more. The comments he's made to me during his last several deliveries have hinted at a contentment I haven't seen in him in quite some time."

"Really?"

Milly frowned. "Except for a little something this morning, actually. He made a delivery to me today instead of yesterday because of the holiday. And he spoke with such a positive tone about both Dylan and Sherry. It was lovely to see. I think you've been such a blessing to that family, dear."

Tina sighed. "They've been a blessing to me." And her throat caught at that. She got hold of her emotions quickly and swallowed them down. She needed to not think about severing her relationship with them.

"But there was something." Milly rested her chin against her hand. "He didn't say anything about it, but I sensed he was carrying a burden. I left a few openings for him to talk, but he didn't step into any of them." Milly set her hand on Tina's for a moment. "I trust you'll keep that to yourself, dear. I only tell you because of your counseling him and the kids. Perhaps he'll talk with you about it, if you ask the right questions. You know how to do that, obviously."

"Usually, yes." Tina played with the edge of her napkin, rolling it in, rolling it out. "But that's actually why I wanted to chat with you. I heard something troubling about Zack this afternoon, and I don't know what to think. I heard something similar awhile ago, but this just doesn't sound like the man I've come to know and—"

She nearly choked on her own words. Mercy, what had she been about to say? Had she really almost said "love" as if it were the most natural fit in her world?

"Can't you just ask him about it?" If Milly noticed Tina's near slip, she didn't let on. "You've never been one to shy away from open communication."

"No, I haven't. But there's a glitch here. I'm dealing with the private testimony of a client."

"Oh? Testimony about Zack? Something negative?"

"Mm-hmm."

Milly shook her head, all but saying the words: *No way is the testimony true.* Instead of speaking, she fussed with the little pot of cream on the table, turning it this way and that.

The two of them sat there, rolling napkins and turning pots, and began a game of twenty questions.

Milly said, "One of your male clients, was it?"

Tina didn't speak. She gave a subtle shake of her head.

"Mmm." Milly set the small porcelain sugar bowl just so, next to the creamer. "I can't imagine anyone calling Zack's business ethics into question."

Tina looked directly into Milly's eyes and delivered another subtle headshake. "No. I can't either."

"Neither can I imagine his being accused of poor moral behavior."

Tina said nothing.

Milly stopped arranging things on the table. She took a breath, released it, and readied herself as if she were about to defuse a bomb. "For example. If a *woman*—"

Tina's gave a barely perceptible nod, and Milly continued.

"—were to tell me Zack had behaved toward her in a less than gentlemanly, respectful manner—"

Tina's eyes widened, ready for Milly's assurance.

In response Milly's own eyes flashed shock and indignation. "Well, I'd say there was definitely a misunderstanding somewhere along the way."

Tina closed her eyes and exhaled with relief. "That's what I figured too."

"Oh, certainly!" Milly leaned forward. "You're certainly right, not telling me who would talk rubbish about Zack. Let me tell you something about that man. I happen to hear plenty, serving tea and savories and going from table to table. I decided long ago that what I heard was other peoples' business to share, not mine. Oh, on the brief occasion I'd share with a husband some wonderful compliment his wife had made about him. Or I'd tell a woman how fondly her girlfriends spoke of her when she was absent from their company. That kind of thing."

"Uplifting comments," Tina said.

"Exactly. But even then I take great care not to be too eager to share anything I hear. And I hear plenty of negative talk. But I can tell you that I hear nothing but praise for Zack. Even when he went through what he did at his wife's hands, he was an absolute gentleman about it."

Tina nodded and reminded herself of how often she had cringed over Stacy's negative take on the world, on her cushy life, and on the people around her. Stacy hadn't really done or said anything that lent credence to the idea of her speaking truthfully or behaving ethically. Tina was no dummy. She knew these things about Stacy. Why had she doubted Zack's integrity for even a moment? What was clouding her judgment?

Milly continued. "You know, it took a stunningly short amount of time after Maya ran off before the single and widowed women in town started in with their casseroles. Not all of them, mind, but enough to overwhelm him. The poor fellow had so much lasagna, I think he started burying it out behind his house. No doubt you've noticed what a handsome young man he is."

Tina looked at her lap and hoped the flush in her cheeks would pass quickly. "Yes."

"I thought at first he held the women at bay in case Maya changed her mind and came back. Then the divorce papers came, and he still didn't take anyone up on their interest in him. That's why he was surprised, I think, when problems started with Dylan and Sherry. He thought he had done everything he could for them. He certainly didn't look out for his own interests, that's for sure. Not his personal, romantic interests."

Tina was surprised by the depth of relief she felt. She wasn't fool enough to think all of that relief was professional. Was that why she questioned

Zack's behavior in the first place? Because she felt she had more at stake than she did with her typical client?

Milly said, "As a matter of fact, you remind me of Zack in that particular regard."

Tina started. "I'm sorry? In what regard?"

"Your romantic interests." Milly's smile, so full of acceptance, acted as assurance that her intentions were to be helpful, not critical. "Maybe your reasons seem different, but I think you and Zack have quite a bit in common, both good and bad."

Tina wasn't sure she wanted to hear the rest of Milly's theory, which made her laugh at herself. The probing counselor, afraid of being analyzed herself. "Well, you know I want to hear what the bad is, right?"

Milly laughed too. "That's probably because the good is so obvious. Both lovely people, inside and out. Both hardworking and ethical. Both kindhearted."

"But?"

Milly's head tilted just slightly. "But both still hurting and scared, thanks to your respective spouses."

Tina couldn't talk at first. There were very few people with whom she discussed what happened with Phil. Milly had been one of them, quite a number of years ago. After all these years she still felt defensive for him.

"There was so much that Phil had no control over."

"Nor did you, dear." Milly placed her hand on Tina's again for a moment. "You know how much I empathize with you. My first husband may not have struggled in the same way Phil did, but he had his own demons to fight. Regardless of our conflicts, I loved Paul. His death devastated me. It took me three years before I could get past the loss enough to consider life with William." She removed her hand but leaned in closer. "Tina, how many years ago did Phil take his life?"

Tina considered it a good sign that the answer didn't spring immediately to mind. "A little more than fourteen. But, Milly, it's not as if I haven't dated in all that time." She lowered her head and pressed her fingers against her brow. "There just hasn't been anyone who has seemed right before now—"

She caught herself too late. Before now? She jerked her head up to find Milly's affectionate, knowing smile.

Milly spoke softly. "Exactly."

FORTY-THREE

Zack was late getting Sherry to the midweek youth group meeting the following evening, so he dropped her off at the front door of the church. Dylan would have driven her and attended himself, but Lorenzo hired him to help paint his newly finished basement. Zack admired Dylan's sense of commitment to Lorenzo—the job had run long, and Dylan chose to stay late and finish.

The drive to church gave Zack and Sherry enough time to discuss Matt and whether or not he had continued to pursue Sherry after she rebuffed his physical advances. He hadn't.

A relieved Zack parked at the entrance to the church long enough for Sherry to jump out of the truck. She came around to his window.

"Thanks, Dad."

"I'll be back for you at eight thirty, sweetie, okay?"

"Could you come maybe fifteen minutes later? Everyone hangs out afterward. Please?" She batted her eyelashes at him and made him laugh.

"Okay. I guess I can do that, on one condition."

"Uh-huh?"

He tapped his cheek and turned it to her.

Sherry tsked and then drew his name out as if it

were two syllables. "Daaaaaad." She planted an amused kiss on his cheek and stepped up to the curb.

"Love you," Zack said.

"Love you too. See you later."

He nodded and pulled the car away from the curb. That was when he saw Tina walking across the church lot, a shoe box in her arms. She smiled when she recognized his truck, and he pulled up next to her.

"Howdy, ma'am." He tipped his baseball cap and spoke like a cowboy. "What brings you to church this fine evenin'?"

She smiled. "Well, sir, I'm fixin' to do sign-ups for summer camp when the youth group is done finished. And I thank you kindly fer askin'."

She was cute as a button. He suddenly didn't want to leave. "Do you have to go right in, or can you talk awhile?" He cocked his head toward his truck's passenger seat.

After a glance at her watch, she eyed the church before walking around to the passenger side.

He put the truck in park. "Oh, I would have opened your door—"

"Nonsense. I'm a big girl." She smiled as she opened the door. "Not that I don't appreciate the gesture." She handed him the shoe box so she could get into the truck more easily.

Zack set the box down next to himself and drove the truck a short distance away from the other

356

cars. "I wanted to let you know about a talk I had with Sherry last night—oh, and she asked how we met, by the way. I told her Milly introduced us."

"Okay. That's certainly true enough."

"Right."

"So," she said. "Your talk last night? A good one?"

"Probably one of the most open talks we've ever had."

Her smile lit up. "Zack, that's great!"

"That's because of you," he said, and then he watched her look down, the very picture of humility.

But her smile remained. "Thanks. I'm not so sure—"

"No, be sure. She even mentioned you. She told me that kid Matt was macking on her, so she—"

"Hang on a second." Tina put her hand up, and he stopped talking. "He was *whating* on her?"

"Macking." He tilted his ball cap back and made a jaunty face at her. "Oh, you don't know the lingo, huh?" He shook his head and pretended disappointment. "My, my, my, counselor. There you are, mingling with the youth of today, and you're this poorly equipped? I'm afraid you're going to have to step it up, missy. Speak their language. The children *are* our future, you know."

Tina's smile slanted and she lifted an eyebrow. "You had to ask Sherry what it meant, didn't you?"

He nodded once. "Yes'm, I did."

"And?"

"That sweaty-palmed ape hit on my baby."

Tina exhaled a short, disgusted breath. "Exactly what you were afraid of."

"Yep. But last night she practically quoted your advice to me. Something about watching the boy's words and hands—"

"And eyes?"

He pointed at her. "That's it. You gave her exactly the info she needed, Tina. You made it simple for her."

"It's not anything a girl doesn't intuitively know on her own, for the most part. But having it verbalized like that helped me when I was Sherry's age, so I thought it might help her too. Those situations can be so difficult for a girl. For women as well, actually. To this day I get terribly uncomfortable when someone comes on to me out of the blue."

Whoa. Suddenly Zack thought of Stacy, and beads of sweat broke out on his forehead. Tina had just described what he experienced at the restaurant. Terribly uncomfortable wasn't the half of it.

"Uh, yeah. You might not believe it, but despite the general, oversexed reputation men have, unwelcome advances are no picnic for us, either."

He expected her to tease him about his claim, but what she did was far different. She looked embarrassed, or maybe shocked. He couldn't imagine she hadn't heard such talk as a therapist. But maybe he had been too frank, considering they were sitting alone in his truck at night.

Then she studied him. She looked into his eyes, and he could swear her thoughts were there but elsewhere as well. It was as if she were remembering something and bringing it in the truck with them. A subtle twinkle of pleasure lit up her eyes, and she said, "No, I believe that." Now the understated curve of a smile. "I believe you."

Somehow he felt a corner of some kind had been turned, and he definitely didn't want her to go into the church just yet.

He slanted the steering wheel upward so he could turn and face more fully in her direction. The gesture seemed to stir her to do something similar. She rested her back against the truck's door.

"Tina, do you mind if I ask you something personal?"

She smiled and shrugged. "Go ahead. I can always plead the Fifth."

"What, exactly, happened with your husband? Did you two divorce? Or—"

She said, "Phil left me two years after we married. I was only twenty at the time."

He raised his eyebrows. "You married young."

"Yeah. High school sweethearts."

"And where is he these days?"

She looked down at her hands before she answered. "Six months after he divorced me, I received word that he had drowned. They ruled it a suicide."

On a swift intake of breath, Zack found himself at a loss for a proper response. Tina didn't seem to notice his awkwardness. As a matter of fact, he thought she looked relieved to have told him. Still, he managed to say, "I'm sorry."

She nodded. "Phil was a musician. Very talented. Guitar, bass, keys. But he struggled with depression, and it wasn't until his moods became more intense that he was diagnosed as bipolar." Her frown made her seem almost confused. "It was hard at times, living with him, because he hated taking his medication. But he was a good man." A shrug and she studied her hands again. "Eventually he made his way to Rehobeth. They think he simply walked into the ocean in the middle of the night and gave up the fight."

Zack removed his baseball cap. "Tina, I'm—"

She looked up and nodded. She didn't need to hear it again. She wasn't crying, but he recognized a certain pain in her eyes. He had seen that over the past few years when he caught himself, unguarded, in the mirror.

Despite their talk about unwanted advances, he still felt driven to do what he did next. He took the sign-up box off the seat, where it separated him from Tina. He placed it on the floor as she watched, unmoving. He slid only slightly closer to her. He took one of her hands, drew it to his lips, and kissed it, just once. He had no idea why, but that felt like the right thing to do.

Then he saw tears spring to her eyes. She removed her hand enough so that she could take hold of his. As if in slow motion, she brought his hand to her face, guided his palm against her cheek, and leaned into it. She held him there and closed her eyes. Her sigh was like a whisper.

The moment was brief, and she left his truck soon after without saying a word.

If he never saw her again, he'd still remember the sweet smile on her face as she leaned against his hand. If he had to, he could live on that for the rest of his life.

FORTY-FOUR

Tina thanked God that her women's group was as boisterous as it was the following morning. For the first time in years she struggled with girlish infatuation and a growing list of what-if questions. Milly's shop was busy, the women's group was lively, and Tina was forced to think about something other than what happened in Zack's truck the night before.

Something similar happened after she left Zack last night. She set up the table in the church fellowship hall, ready to handle youth camp sign-ups, as planned. A number of parents milled about, early to pick up their teens. Their interest in camp information temporarily distracted her from thoughts of Zack. And Phil. And the fear she realized she still carried after so tragic a loss of love fourteen years ago. She had been of the impression that the counseling she received following Phil's death had helped her get beyond the effects of loss and grief. She had been so impressed she went back to school to become a counselor herself.

But when her fondness for Zack emerged, it was as if she were experiencing the loss all over again. She was doing exactly what she cautioned cute little Brandy against. She was projecting. What would it feel like to lose Zack if she became personally involved with him? Much better to stay removed, to prevent the relationship from becoming more than it was.

And all this time she thought she was simply demonstrating high professional ethics.

Meredith's voice was the first to break through Tina's reverie in the tea shop. That, in itself, was a marvel. Timid Meredith pitched her voice with an assurance Tina had never heard before.

"Well, I have something to announce, ladies." Meredith grinned and sat up with marked self-respect.

Gerry broke into a smile and almost stole her thunder. Tina gently rested her hand on Gerry's arm to still her. This was Meredith's moment.

She had their attention, and she looked at each of them before she spoke. "I got my raise."

Their cheers turned a few heads before they hushed themselves.

"And the best part," Meredith said, "was that I worked up the nerve to ask for it myself."

"Meredith, that's wonderful, honey," Sally said.

"I'm so proud of you." Tina wanted to hug her.

Meredith nodded and launched back into her story. "I don't know if I've ever been that nervous before! I told my boss, I said, 'Mr. Kingston, I'd like to draw your attention to something. I like

Aaron and think he does a fine job, but you have to understand that this is a small office and people talk. So I know Aaron receives a bigger paycheck than I do, and we both do the exact same work. I think it's only fair that my pay be increased to match his.'"

Gerry laughed. "You go, girl!"

"I did!" Meredith said. "I went!" She made them all laugh. "And Mr. Kingston grumbled something about seniority, and I reminded him that Aaron and I both started at the same time. And you know what happened?"

They all leaned in.

"Aaron! He was listening, I guess. He actually poked his head in, said 'Excuse me,' and told Mr. Kingston I was right. About all of it. He said . . ." Her voice softened. "He said he remembered seeing me that first day like it was yesterday."

No one said anything for a moment, and Meredith's cheeks turned crimson.

Gerry looked from Meredith to Tina, who wiggled her eyebrows.

Carmella sat back. "Well, what a cool guy he turned out to be."

Sally rested her chin on her hand. "Kind of a hero, huh?"

Tina said, "Is there something else you wanted to share, Meredith? You have . . . more news, maybe?"

The shy Meredith had returned. She quickly

shook her head and looked down. But a secret smile emerged. Without looking up, she spoke. "Maybe later."

Milly approached the table. "My favorite group of ladies! Sorry to make you wait. What are we craving this morning?"

Gerry murmured to Tina. "Aaron, from the looks of it." But she was mercifully drowned out by Carmella's questions about the day's pastry specials.

Tina smacked softly at Gerry. "Behave yourself, miss."

"Tina sampled one of my latest creations not too long ago." Milly glanced at Tina.

"Oh! Yes, the chocolate malt . . ."

"Malted Chocolate Mousse Cake." Milly surveyed the table. "How naughty do you ladies want to be? Dessert or simple breakfast?"

Carmella sighed. "Milly, why do you always assume it's either-or?"

"How about we try the mousse cake." Tina grinned at Carmella. "For starters, anyway."

Carmella nodded.

"And I'm going to bring you a simple Earl Grey tea with that." Milly looked around the table. "All right with everyone?"

She received no arguments before she headed back to the kitchen.

Carmella said, "Speaking of heroes, my girl Faye was mighty impressed with that little gal

Sherry this past week at the Fourth of July show in Leesburg."

"My Sherry?" Tina spoke without thinking. The group all smiled at what sounded like maternal pride. Tina realized that was exactly what she felt. Of course, she would be pleased when anyone she counseled ended up doing well. But this was more than that. And it was new. A lovely sentiment.

Carmella smiled. "Well, *Zack's* Sherry, so I guess, yeah, she's kind of your Sherry by—"

"By the fact that you're dating Daddio." Gerry lifted her eyebrows at Tina. "Right?"

"We're not dating!" Tina exclaimed, but she had to laugh as she said it. Even she wouldn't have believed her if she were them. "Anyway. How did Sherry impress Faye, Carmella?"

"First of all *I'm* impressed, because she managed to get Faye's mind off of that cute brother of hers, Dylan. She must have told Faye stuff that brought him down to earth with the rest of us mortals. At least now Faye talks about him like he's a regular friend instead of some teen heartthrob or something."

"That's a healthy development," Tina said.

"Right. So here's the Sherry thing. The night of the Fourth, this kid starts hanging around. Sherry and her friends had set up their chairs and blankets near us to watch the fireworks. And this boy comes and sits next to Sherry, just being friendly at first. But Faye said he was kind of foul-mouthed, and a few times she watched him when Sherry wasn't looking at him. I did too." Carmella looked at the rest of the group. "She's really a cute little thing. And he was eyeballing her all creepy-like when she wasn't looking."

Even though Tina knew about the incident, listening to this story incensed her. She was glad Zack wasn't around to hear it.

"Then he not only puts his arm around her, but he rests his hand—or tries to rest his hand—where it most definitely does not belong." She laughed. "Girlfriend apparently has some sharp elbows and *knows* how to use them! She didn't break any of his ribs, but he seemed to think she did that night. Faye told me later she was so impressed because Sherry had been pretty enamored of this kid before, but now she has him figured out."

Tina sighed. "Well, I have to thank Faye for her influence. She and the rest of the youth group have made my job so much easier—"

Oh, mercy. What was she saying? Had she lost her mind? She couldn't be telling this group she was counseling Sherry.

Sally frowned, her confusion obviously innocent. "Your job? Is Sherry one of your patients?"

Tina shook her head. "I don't have patients. I have clients."

"So, she's a client?" Meredith asked. "Is her father also a—"

"No." Oh, this wasn't good. "Look, ladies, I

can't talk about that. Carmella, I'm so happy to hear about how the girls are doing. Please thank Faye for being such a good friend to Sherry."

"I will, I will. But you said you weren't dating Zack. So he's not your boyfriend. And he's not a client or the father of your client."

Meredith and Sally both talked at once.

"I thought—"

"But how come everyone said—"

Gerry leaned in and tapped on the table to snap everyone out of it. "Ladies. She doesn't want to talk about it."

The questions immediately stopped.

Tina lifted her eyebrows at Gerry. "Well, thank you, Gerry."

Gerry shrugged. "I figure time will tell. You don't have to."

Milly arrived just then, and she smiled at the oohs and aahs in reaction to the decadent cake. "You'll all have to tell me what you think."

Again, Gerry murmured to Tina. "*I* think you're smitten, is what I think." For that she received another quick swat—and a subtle smile—from Tina.

Carmella still had the floor and moved from her pleasure about Faye to her pride in having avoided sugar since their last meeting. Then she helped herself to a slice of mousse cake and turned the discussion away from talk of Sherry, Zack, and their relationship with Tina.

Tina allowed the topic to be carried away, but she knew it would emerge again in her own mind once the session ended. She could see that her usefulness to Zack's kids was running thin. Before he asked for her help, both kids just needed a little more guidance than he was able to give. Zack had simply required another set of proverbial hands to set them in the right direction. They seemed to be heading in that direction now. He wasn't going to need her counsel much longer.

Gerry was good for a tease, but Tina knew, especially after last night, that her last quip had landed awfully close to the mark.

FORTY-FIVE

"Eleven weeks down, almost. Only twenty-nine more to go." Brandy made her announcement at the close of her session with Tina that afternoon. "I'm almost into the second trimester. I hardly ever feel sick in the mornings anymore." She rested her hand against her stomach. "And only about eight more weeks till they can tell us the gender."

Tina walked with her to the door. "So you decided you want to know if you're having a boy or girl?"

"Yeah. Mike was right. There's no way I'd be able to wait until the delivery. You know me. I'm obsessing about every detail. What made me think I wouldn't do the same about the gender? That's okay, isn't it?"

"That's just eager curiosity, Brandy, not obsession. If you learn the gender and find a reason to chronically worry about it after that, we'll talk obsession."

Brandy opened the door. "I'm already dying to get the nursery set up. And since we're going to visit my parents for a week next month, I'd kind of like to hire someone to do the painting while we're gone. You know, just to play it safe with being around paint fumes and stuff."

Tina put her hand on Brandy's shoulder. Not only was this sweet girl taking special care with her bipolar meds, she was showing such responsibility with other exposures, like paint fumes, caffeine, alcohol, and such. Brandy had been smart but flighty when she first came to Tina two years ago.

"I'm so proud of you."

Brandy paused at the door and grinned. "Thanks! What did I do?"

"You've grown so much."

"Yeah, and now it's not just from behind." Brandy flattened her shirt against her stomach. "See?"

Tina laughed. "That wasn't what I meant."

"I know. I'm playing witcha." Brandy suddenly gave her a quick hug. "See you next week, Tina."

The embrace tugged at Tina's heart as she walked back into her office. But she barely had time to get a lump in her throat before her heart lurched at what happened next.

Stacy Sumner stormed in as if it were all about her everywhere in the world. "I need to talk with you immediately, Tina."

Tina's hand went reflexively to her hip. "Excuse me? Stacy, no. I've just seen my last client for the day. And I made it clear you weren't to come back here without George."

"He's not going to come with me!" Stacy nearly shouted, so Tina shut her door to avoid disturbing other people in the building. She hated the fact that doing so gave Stacy the impression she was willing to counsel her.

"Did you even ask him?"

Stacy's laugh was oozing bitterness. "Not yet. Maybe I'll have my attorney ask his attorney."

Tina's brows furrowed. "What do you mean?"

"He caught us. He caught us together, and it's all over. He was supposed to go out of town this morning, but he forgot some paperwork and came back to the inn."

Us? Tina struggled with the disorientation attacking her mind with that one word. There was just no way. If she and everyone else had read Zack that poorly, *nothing* made sense. "Us? You and . . . and . . ."

"Ferguson." She plopped down on Tina's loveseat as if her legs were suddenly useless. "Our insurance rep."

Tina fell into her chair too, similarly drained. So someone else had taken Stacy up on her advances. Relief flooded through Tina and brought her energy swiftly back. How could she have even thought of Zack for a moment in this scenario?

Stacy started to cry. "What's going to happen to me now? How could I have been so stupid? Ferguson doesn't care about me." She flipped her hand at the air as if swatting a fly from her face. "What am I saying? I don't care about him either. It's George I care about. And now—"

Tina bolted upright. "Hang on. George? Boring George, the man you've complained to me about nonstop as long as you've been coming here? The man behind whose back you've . . . Stacy, I'm not a fan of divorce by any means, but two days ago you sat right here and said maybe you needed a divorce. Is that the George you care about?"

"How can you be so mean to me at a time like this? All marriages have difficulties, don't they? Don't all husbands and wives complain once in awhile about their spouses? You know, don't they get bugged about the little things?"

Wow. Had Stacy started off complaining about "the little things" and failed to notice how big, how dangerous her complaints had become? Certainly she had used her complaints to justify whatever behaviors had led to her sitting here now, on Tina's loveseat, apparently on the brink of divorce.

If Tina were ever blessed by marriage again, she had to remember this moment, especially when tempted to complain too bitterly about "the little things."

She stood and went to her desk. She pulled open the top drawer and removed a business card, which she brought over to Stacy.

"Here. You need to give this lady a call as soon as possible." She sat back down across from her.

Stacy wiped her tears and mascara across her

cheeks and read the card. "Who's this?"

"Her specialty is marriage restoration. If you really care about George, I suggest you give her a call, get an appointment as soon as you can, and ask for her help in repairing your marriage."

Stacy frowned and let her lips curl as if she had tasted something unpalatable. "Wait a second. Isn't that what I pay you for?"

Deep breath in, deep breath out. Tina hadn't even billed her for the last appointment. "I can't counsel you anymore, Stacy. Not only is couple's counseling not my strength, I . . ."

What could she say? She couldn't counsel Stacy because she'd rather wring her neck for lying about Zack? She hated that Stacy was after the man she . . . ? She what? What did she feel for Zack? And what did he feel for her?

Stacy snapped her fingers in Tina's face. "Hello? Are you even listening to me? So you're quitting on me too, then? Is that what you're telling me?" Then, with a voice full of venom, she called into question Tina's virtue and character, using words that demonstrated her own failing in that very regard.

Tina managed to muster a calm smile as she stood and walked to her office door. She opened it and spoke as pleasantly as if she were ordering tea and crumpets at Milly's.

"No, I'm not quitting on you, Stacy. What I'm doing is kicking you out."

• • •

Tina had never been one for ugly confrontations. It was one of the reasons she and Phil struggled so when his manic moods turned angry. Her avoidance seemed to fuel his determination to engage her in a fight. So her heartbeat raced after Stacy thundered out of the office, dropping curse words like ice in a hailstorm.

But she knew the drumming in her chest was about more than the scene with Stacy.

She was scared to death. About Zack.

For fourteen years she had functioned perfectly well on her own. Her need for male companionship and light romance had been satisfied well enough by casual dating. She had carried on, contented. But now she knew her contentment had been planted in the deep certainty that real love would come along eventually.

If that's what grew in her heart now—real love—how would she handle it if Zack didn't feel the same way? One compassionate kiss on the hand didn't necessarily translate to anything more than empathy.

Mercy. Was there any quality she found more attractive than empathy?

She groaned in frustration.

There was no way around it. Regardless of how he felt, and regardless of whether or not she could trust her own emotions, she needed to tell him she couldn't counsel him about Dylan and Sherry anymore. She was too emotionally involved. She had lost her grip on all sense of detached professionalism with regard to the entire family. If Zack wasn't serious about her and ended up dating another woman, she didn't want to be around for that. And she didn't want to get any closer to Dylan and Sherry if they weren't going to be a part of her life.

She knew she was projecting again, but in this case there was a practical, ethical reason for it. She needed to remove herself from her position as counselor before any further complications arose. If she waited too late, she could actually cause pain by stepping away when they came to her for counsel.

That was it. Her responsibility was to do the right thing by those kids and trust in God's plan for the rest. She remembered the verse she and Edie had embraced at church last month. God knew what His plan was for her, and it was for her own good. She'd just have to believe that.

She had fallen into pacing back and forth in her office. It wouldn't be dark for a few hours, but the early evening would probably be cooler now than the day had been. She had been indoors since returning from her women's group meeting this morning. The four walls and Stacy's visit were stifling. Yet Tina didn't feel like getting in her car and heading home just yet.

She grabbed her keys, locked up the office, and went outside for a walk. She would clear her head and give time and thought to what she'd say to Zack.

At least that was the plan before she reached the corner, saw Zack walking across the street toward her, and stepped in front of an oncoming car.

FORTY-SIX

Zack cried out when he saw the car driving toward Tina. He didn't even use words, just a shout of alarm, as if he'd been shot. By the sheer grace of God, the driver had her window open and hit the brakes in reaction to his voice or to the sudden awareness that she was about to hit someone.

Someone.

Tina.

She had gone down, but Zack saw it all. The car didn't hit her. He ran the rest of the way across the street, lifted her instantly from the ground, and carried her to safety. A wrought-iron bench sat beside the corner shop, and he set her down there, even while maintaining his hold on her, in case she fainted. A small crowd of people gathered, and the driver joined them.

"Oh my heavens, are you all right?" She had a New Jersey accent and spoke as fast as an auctioneer. "I'm so sorry! I didn't hit you, did I? You just stepped out so suddenly that I didn't see . . . should we call the police? An ambulance? I'm sorry. I don't know my way around here. I was confused. I'm so, so sorry."

Zack could feel Tina shaking. She looked at the

woman blankly for a moment and then looked at him. Her breathing was as fast as a puppy's.

"Try to take deeper breaths, Tina." He looked at the driver. "Yeah, could you call an ambulance, please?"

"No," Tina said. She looked at the woman again, and Zack felt her cold hand on his arm. "No, don't do that. I'm okay. Just scared."

The crowd thinned, but the woman stayed put. "What can I do for you, then? I can't just leave." She put up a finger. "Hold on a second." She went back to her car. "Hold on," she called over her shoulder.

As if they were going to jump up and skip on down the street.

She came swiftly back with her purse, through which she dug for something. She pulled a little silver cardholder out and removed a business card. "Here. This is me. Erma Blumberg. Realtor." She gave it to Zack. "I was on my way to the airport to go back home. You call me if there's anything I can do." She looked at Tina. "You sure you don't want to go to the hospital, honey? I'll take another flight, no problem."

Tina already seemed more herself. She almost smiled for the woman. "I'm sure. I'm perfectly fine. You didn't hit me. I just fell because I was scared. Really."

When the woman remained, Tina waved her off. "Catch your plane."

Erma approached her and reached out as if she were going to touch Tina's cheek with affection. She stopped herself and said, "You're a dear woman to let this go."

Tina said, "Listen, you're probably as shaken up by this as I am, even if you don't yet realize it. Take care with your drive to the airport, okay? Focus. And don't worry about me."

She amazed Zack. Even in this moment she managed to think like a therapist.

Erma drove away, and Tina was right. She looked frightened there behind the wheel, as if she feared someone would step in front of her again.

Tina took a deep breath, and when she released it, Zack heard a quiver. Without thought he placed his hand at the base of her head, much like he did to Sherry when she needed comfort.

For some reason the gesture prompted her tears. She softly laughed at herself and blew out another breath of relief. "That was close."

"Yes." He thought about how differently this might have turned out, and tears came to his eyes too.

"Well." Tina breathed a hearty breath again. "I know for sure now. I am *not* ready to die." She wiped at her tears.

He realized he was stroking her hair. He stopped and rested his hand on the bench back, behind her.

She looked at him. "Where were you headed when I saw you?"

"I was coming to see you. I was in town and hoped I might catch you. There's something I want to talk about with you."

She nodded. "Well, you have my complete attention now." She smiled and wiped away the last of her tears. "I actually wanted to talk with you about something too."

"Ladies first, then."

She shook her head as if she was going to ask him to speak, but then she stopped. "You know what? I almost bought the farm just now—not your farm, just the proverbial farm—"

He smiled.

"And there's something about coming that close to death that makes it easier to be frank. Zack, I can't counsel you and the kids anymore."

That took him aback, and he felt his smile fall. "Oh."

"I just don't feel I can be objective now, if I ever really was. I've become too wrapped up in the kids. I care too much about them. I mean, I've started to think of them as if they're my own kids rather than my clients." She sighed. "And then there's you." She chuckled at herself. "I definitely don't think of you as a client. Not even a gorgeous . . ."

Her voice trailed off and she looked directly into his eyes. "Not even a gorgeous, kindhearted one. So, you see, as much as I hate to, I have to quit."

He swallowed. Gorgeous. Kindhearted. He

could probably get away with giving her a kiss right about now. Then she spoke again.

"What did you want to talk with me about?"

"Hmm?"

"You said you were coming to talk with me." She had another tear, right on the edge of her eye. She was the cutest little thing he'd ever seen.

"Oh. That." He put his hand at the back of her head again and leaned toward her. "I wanted to tell you . . ." He grazed her lips with his and whispered his words. "You're fired."

And then he kissed her. Zack never claimed to be an expert in such things, but there was no denying it. She was kissing him right back.

The honk of a horn startled both of them. Edie sat in her police cruiser, the windows open. She looked as happy as he'd ever seen her.

"Have you two loiterers been here long enough to see what happened with the car that almost hit a lady? Someone called."

Zack pointed at Tina, who raised her hand. "I would be said lady, yes."

Edie gasped. "Oh, my goodness, it was *you,* Tina? Are you okay? Do I need to go after the driver?"

Tina shook her head and waved for Edie to join them. "No, no. I'm perfectly fine. I sent her away. She didn't actually hit me."

Edie turned off the engine, yanked the brake on the cruiser, and then got out of her car and came over to them. "Was it someone you knew? Some crazy client?"

"As always, not funny."

Zack said, "She was a Realtor." He pulled the card from his shirt pocket. "From Trenton. On her way to the airport. She seemed nice enough for a terrible driver."

"Agreed." Tina smiled at him. They were still turned toward each other, and he kept his arm across her shoulders.

Edie took it all in, and then she lifted her eyebrows and gave Tina a direct gaze. "I think you need to call me. *Real* soon. Yes?"

"Yes. Will do."

As Edie walked back to the car she spoke over her shoulder. "You've had quite a week, Miss Tina. Getting arrested. Getting run over. I don't know what kind of call I'm going to get about you next." She got in the car and repeated that pointed gaze at Tina. "But I know what kind of call I *expect* to get from you. I'll be home tonight, as a matter of fact." She slipped her sunglasses on, started the car, and gave a quick nod to each of them before she pulled away.

Zack looked at Tina, who had a bit of a sheepish look about her.

"She wants to know about us, doesn't she?"

She nodded. "She does."

"And what do you plan to tell her?"

She took a big breath and released it. "You

know, the usual. You fired me and had to come up with an attractive severance package."

"Wait—did she just say you were arrested this week?"

She grimaced. "You heard that, did you?"

"Mm-hmm. *Arrested,* arrested?"

"Not really. Not officially. Just . . . it was just Bucky being a goof. He was angry with me and got carried away."

He sat up straighter. "Did this have anything to do with your laying into him for how he was treating Dylan?"

"Only everything." She gave him a sweet smile.

He shook his head. That guy was a complete idiot. But what Tina did! And she didn't even mention it. He turned admiring eyes on her.

"You did that for Dylan? For me?"

She shrugged. "Well, I didn't go down to the station with the intention of getting arrested."

"That was just a bonus, huh?"

"Yes." She spoke with melodrama. "I was afforded the privilege of suffering the shackles of persecution for my man."

He felt a flip in his heart. "Is that who I am?"

Her cheeks flushed. The frankness she professed seemed to be wearing off. She spoke softly. "If you're interested, the job is open."

"I'll take it." He stood and held his arm out for her, in case she still felt wobbly. "How about we leave your car here for now? Come have dinner with me and the kids, and then I'll drive you home. Dylan and I can get your car to your place."

"That's such trouble for you and Dylan. I can drive, Zack." She took his arm and stood, but she wavered slightly until she found firm footing.

"I'm sure you can. But let's just give you a night's rest before you do. For me?"

She smiled. "All right. Thanks. I need to get some stuff from my office."

They walked arm in arm down the street. Zack gave her a sideways glance. "Now that we don't have to masquerade in front of the kids anymore, how are we going to keep this relationship interesting?"

She looked into his eyes. Hers were still playful, but there was no mistaking a serious, deeper emotion there. "We'll put our heads together." She made him stop, and she reached up and brushed his hair away from his eyes. She gently pulled him toward her and smiled, ready to kiss him again. "I'm sure we'll come up with something."

DISCUSSION QUESTIONS

1. At the very beginning of the book, the point is made that Zack differs from the typical male in one respect. What is that difference? What does that tell you about him?

2. Are there men in your life who typify the male stereotype with regard to compartmentalizing work issues and personal issues? Are there men in your life more like Zack in that regard? How do/would those temperaments affect you?

3. What experience has Tina carried with her for the past 14 years? How do you think it has affected her romantic relationships? If you can pinpoint a past experience (positive or negative) that still colors your romantic relationships today, express what that effect is.

4. Dylan and Sherry rebel in ways many teens do. How do you think their behavior might have differed if their mother were still around? Would it be better? Worse?

5. Why was Dylan drawn to the pastors and youth group at Tina's church? How does that compare to your experience with evangelism?

6. Officer Bucky Reynolds exhibits a number of differing personality traits throughout the book. Tina's friend Edie insists he's "a good cop." Why does Bucky make some of the poor decisions he makes in this story?

7. Tina assures Milly she could never be nosy. What do you think of Milly's suggestions about Zack and Tina getting together? Does she have matchmaking in mind, or is she only thinking of the kids?

8. Speaking of nosy, consider Tina's women's group. Does Tina allow them too much familiarity with her, or is the counselor-client relationship a healthy one? Would you be more comfortable in Tina's group or in one with a more formal environment?

9. What do you think about the method Tina and Zack used to encourage Dylan and Sherry to comfortably talk with Tina?

10. What was it that initially turned Zack to Christ when he was a young man? What are your thoughts about whether or not he should

share that particular information with Dylan and/or Sherry?

11. What do you think of Tina's ultimate decision with regard to counseling Stacy Sumner? Was she fair or not? How would you have handled that final meeting?

12. In the final scene, what happened to cause Tina to feel more open and frank with Zack than she had ever been before? What kept her from being that honest with him (and herself) before then?

Apple-Cranberry Scones

Ingredients
2 cups flour
4 teaspoons baking powder
¼ teaspoon salt
½ cup sugar
4 tablespoons butter
2 tablespoons Crisco
1 egg
¾ cup heavy cream
½ cup chopped apple
⅓ cup dried cranberries
¾ cup powdered sugar

Directions
Heat oven to 375 degrees.

Mix flour, baking powder, salt, and sugar in a large mixing bowl.

Cut in butter and shortening.

In another bowl, beat egg. Add cream and mix. Add this mixture to dry ingredients.

Add apple and cranberries.

Turn dough out onto a floured surface and knead four to six times. Handle as little as possible to keep dough light.

Roll out to a round 1-inch thick.

Cut circle in half, and then cut each half into four wedges.

Use a spatula to place wedges on an ungreased cookie sheet.

Bake for 17 minutes.

Let cool on cookie sheet for two minutes. Meanwhile, place a sheet of wax paper under a cooling tray.

Use a spatula to move scones to a tray.

In a small bowl add just enough water to the powdered sugar to create a thin white glaze. Drizzle the glaze over the tops of the scones. Serve warm.

Ham Salad Tea Sandwiches

Ingredients
½ pound cooked low-sodium ham
1 tablespoon slivered almonds
5 large pimento-stuffed green olives
1 hard-boiled egg
¼ cup mayonnaise
12 slices thin sandwich bread (Pepperidge Farm White Sandwich Bread works well for tea sandwiches)

Directions
Place ham, almonds, olives, and egg in a food processor and pulse until just finely chopped (not pureed).

Add mayonnaise (you only want to moisten the mixture, not overwhelm it—if your ham is already moist, go easy on the mayonnaise).

Spread the mixture evenly on 6 slices of bread and cover with remaining slices.

Gently cut crust from sandwiches and slice each sandwich into fours. Can be sliced diagonally to make four little triangles or sliced straight to make three rectangular "fingers."

Makes 18-24 tea sandwiches.

Lemon Cream Tea Cakes

Tea Cake Ingredients
3 tablespoons butter, softened
1 cup sugar
2 small eggs
½ teaspoon vanilla
2½ cups flour
1 teaspoon baking powder
½ teaspoon baking soda
1/8 teaspoon salt
½ cup buttermilk

Directions
Preheat oven to 350 degrees.

Beat butter and sugar together on medium setting. Beat in eggs, one at a time, and then add vanilla.

Combine flour, baking powder, baking soda, and salt. Alternate between adding these dry ingredients and the buttermilk to the butter/sugar/egg mixture.

Wrap and refrigerate overnight.

Dust working surface with flour, empty mixture onto flour, and roll to approximately ¼-inch thickness.

Cut with 2½-inch wide juice glass or cookie cutter and place one inch apart on baking sheets.

Bake for 9 minutes or until very lightly browned.

Remove to cooling trays and cool completely before use in this recipe. Then carefully slice through each cake horizontally, spread layer of lemon cream on bottom half, and replace top on cake. You can put a dollop of cream on top too.

Makes approximately 24 tea cakes.

Lemon Cream Ingredients

¼ cup butter
⅔ cup sugar
2 tablespoons lemon juice
1 tablespoon grated lemon rind
2 eggs
1 cup heavy cream

Directions

Melt butter in microwave. Mix with sugar, juice, and rind in saucepan. Whisk in eggs.

Cook over medium-low heat, stirring, approximately 10 minutes. Mixture should thicken enough to coat spoon. Do not let boil.

Strain through a sieve into a bowl, place sheet of plastic wrap directly on top of mixture, and place in refrigerator for two hours.

Beat heavy cream in a bowl until soft peaks form.

Uncover lemon mixture and fold into heavy cream.

Chicken Curry Tea Sandwiches

Ingredients
2 cups cooked chicken breast, finely chopped
⅓ cup finely chopped celery
½ cup chopped cashews
½ cup golden raisins
¼ cup chopped scallions (include the green stems)
½ cup mayonnaise
½ cup sour cream
1 teaspoon curry powder
1 tablespoon lemon juice
Salt, pepper, and hot sauce to taste
16 slices thin sandwich bread (Pepperidge Farm White Sandwich Bread works well for tea sandwiches)
Butter for bread

Directions
In a bowl combine chicken, celery, cashews, raisins, and scallions.

In another bowl combine mayonnaise, sour cream, curry powder, and lemon juice.

Add the creamy dressing to the chicken mixture and mix well.

Add salt, pepper, and hot sauce to taste.

Butter slices of bread. Spread filling on eight slices and cover with remaining slices.

Gently cut crusts away and cut sandwiches into triangles.

Makes 32 tea sandwiches.

Malted Chocolate Mousse Cake

Ingredients
10 ounces dark chocolate, chopped
2 eggs (room temperature)
¼ cup caster sugar (very fine granulated sugar)
¾ cup heavy cream, whipped
6 ounces crushed malt balls
1 8.8-ounce container mascarpone cheese
7 ounces heavy cream, whipped
3 7-ounce packages white chocolate-and-macadamia
  nut cookies
1 cup Bailey's Irish cream liqueur (for nonalcoholic
  version, use Irish Crème coffee creamer)

Directions
Make chocolate mousse—

In a microwave-safe bowl, microwave chopped chocolate until almost melted, stirring after each minute. Set aside to cool slightly.

Beat eggs and caster sugar with electric beater for five minutes.

Stir in cooled chocolate.

Fold in ¾ cup whipped cream.

Refrigerate until needed.

Set aside ¼ cup crushed malt balls.

Fold together the remaining malt balls, mascarpone, and whipped cream. Remove the base of an 8-inch spring form pan and place the ring on a large serving plate (ring will serve as a mold for the cake). Cut a strip of parchment paper and line side of ring. Dip cookies, one at a time, into the liqueur or creamer and place in single layer in the ring to make a base for the dessert. Spread half the mascarpone mixture over cookies. Top with another layer of cookies dipped in the liqueur or creamer.

Spread the chocolate mousse over cookies. Top with one more layer of cookies dipped in liqueur. Spread remaining mascarpone mixture over cookies and sprinkle with the ¼ cup reserved malt balls.

Cover and refrigerate overnight. Then remove spring form ring, peel away the parchment paper, cut, and serve.

ABOUT THE AUTHOR

Trish Perry is the author of numerous novels, including *The Guy I'm Not Dating*, *Beach Dreams*, and *Sunset Beach*. She is also an award-winning writer and former editor of *Ink and the Spirit*, a quarterly newsletter of the Capital Christian Writers organization in the Washington DC area. In addition to writing novels, Trish has published numerous short stories, essays, devotionals, and poetry in Christian and general market media, and she is a member of the American Christian Fiction Writers group.

Center Point Publishing
600 Brooks Road ● PO Box 1
Thorndike ME 04986-0001 USA

(207) 568-3717

US & Canada:
1 800 929-9108
www.centerpointlargeprint.com